Mermaids on the Golf Course

Patricia Highsmith was born in Fort Worth, Texas, in 1921. Her parents moved to New York when she was six, and she attended the Julia Richmond High School and Barnard College. In her senior years she edited the school magazine, having decided at the age of sixteen to become a writer. Her first novel, *Strangers on a Train*, was filmed by Alfred Hitchcock and her third, *The Talented Mr Ripley*, was awarded the Edgar Allan Poe Scroll by the Mystery Writers of America. She has commented that she is 'interested in the effect of guilt on my heroes'. Miss Highsmith enjoys gardening and carpentering, painting and sculpture; some of her works have been exhibited. She now lives in Switzerland.

Patricia Highsmith's books include *Deep Water*, *A Dog's Ransom*, *The Cry of the Owl*, *The Glass Cell*, *The Suspension of Mercy*, *This Sweet Sickness*, *Edith's Diary*, *The Boy Who Followed Ripley*, *People Who Knock on the Door* and several collections of short stories, *Eleven*, *The Animal-Lover's Book of Beastly Murder*, *Little Tales of Misogyny*, *The Black House* and *Slowly, Slowly in the Wind* (all published in Penguins).

Mermaids on the Golf Course

PATRICIA HIGHSMITH

PENGUIN BOOKS

Penguin Books Ltd, Harmondsworth, Middlesex, England
Viking Penguin Inc., 40 West 23rd Street, New York, New York 10010, U.S.A.
Penguin Books Australia Ltd, Ringwood, Victoria, Australia
Penguin Books Canada Limited, 2801 John Street, Ontario, Canada L3R 1B4
Penguin Books (N.Z.) Ltd, 182–190 Wairau Road, Auckland 10, New Zealand

This collection first published by William Heinemann Ltd 1985
Published in Penguin Books 1986
Reprinted 1986

The following stories included in this collection have been
previously published in English: "Where the Action Is"
(*Company*, London, 1984), "Not in this Life, Maybe the Next"
(under the title "The Nature of the Thing", *Ellery Queen's
Mystery Magazine*, New York, 1970), "The Romantic" (*Cosmopolitan*,
London, 1983

Made and printed in Great Britain by
Richard Clay (The Chaucer Press) Ltd,
Bungay, Suffolk

Contents

Mermaids on the Golf Course

Friday, 15th of June, was a big day for Kenneth W. Minderquist and family, meaning his wife Julia, his granddaughter Penny, aged six and the apple of his eye, and his mother-in-law Becky Jackson, who was due to arrive with Penny.

The big house was in top notch order, but Julia had double-checked the liquor supply and the menu — canapés, cold cuts, open-face sandwiches, celery, olives — a real buffet for the journalists and photographers who were due at eleven that morning. Last evening, a telegram had arrived from the President:

> CONGRATULATIONS, KEN. HOPING TO LOOK IN FRIDAY MORNING IF I CAN. IF NOT, BEST WISHES ANYWAY. LOVE TO YOU AND FAMILY. TOM.

This had pleased Minderquist and made Julia, always a rather nervous hostess, check everything again. Their chauffeur–butler Fritz would be on hand, of course, a big help. Fritz had come with the house, as had the silverware and the heavy white napkins and the furniture and in fact the pictures on the walls.

Minderquist watched his wife with a cool and happy confidence. And he could honestly say that he felt as well now as he had three months ago, before the accident. Sometimes he thought he felt even better than before, more cheerful and lively. After all, he had had weeks of rest in the hospitals, despite all their tests for this and that and the other thing. Minderquist considered himself

3

one of the most tested men in the world, mentally and physically.

The accident had happened on St Patrick's Day in New York. Minderquist had been one of a couple of hundred people in a grandstand with the President, and after the parade was over, and everyone in the grandstand had climbed down and were dispersing themselves in limousines and taxis, gunshots had burst out — four of them, three quick ones and one following — and quite fortuitously Minderquist had been near the President when he had seen the President wince and stoop (he had been shot in the calf), and not even thinking what he was doing, Minderquist had hurled himself on to the President like a trained bodyguard, and both of them had fallen. The last shot had caught Minderquist in the left temple, put him into a coma for ten days, and kept him in two hospitals for nearly three months. It was widely believed that if not for Minderquist's intervention, the last bullet would have hit the President in the back (newspapers had printed diagrams of what might have happened with that last shot), perhaps severing the spinal cord or penetrating his liver or what not, and therefore Minderquist was credited with having saved the President's life. Minderquist had also suffered a couple of cracked ribs, because bodyguards had hurled themselves on *him* after he had covered the President.

To express his gratitude, the President had presented the Minderquists with 'Sundocks', the handsome house in which they now lived. Julia and Fritz had been here a month. Minderquist had come out of the Arlington hospital, his second, ten days ago. The house was a two-storey colonial, with broad and level lawns, on one of which Fritz had set up a croquet field, and there was also a swimming pool eighteen by ten yards wide. Somehow their green Pontiac had been exchanged for a dark blue Cadillac, which looked brand new to Minderquist. Fritz had driven Minderquist a couple of times in the Cadillac to a golf course nearby, where Minderquist had played with his old set of clubs, untouched in years. His doctors said mild sports were good for him. Minderquist thought he was in pretty good shape, but he had added a few inches to his waistline during the last weeks in the hospital.

Today, for the first time since he had emerged from the Arlington hospital, on which day there had been only a few photographers taking shots, Minderquist was to face the press. In the months before the 17th of March mishap, Minderquist had been in the public eye because of his closeness to the President in the capacity of economic advisor, though Minderquist held no official title. Minderquist had a Ph.D. in economics, and had been a director of a big electrical company in Kentucky, until six months ago when the President had proposed a retaining salary for him and offered him a room in the White House in which to work. One of the President's aides had heard Minderquist speak at Johns Hopkins University (Minderquist had been invited to give a lecture), and had introduced him to Tom, and things had gone on from there. *A man who talks simple and straight*, a newspaper heading had said of Minderquist earlier that year, and Minderquist was rather proud of that. He and the President didn't always see eye to eye. Minderquist presented his views calmly, with a take-it-or-leave-it attitude, because what he was saying was the truth, based on laws of economics of which the President knew not much. Minderquist had never lost his temper in Washington, D.C. It wasn't worth it.

Minderquist hoped that Florence Lee of the *Washington Angle* would be coming today. Florrie was a perky little blonde, very bright, and she wrote a column called 'Personalities in Politics'. Besides being witty, she had a grasp of what a man's or woman's job was all about.

"Hon—*ey*?" Julia's voice called. "It's after ten-thirty. How're you doing?"

"Fine! Coming!" Minderquist called back from the bedroom where he was checking his appearance in the

5

mirror. He ran a comb through his brown and grey hair, and touched his tie. On Julia's advice, he wore black cotton slacks, a blue summer jacket, a pale blue shirt. Good colours for TV, but probably there would be none today, just journalists and a few cameras snapping. Julia was not as happy as he in 'Sundocks', Minderquist knew, and maybe in a few weeks they would move back to their Kentucky place, after he and Julia discussed the matter further. But now for the President's sake, for the sake of his future in Washington, which was interesting and remunerative, and for the pleasure of the media, the Minderquists had to look as if they appreciated their new mansion. Minderquist strode out of the bedroom.

"Penny and Becky aren't here yet?" he said to his wife who was in the living room. "Ah, maybe that's them!" Minderquist had heard car tyres in the driveway.

Julia glanced out of a side window. "That's Mama's car. — Doesn't it look nice, Ken?" She gestured towards the long buffet table against a wall of the huge living-room.

"Great! Beautiful! Like a wedding or something. Ha-ha!" Glasses stood in sparkling rows, bottles, silver ice buckets, plates of goodies. Minderquist was more interested in his granddaughter, and headed for the front door.

"Ken!" said his wife. "Don't overdo it today. Keep calm — you know? And careful with your language. No four-letter words."

"Sure, hon." Minderquist got to the front door before Fritz, and opened it. "Hel-lo, Penny!" He wanted to pick the little fair-haired child up and hug her, but Penny shrank back against Becky and buried her face shyly in her great-grandmother's skirt. Minderquist laughed. "Still afraid of me? 'S matter, Penny?"

"You scared her — coming at her so fast, Ken," said Becky, smiling. "How are you? You're looking mighty handsome today."

Chit-chat between the women in the living-room.

6

Minderquist slowly followed the child — his only grandchild — towards the hall that led to the kitchen, but Penny darted down the hall as if running for her life, and Minderquist shook his head. His glimpse of the child's blue eyes lingered in his mind. She had used to leap into his arms, confident that he would catch her. Had he ever let her down, let her drop? No. It was since he had come out of the hospitals that Penny had decided to be 'afraid' of him.

"Kenny? Ken?" said Julia.

But Minderquist addressed his mother-in-law. "Any news from Harriet and George, Becky?"

Harriet was the Minderquists' daughter, mother of Penny, and Harriet and her husband George had parked Penny at 'Sundocks', much to Minderquist's delight, while they took a three-week vacation in Florida. But Penny had started acting strangely towards Minderquist, crying real tears for no reason, having a hard time getting to bed or to sleep at night, so Becky, who lived twenty miles away in Virginia, had taken the child to her house a few days ago.

Minderquist never heard Becky's answer, if she made any, because the press was arriving. Two or three cars rolled up the drive. Julia summoned Fritz from the kitchen, then went to open the front door herself.

There were at least fifteen of them, maybe twenty, mostly men, but five or six were women. Minderquist's eyes sought Florrie Lee and found her! His morale rose with a leap. She brought him luck, put him at his ease. Not to mention that it was a pleasure to look at a pretty face! Minderquist looked at her until her eyes met his and she smiled.

"Hello, Ken," she said. "You're looking well. Glad to see you up and around again."

Minderquist seized her slightly extended hand and pressed it. "A pleasure to see *you*, Florrie."

Minderquist greeted a few other people politely, recognizing some of the faces, then steered those who wanted refreshments towards the buffet table where Fritz in his white waistcoat was already busy taking orders. A couple of cameras flashed.

"Mr Minderquist," said an earnest, lanky young man with a ballpoint pen and a notepad in one hand. "Can I have a couple of minutes with you later in private? Maybe in your study? I'm with the Baltimore *Herald*."

"Cain't promise you, son, but Ah'll try," Minderquist replied, putting on his genial southern drawl. "Meanwhile come over here and par—take."

Julia was pulling up chairs for those who wanted chairs, making sure that people had the drink or fruit juice that they wished. Her mother, Becky, who Minderquist thought looked very trim and well done up today, was helping her. Becky managed a nursery in Virginia, not for children, Minderquist remembered he had said a few times to the media, when they asked him about family life, but for plants.

"Ah, tell 'em to shove it!" Minderquist said with a grin, in reply to a journalist's question, were the rumours true that he was going to retire. Minderquist was gratified by the ripple of laughter that this evoked, though he heard Julia say: "Such language, Ken!"

Minderquist had not sat down. "Where's Penny?" he asked his wife.

"Oh —" Julia gestured vaguely towards the kitchen.

"Going back to Washington again soon then, sir?" asked a voice from among the seated people. "Or maybe Kentucky? Lovely place you've got here."

"Bet yer ass — Washington!" Minderquist said firmly. "Julia, honey, isn't there a beer for me anywhere? Where's Fritz?" Minderquist looked for Fritz, and saw him heading for the kitchen with an ice bucket.

"Yes, Ken," Julia replied, and turned to the buffet table.

He wasn't supposed to drink anything alcoholic, because of some pills he still had to take, but he treated himself to a beer on rare occasions, such as his fifty-ninth birthday just after he had left the second hospital, and this was another rare occasion, meeting the press with his favourite female journalist, Florrie Lee, sitting just two yards away from where he stood. Minderquist ignored one boring question, as he saw Becky leading his granddaughter in from the kitchen hall, holding Penny by the hand. Penny hung back, squirming at the sight of so many people, and Minderquist's smile grew broader.

"Here comes the sweetest little granddaughter in the world!" Minderquist said, but maybe nobody heard him, because several of the photographers started clamouring for Minderquist to pose for a shot with Penny.

"Out by the pool!" someone suggested.

They all went out, Julia too. Minderquist placed his beer glass which someone, not Julia, had put into his hand a few seconds ago, by a big flowerpot on the blue-tiled border of the pool, frowned into the bright sunlight, and kept his smile. But Penny refused to take his hand, and evaded like an eel his efforts to grasp her. Becky managed to catch Penny by the shoulders, and they grouped themselves, Minderquist, Julia, Becky and Penny, for several shots, until Penny ducked and escaped, running the length of the pool's side, and everyone laughed.

Back in the living-room, the questions continued.

"Any pains now, Mr Minderquist?"

Minderquist was staring at Florrie, who he thought was giving him a special smile today. "Na-ah," he answered. "If I get any pains —" He did get headaches sometimes, but he didn't want to mention that. "Not to mention, no. I'm feeling fine, doing a little golfing —"

"When do the doctors say you can be back on the job?"

"I'm back at work now, you might say," Minderquist replied, smiling in the direction of the question. "Yes. I get — you know — memos from the President — make decisions." Where was Tom? Minderquist looked over his shoulder, as if the President's car might be slipping

9

up the driveway, or more likely a helicopter would be landing on the big lawn out there, but he had heard nothing. "Tom said he might look in. Don't know if he can today. Does anybody know?"

Nobody answered.

"Don't you want to sit down, Ken?" Julia asked.

"No, I'm fine, thanks, hon."

"You swim on your own out in the pool?" asked a female voice from somewhere.

"Sure, on my own," Minderquist said, though Fritz was always in the pool with him when he swam. "Think I've got a lifeguard out there? Or a mermaid to hold me up? Wish I had, I'd like that!" Minderquist guffawed, as did a few of the journalists. Minderquist glanced at his wife just in time to see her make a gesture which said, "Watch it," but Minderquist thought he was doing pretty well. A few laughs never hurt. He knew he looked full of energy, and the press always liked energy. "Ah really would like to ride on a mermaid," he went on. "Now on the *golf* course —" Minderquist had been going to indulge in a little fantasy about mermaids on the golf course, but he noticed a murmur among the assembled, as if the journalists were consulting one another. Mermaids who graced the links and flipped their tails to send the balls to a more convenient position for the golfer, Minderquist had been going to say, but suddenly three people put questions to him at once.

The questioners wanted to get back to the accident, the attempted assassination of the President.

"Just how you think of it now," a male voice said.

"Well, as I always said — it was a clear day. Peaceful, sunny. Fun. On that grandstand near the street. Till we climbed down." Minderquist glanced at Florrie Lee who was looking straight at him, and he blinked. "When I heard the shots —' Minderquist's mind went into a fog suddenly. Maybe he'd told the story too many times. Was that it? But the show had to go on. "I didn't know what the shots were, you know? Could've been firecrackers or a car backfiring. Then when I saw Tom bend forward, grabbing for his leg, I somehow knew. I was standing so near the President — there was only one thing to do, so I did it," Minderquist concluded with a chuckle, as if he had just related a funny story. He touched the dent in his left temple absently, as he watched the journalists scribbling, though some of them had tape recorders. He looked across the room at Julia, and saw her nod at him with a faint smile, meaning she thought he had said all that pretty well.

"You were talking about recreation, Mr Minderquist," said another male voice. "You play golf now?"

"Sure do. Fritz drives me over. Quite a few mermaids on the golf course, I must say!" Minderquist was thinking of the pretty teen-aged girl golfers in their shorts and halters, flitting about like butterflies. Just kids, but they were decorative. Not so attractive as Florrie Lee though, who Minderquist realized was not only more approachable than the teen-agers (one of whom had declined his offer of a soft drink at the clubhouse last week), but seemed to be inviting an approach from him this morning. Never had he seen her look at him like this, fixedly and with a subtle smile from her front-line position among the media in their chairs.

Someone laughed softly. Minderquist saw the laughter, a young man with dark-rimmed glasses, who had turned to the man beside him and was whispering something.

"*Mermaids* on the golf course?" asked a woman, smiling.

"Yes. I mean all the pretty girls." Minderquist laughed. "Wish there *were* mermaids, all blond with long hair and bare bosoms. Ha-ha! By the way, I know a mermaid joke." Minderquist tugged the sides of his jacket together, but he knew the jacket wouldn't button, and he didn't try. "You all know the one about the Swedish mermaid who spoke only Swedish and got picked up by some English fishermen? They thought she was saying —"

11

"Ken, *don't!*" came Julia's voice clearly from Minderquist's left. "Not that one."

More laughter from the assembled.

"Let's have it, Ken!" someone said.

And grinning, Minderquist would gladly have continued, but Julia was beside him, gripping his left arm, begging him to stop, but smiling also to put a good face on it. Minderquist folded his arms with husbandly resignation. "Okay, not that one, but it's one of my best. Anything to please the ladies."

"You and your wife play Scrabble, sir? I noticed a Scrabble set on the table over there," said a man.

The word "Scrabble" was like a small bomb exploding in Minderquist's mind or memory. He and Julia didn't play any more. The fact was, Minderquist couldn't concentrate or didn't want to. "Oh-h, sometimes," he said with a shrug.

Then Minderquist was aware of whispering again among a few people. He looked for Julia, and saw her taking someone's glass to replenish it. Yes, at least six heads, including even Florrie Lee's, were bent as people murmured, and Minderquist had the feeling they were picking at him, maybe saying he wasn't his old self, just trying to act as if he were. Maybe they even suspected that he was impotent now (how long would that last?), and could they know this from the doctors to whom he had spoken? But doctors weren't supposed to disclose information about their patients. *Steady improvement every day*, the newspapers had said during the coma days and after, during the days when the President had looked in to be photographed with him when he had been confined to his bed, and he was better and better up to this moment, in fact, if the newspapers took the trouble to print anything about him, and they did every couple of weeks. . . . *sitting up in bed cracking jokes* . . . Sure, sometimes he felt like joking, and at other times he knew he was a changed man, made over into someone else almost, as changed as his abdomen, now bulging, or as his face

12

which looked bloated and sometimes a bit swimmy to him. Minderquist had heard about lobotomy, and suspected that this was what had happened to him with that bullet through his temple, but when he had asked his chief doctor, and the next doctor under him, both had emphatically denied it. "Phoneys," Minderquist murmured with a quick frown.

"What? How's that, Mr Minderquist?"

"Nothing." Minderquist shook his head at a plate of canapés that Fritz extended.

"Sit down for a while, Ken," said Julia who was beside him again.

"Going okay?" he whispered.

"Just fine," she whispered back. "Don't worry about anything. It's nearly over." She went away.

"Delicious liverwurst, Kenneth. Have one." It was Florrie Lee at his side now, holding a round plate with little round liverwurst canapés on it.

"Thank you, ma'am." Minderquist took one and shoved it into his mouth.

"You did well, Ken," Florrie said. "And you're looking well, too."

He was aware of her nearness, her scent that suggested a caress, and he wanted to seize her and carry her away somewhere. Impulsively, he took her free hand. "C'mon, let's go out in the sun," he said, nodding towards the wide open doors on the lawn and the swimming pool.

"Could we possibly see your study, Mr Minderquist? Maybe take a picture there?"

Damn the lot of 'em, Minderquist thought, but he said, "Sure. Got a nice one here. It's this way." He led the way, smiling a small but real smile, because Florrie had given him a mischievous look, as if she knew he hated to turn loose of her hand. He glanced behind him and saw that Florrie was coming too, along with God knew how many others.

His study or office was book-lined, the books being all from the Kentucky house, and the square room looked orderly to say the least. His new desk had a green blotter, a letter-opener, a pen-and-pencil set, a brown leather folder (what was that for?), a heavy glass ashtray, and no papers at all on it. The wastebasket was empty. Minderquist obligingly leaned against his desk, hands gripping its edge.

Flash! Click! Click! Done!

"Thanks, Ken!"

"When do the doctors say you can go back to Washington, Ken?"

Minderquist kept his smile. "Well — ask the doctors. Maybe next week. I dunno why not."

Minderquist left his study as the others did, feeling relief because it was after twelve noon, the media would be thinking about lunch, and taking off. So was Minderquist thinking about lunch, and he meant to invite Florrie Lee out somewhere. Fritz could drive them anywhere. There were charming hostelries in the area, old taverns with cosy nooks and tables. And then? With Florrie, he wouldn't have any problems, he was sure.

"'Bye, Mr Minderquist. Many thanks!"

"Keep well, sir!"

Cars were taking off.

Minderquist's eyes met Florrie's once more as he poured himself a scotch on the rocks at the buffet table. He deserved this one drink. He took a sip, then set the glass down. Florrie had that come-hither look again: she liked him. Minderquist moved towards her, with the intention of bowing, and proposing that he and she have lunch together somewhere.

But Florrie turned quickly away.

Minderquist grabbed her hand. She undid his grasp with a twisting movement, and walked towards the big open doors, Minderquist behind her. "Florrie?"

"Take . . ." The rest of what Florrie said was lost.

But Florrie wasn't gone. In the sunshine, her light dress and her hair seemed all golden, like the sun itself. Minderquist followed her along the border of the pool, where Penny had run a few minutes ago.

14

"Ken, stop it!" Florrie called, laughing now, and she stepped behind a round table, which she plainly intended to circle if he came any closer.

Minderquist darted, choosing the left side of the table. "Florrie — just for *lunch*! I —"

"Ken!"

Had that been his wife's voice? Grinning, trotting, loping, Minderquist chased Florrie down the other side of the pool, the long side, Florrie turned the corner, her little high heels flying, Minderquist leapt the corner, and fell short. His foot struck the blue-tiled edge, and suddenly he was falling sideways, towards the water.

A thud of water in Minderquist's ears blocked yelps of laughter which for a few seconds he had heard. Minderquist gulped and inhaled water, then his head poked above the surface, barely. Hands reached for him from the edge of the pool.

"You okay, Ken?"

"Good diving there! Ha-ha!"

Minderquist struggled to get up to the rim of the pool. People pulled at his arms, his belt. Someone produced a towel. Where was Florrie? Even when Minderquist had wiped his eyes, he couldn't see her anywhere, and she was all that mattered.

"Didn't hurt yourself, did you, Mr Minderquist?" asked a young man.

"No, no, Chris' sake! — What's happened to Florrie?"

"Ha-ha!"

More laughter. One man even bent double for an instant.

"'Bye, Mr Minderquist. We're taking off."

Minderquist strode towards the house, head high, wiping the back of his neck with the towel. He was still host in his house. He wanted to see if Florrie was all right. Minderquist looked around in the big living-room, which was eerily empty. A car was pulling away down the driveway. Minderquist thought he heard his wife's voice from the direction of the hall across the living-room.

"You will *not*," Julia said.

"But this is — This can be *funny*," said a man's voice. "It's harmless!"

Minderquist reached the threshold of his and his wife's bedroom, whose door was open. Julia stood with a revolver in her hand, the gun that Minderquist knew lived in the top drawer of the chest of drawers to Julia's left, and Julia was pointing it at a man whose back was to Minderquist.

"Drop that thing on the floor or I'll shoot it to pieces," Julia said in a shaking voice.

The man obediently pulled a strap over his head and let his camera sink to the carpet.

"Now get out," Julia said.

"I wouldn't mind having that camera back. I'm with the Baltimore —"

"What the hell's going on here?" Minderquist asked, walking into the room.

"I want those pictures. Simple as that," Julia said.

"Just pictures of you and Florrie by the pool, sir!" the young man said. "Nothing wrong. A little action!"

"Of Florrie? *I* want them!" Minderquist said.

The young man smiled. "I understand, sir. Well, y-you've sure got the pictures and the camera too. Unless you want me to get 'em developed for you."

"No!" Julia said.

"Why not? Might be quicker," said Minderquist.

"Empty that camera now." Julia pointed the gun at the young man.

Two men stood in the hall, gawking.

The photographer wound up the rest of his roll, opened the camera, and laid the roll on top of the chest of drawers.

"Thanks," Minderquist said, and put the roll into his jacket pocket, realized that the pocket was sopping wet, and pulled the roll out and held it in his hand.

" 'Bye, Mrs Minderquist," said one of the men in the hall. "And thank you both."

" 'Bye, and thanks for coming," Julia said pleasantly, both hands behind her.

The photographer put his strap around his neck again. "Goodbye and good luck, Mr Minderquist!" He stumbled a little getting out of the doorway.

"Let me have that roll, Ken," Julia said quietly.

"No, no, *I* want it," Minderquist said, knowing his wife would destroy the thing if she could, just because Florrie was on it.

"I'll shoot you if you don't." She levelled the gun at him.

Minderquist pressed his thumb against one flat end of the roll in his hand. He'd have pictures of Florrie of his own, maybe a couple of good ones that he could have blown up. "You go ahead," he replied.

Julia bent towards the chest of drawers, holding the gun in both hands as if it weighed a lot suddenly. She put the revolver back into the top drawer.

The Button

Roland Markow bent over his worktable in the corner of his and his wife's bedroom, and again tried to concentrate. Schultz had neglected to report his Time Deposit gains for the end of the year. Roland was now looking at Schultz's December totals, and all Schultz's papers were here, earnings and bills paid for the twelve months of the year, but did he have to go through all those to find Schultz's Time Deposits and God knew what else — a few stocks, Roland knew — himself? Schultz was a freelance commercial artist, considered himself efficient and orderly, Roland knew, but that was far from the truth.

"Goo-*wurr*-kah!" came the mindless voice again, loudly, though two doors were shut between the voice and Roland.

"Goo-woo-*woo*," said his wife's voice more softly, and with a smile in it.

Sickening, Roland thought. One would think Jane was encouraging the idiot! The *child*, Roland corrected himself, and bent again over Schultz's tax return.

It was a tough time of the year, late April, when Roland habitually took work home, as did his two colleagues. The Internal Revenue Service had its deadlines. *Fake it*, Roland thought in regard to Schultz's Time Deposit interest. He could estimate it in his head within a hundred dollars or so, but Roland Markow wasn't that kind of man. By nature he was meticulous and honest. He was convinced that his tax clients came out better in the long run if he turned in meticulous and honest income

21

tax return forms for them. He couldn't phone Schultz and ask him to do it, because all Schultz's papers were here in twelve envelopes, each labelled with the name of the month. He'd have to go through them himself. And it was almost midnight.

"Goo-*wurr*-kah-*wurr-r*—kah!" screamed Bertie.

Roland could stand it no longer and leapt up, went to the door, crossed the little hall, and knocked perfunctorily before he opened the door to Bertie's room half way.

Jane was on the floor on her knees, sitting on her heels, smiling as if she were having a glorious time. Her eyes behind the black, round-rimmed glasses looked positively merry, and her hands on her thighs were relaxed.

Bertie sat in a roundish heap before her, swimmy-eyed, thick tongue hanging out. The child had not even looked Roland's way when the door opened.

"How's the work going, dear?" Jane asked. "Do you know it's midnight?"

"I know, can't be helped. Does he have to keep saying this 'Guh-wurka' all the time? What *is* this?"

Jane chuckled. "Nothing, dear. Just a game. — You're tired, I know. Sorry if we were loud."

We. A crazy anger rose in Roland. Their child was a mongoloid, daft, hopelessly brainless. Did she have to say "we"? Roland tried to smile, pushed his straight dark hair back from his forehead, and felt a film of sweat, to his surprise. "Okay. Just sounded like Gurkha to me. You know, those Indian soldiers. Didn't know what he was up to."

"G'wah-h," said Bertie, and collapsed sideways on to the carpet. He wasn't smiling. Though his slant eyes seemed to meet Roland's for an instant, Roland knew they did not. Epicanthal folds was the term for this minor aberration.

Roland knew all the terminology for children — organisms — who had Down's syndrome. He had of course read up on it years ago, when Bertie had been born. The complicated information stuck, like some religious rote he had learned in childhood, and Roland hated all this information, because they could do nothing about Bertie, so what good was knowing the details?

"You are tired, Rollie," said Jane. "Mightn't it be better to go to bed now and maybe get up an hour earlier?"

Roland shook his head wearily. "Dunno. I'll think about it." He wanted to say, "Make him shut *up*!" but Roland knew Jane got a pleasure out of playing with Bertie in the evenings, and God knew it didn't matter when Bertie got to sleep, because the longer he stayed up, the longer he might sleep and keep quiet the next morning. Bertie had his own room, this room, with a low bed, a couple of heavy chairs that he couldn't tip over (he was amazingly strong), a low and heavy wooden table whose corners had been rounded and sanded by Roland, soft rubber toys on the floor, so that if Bertie threw them against the window, the glass wouldn't break. Bertie had thin reddish hair, a small head that was flat on top and behind, a short flat nose, a mouth that was merely a pink hole, ever open, with his oversized tongue usually protruding. The tongue had ugly ridges down it. Bertie was always drooling, of course. The awful thing was that they were going to be stuck with him for the next ten or fifteen years, or however long he lived. Mongoloids often died of a heart condition in their teens or earlier, Roland had read, but their doctor, Dr Reuben Blatt, had detected no weakness in Bertie's heart. Oh no, Roland thought bitterly, they weren't that lucky.

Roland pressed the ballpoint pen with the fingertips of his right hand, pressed it against his palm. The worst thing was that Jane had completely changed. He watched her now, bending forward, smiling and cooing at Bertie again, as if he weren't still in the room. Jane had gained weight, she wore sloppy espadrilles around the house all the time, even to go shopping, if the weather permitted. They'd lost nearly all their friends over the past four or five years, all except the Drummonds, Evy and Peter, who Roland felt kept on seeing them out of morbid curiosity about Bertie. They never failed to ask "to see Bertie for a few minutes", when they came for drinks or dinner, and they usually brought Bertie a little toy or some candy, to be sure, but their avid eyes as they looked at Bertie Roland could never forget. The Drummonds were fascinated by Bertie, as one might be fascinated by a horror film, something out of this world. And Roland always thought, out of this world, no, out of his own loins, as the Bible said, out of Jane's womb. Something had gone wrong, one chance in seven hundred, according to statistics, providing the mother wasn't over forty, which Jane had not been, she'd been twenty-seven. Well, they had hit that one in seven hundred. Roland remembered as vividly as if it had been yesterday or last week the expression on the obstetrician's face as he had come out of the labour ward. The obstetrician (whose name Roland had forgotten) had been frowning, with his lips slightly parted as if he were mustering the right words, as indeed he had been. He had known that the nurse had already given the anxiously waiting Roland a fuzzy and rather alarming announcement.

"Ah, yes — Mr Markow? — Your child — It's a boy. He's not normal, I'm sorry to say. May as well tell you now."

Down's syndrome. Roland hadn't at once connected this with mongolism, a term he was familiar with, but seconds later, he had understood. Roland recollected his puzzlement at the news, a stronger feeling than his disappointment. And was his wife all right? Yes, and she hadn't seen the child.

Roland had seen the child an hour or so later, lying in a tiny metal box, one of thirty or so other metal boxes visible through a glass wall of the sterile and specially heated room where the newborns lay. No one had needed to point out his son to him: the miniature head with its flat top, the eyes that appeared slanted though they were

24

closed when Roland had seen them first. Other babies stirred, clenched a little fist, opened their mouths to breathe, yawn. Bertie didn't stir. But he was alive. Oh yes, very much alive.

Roland had read up on mongoloids, and had learned that they were singularly still in the womb. "No, he's not kicking as yet!" Roland remembered Jane saying half a dozen times to well-meaning friends who had inquired during her pregnancy. "Maybe he's reading books already," Jane had sometimes added. (Jane was a great reader, and had been a scholarship student at Vassar, where she had majored in political science.) And how different Jane had looked then! Roland realized that he could hardly have recognized her as the same person, Jane five years ago and Jane now. Slender and graceful, with lovely ankles, straight brown hair cut short, an intelligent and pretty face with bright and friendly eyes. She still had the lovely ankles, but even her face had grown heavier, and she no longer moved with youthful lightness. She had concentrated herself, it seemed to Roland, upon Bertie. She had become a kind of monument, something mostly static, heavy, obsessed, concentrating on Bertie and on caring for him. No, she didn't want any more children, didn't want to take a second chance, she sometimes said cheerfully, though the chances were next to nil. Both Roland and Jane had had their blood cultures photographed for chromosome count. Usually the woman was "the carrier", but Jane was not deficient of one chromosome, and neither was he. By no means had she a chromosome missing, which might have meant that one of the forty-five she did have carried the "D/G translocation chromosome" which resulted in a mongoloid offspring in one in three cases. So if he and Jane did have another child, they would be back to the one in seven hundred odds again.

It had more than once crossed Roland's mind to put Bertie down, as they said of dogs and cats who were hopelessly ill. Of course he'd never uttered this to Jane or to anyone, and now it was too late. He might have asked the doctor, just after Bertie's birth, with Jane's consent, of course. But now as Jane frequently reminded Roland, Bertie was a human being. Was he? Bertie's I.Q. was probably 50, Roland knew. That was the mongoloid average, though Bertie's I.Q. had never been tested.

"Rollie!" Smiling, Jane lay on her back now, propped on her elbows. "You do look exhausted, dear! How about a hot chocolate? Or coffee if you've really got to stay up? — Chocolate's better for you."

Roland mumbled something. He did have to work another hour at least, as there were two more returns to wind up after Schultz's. Roland stared at his son's — yes, his *son's* — toadlike body, on its back now: stubby legs, short arms with square and clumsy hands at their ends, hands that could do nothing, with thumbs like nubbins, mistakes, capable of holding nothing. What had he, Roland, done to deserve this? Bertie was of course wearing a diaper, rather an oversized diaper. At five, he looked indeed like an oversized baby. He had no neck. Roland was aware of a pat on his arm as his wife slipped past him on the way to the kitchen.

A few minutes later, Jane set a steaming mug of hot chocolate by his elbow. Roland was back at work. He had found Schultz's Time Deposit interest payments, which Schultz had duly noted in April and in October. Roland finished Schultz and reached for his next dossier, that of James P. Overland, manager of a restaurant in Long Island. Roland sipped the hot chocolate, thinking that it was soothing, pleasant, but *not* what he needed, as Jane had informed him. What he needed was a nice wife in bed, warm and loving, even sexy as Jane had used to be. What they both needed was a healthy son in the room across the hall, reading books now, maybe even sampling Robert Louis Stevenson by now, as both Roland and Jane had done at Bertie's age, a kid who'd try to hide the light after lights-out time to sneak a few more pages of adventure. Bertie would never read a corn flakes box.

Jane had said she would sleep on the sofa tonight, so he could work at his table in the bedroom. She couldn't sleep with a light on in the bedroom. She had often slept on the sofa before — they had a duvet which was simple to put on top of the sofa — and sometimes Roland slept there too, to spell Jane on the nights when Bertie appeared restless. Bertie sometimes woke up in the night and started walking around his room, butting his head against the door or one of his walls, and one or the other of them would have to go in and talk to him for a while, and usually change his diaper. The carpet would look a mess, Roland thought, except that its very dark blue colour did not show the spots that must be on it. They had sedatives for Bertie from their doctor, but neither Roland nor Jane wanted Bertie to become addicted.

"Damn the bastard!" Roland muttered, meaning James P. Overland, whose face he scarcely remembered from the two interviews he had had with Overland months ago. Overland hadn't prepared his expenses and income nearly as well as the commercial artist Schultz, and Roland's colleague Greg MacGregor had dumped the mess on him! Of course Greg had his hands full now too, Roland thought, and was no doubt burning the midnight oil in his own apartment down on 23rd Street, but still — Greg was junior to Roland and should have done the tough work first. Roland's job was to do the finishing touches, to think of every legitimate loophole and tax break that the IRS permitted, and Roland knew them all by heart. "I'll settle Greg's hash tomorrow," Roland swore softly, though he knew he wouldn't. The matter wasn't that serious. He was just goddamned tired, angry, bitter.

"Guh—*wurrr-rr*-kah!"

Had he heard it, or was he imagining? What time was it?

Twenty past one! Roland got up, saw that the bedroom door was closed, then nervously opened the door a little. Jane was asleep on the sofa, he could just make out the

27

paleness of the blue duvet and the darker spot which was Jane's head, and she hadn't wakened from Bertie's cry. She was getting used to it, Roland thought. And why not, he supposed. Before "Goo-*wurr*-kah" it had been "Aaaaagh!" as in the horror films or the comic strips. And before that?

Roland was back at his worktable. Before that? He was staring down at the next tax return after Overland (to whom he had written a note to be read to Overland by telephone tomorrow if a secretary could reach him), and actually pondering what Bertie had used to utter before "Aaaaagh!" Was he losing his mind? He squirmed in his chair, straightened up, then bent again over the nearly completed form, ballpoint pen poised as he moved down a list of items. It was not making any sense. He could read the words, the figures, but they had no meaning. Roland got up quickly.

Take a short walk, he told himself. Maybe give it up for tonight, as Jane had suggested, try it early tomorrow morning, but now a walk, or he wouldn't be able to sleep, he knew. He was wide awake and jumpy with nervous energy.

As he tiptoed through the dark living-room towards the door, he heard a low, sleepy wail from Bertie's room. That was a mewing sort of cry that meant, usually, that Bertie needed his diaper changed. Roland couldn't face it. The mewing would eventually awaken Jane, he knew, and she could handle it. She wasn't going to a job tomorrow. Jane had given up her job with a U.N. research group when Bertie had been born, though she wouldn't have given it up, Roland found himself thinking for the hundredth time, if Bertie hadn't had Down's syndrome. She would have gone back to her job, as she had intended to do. But Jane had made an immediate decision: Bertie, her little darling, was going to be her full-time job.

It was a relief to get out into the cool air, the darkness. Roland lived on East 52nd Street, and he walked east. A pair of young lovers, arms around each other's waist, strolled slowly towards him, the girl tipped her head back and gave a soft laugh. The boy bent quickly and kissed her lips. They might have been in another world, Roland thought. They were in another world, compared to his. At least these kids were happy and healthy. Well, so had he and Jane been — just like them, Roland realized, just about six years ago! Incredible, it seemed now! What had they done to deserve this? Their fate? What? Nothing that Roland could think of. He was not religiously inclined, and he believed as little in prayer, or an afterworld, as he did in luck. A man made his own destiny. Roland Markow was the grandson of poor immigrants. Even his parents had had no university education. Roland had worked his way through CUNY, living at home.

Roland was walking downtown on First Avenue, walking quickly, hands in the pockets of his raincoat which he had grabbed out of the hall closet, though it wasn't raining. There were few people on the sidewalk, though the avenue had a stream of taxis and private cars flowing uptown in its wide, one-way artery. Now, out of a corner coffee shop, six or eight adolescents, all looking fourteen or fifteen years old, spilled on to the sidewalk, laughing and chattering, and one boy jumped twice, as if on a pogo stick, rather high in the air before a girl reached for his hand. More health, more youth! Bertie would never jump like that. Bertie would walk, could now in a way, but jump for joy to make a girl smile? Never!

Suddenly Roland burnt with anger. He stopped, pressed his lips together as if he were about to explode, looked behind him the way he had come, vaguely thinking of starting back, but really not caring how late it got. He was not in the least tired, though he was now south of 34th Street. He thought of throttling Bertie, of doing it with his own hands. Bertie wouldn't even struggle much, Roland knew, wouldn't realize what was happening, until it was too late. Roland turned and headed uptown, then crossed the avenue eastward at a red light. He didn't care if he roamed the rest of the night. It was better than lying sleepless at home, alone in that bed.

A rather plump man, shorter than Roland, was walking towards him on the sidewalk. He wore no hat, he had a moustache, and a slightly troubled air. The man gazed down at the sidewalk.

Suddenly Roland leapt for him. Roland was not even aware that he leapt with his hands outstretched for the man's throat. The suddenness of Roland's impact sent the man backwards, and Roland fell on top of him. Scrambling a little, grasping the man's throat ever harder, Roland tugged the man leftward, towards the shadow of the huge, dark apartment building on the left side of the sidewalk. Roland sank his thumbs. There was no sound from the man, whose tongue protruded, Roland could barely see, much like Bertie's. The man's thick brows rose, his eyes were wide — greyish eyes, Roland thought. With a heave, Roland moved the fallen figure three or four feet towards a patch of darkness on his left, which Roland imagined was a hole. Not that Roland was thinking, he was simply aware of a column or pit of darkness on his left, and he had a desire to push the man down it, to annihilate him. Panting finally, but with his hands still on the man's throat, Roland glanced at the darkness and saw that it was an alleyway, very narrow, between two buildings, and that part of the darkness was caused by black iron banisters, with steps of black iron that led downwards. Roland dragged the man just a little farther, until his head and shoulders hung over the steps, then Roland straightened, breathing through his mouth. The man's head was in darkness, only part of his trousered legs and black shod feet were visible. Roland bent and grabbed the lowest button of the man's grey plaid jacket and yanked it off. He pocketed this, then turned and walked back the way he had come, still breathing

30

through parted lips. He paid no attention to two men who walked towards him, but he heard some words.

". . . told her to go to *hell*! — Y'know?" said one.

The other man chuckled. "No kidding!"

At First Avenue, Roland turned uptown. Roland's next thought, or rather the next thing that he was aware of, was that he stood in front of the mostly glass doors of his apartment building, for which he needed his key, but in his left side trousers pocket he had his keys, as always. He glanced behind him, vaguely thinking that the taxi that had brought him might just be pulling away. But he had walked. Of course, he had gone out for a walk. He remembered that perfectly. He felt pleasantly tired.

Roland took the elevator, then entered the apartment quietly. Jane was still asleep on the sofa, and she stirred as he crossed the living-room, but did not wake up. Roland tiptoed as before. The lamp was still on, on his worktable. Roland undressed, washed quietly in the bathroom, and got into bed. He had killed a man. Roland could still feel the slight pain in his thumbs from the strain of his muscles there. That man was dead. One human being dead, in place of Bertie. That was the way he saw it, now. It was a kind of vengeance, or revenge, on his part. Wasn't it? What had he and Jane done to deserve Bertie? What had all the healthy, normal people walking around on the earth, what had *they* done to deserve their happy state? Nothing. They'd simply been born. Roland slept.

When Jane brought him a cup of coffee in bed at half past seven, Roland felt especially well. He thanked her with a smile.

"Thought I'd let you sleep this morning no matter what," Jane said cheerfully. "No tax returns are worth your *health*, Rollie dear." She was already dressed in one of her peasant skirts that concealed the bulk of her hips and thighs, a blue shirt which she had not bothered to tuck into the skirt top, her old pale blue espadrilles. "Now what for breakfast? Pancakes sound nice? Batter's all

31

made, because Bertie likes them so much, you know. Or
—bacon and eggs?"

Roland sipped his coffee. "Pancakes sound great. With
bacon too, I hope."

"You bet, with bacon! Ten minutes." Jane went off to
the kitchen.

Roland felt in good spirits the entire day. Jane
remarked on it before he left the apartment that morning,
and Greg at the office said: "Miracle man! Did you win
on the horses or something? Did you see that pile of stuff
on your desk?"

Roland had, and he had expected it. Greg had worked
till two-thirty in the morning, he said, and he looked it.
The telephones, four of them, rang all day, clients calling
back after having had questions put to them by Roland
or Greg by telephone or by letter. Roland did not feel so
much cheerful as confident that day. He felt calm, really,
and if he looked consequently cheerful, that was an
accident. He could remind himself that the office had
gone through last year's deadline, and the year's before
that, in the same state of nerves and overwork, and they'd
always made it, somehow.

Roland wore the same trousers, and the button was in
the right-hand pocket. He pulled it out in a moment
when he was alone in his office and looked at it in the
light that came through his office window. It was greyish
brown, with holes in which some grey thread remained.
Roland pulled the thread out and dropped the bits into
his wastebasket. Had he really throttled a man? The idea
seemed impossible at ten past four that afternoon, as he
stood in his pleasant office with its green carpet, pale
green curtains and white walls lined with familiar books
and files. The button could have come from anywhere,
Roland was thinking. It could have fallen off one of his
own jackets, he could have shoved it into his pocket with
an idea of asking Jane to sew it on, when she found the
time.

It did cross Roland's mind just after five o'clock (the

office including the two secretaries was working till seven)
to look at the *Post* tonight for the discovery of a body on
— what street? A man of forty or so with moustache,
named — Strangled. But Roland's mind just as quickly
shied away from this idea. Why should he look in the
newspapers? What had it got to do with him? There
wouldn't be a clue, as they said in mystery novels. Sheer
fantasy! All of it. A corpse lying on East 40th Street or
45th Street or wherever it had been? Not very likely.

In four days, the office work had greatly let up. Some
clients were going to be a little late (their own fault for
not having their data all together), and would have to
pay small fines, but so be it. Fines weren't life or death.
Roland ate better. Jane was pleased. Roland showed
more patience with Bertie, and he could laugh with the
child now and then. He sat on the floor and played with
him for fifteen and twenty minutes at a time.

"That'll help him, you know, Rollie?" said Jane, watching them arrange a row of soft plastic blocks. Jane spoke
as if Bertie couldn't understand a word, which was more
or less true.

"Yep," said Roland. The row of blocks had a space
between each block and the next and Roland began setting more blocks on these gaps with the objective of
building a pyramid. "Why don't we ask the Jacksons
over soon?" He looked up at Jane. "For dinner."

"Margie and Tom! I'd love to, Rollie!" Jane was beam-
ing, and she brought her hands down on her thighs for
emphasis. "I'll phone them tonight. It was always you
who didn't want them, you know, Rollie. *They* didn't
mind. I mean — about Bertie. Bertie was always locked
up in his room, anyway!" Jane laughed, happy at the
idea of inviting the Jacksons. "It was always you who
thought Bertie bothered *them*, or they didn't like Bertie.
Something like that."

Roland remembered. The Jacksons, like most people,
were disgusted by Bertie, a little afraid of him for all
Bertie's smallness, as normal people were always afraid

33

of idiots, unpredictable things that might do them harm. Now Roland felt that he wouldn't mind that. He knew he would be able to laugh, make a joke, put the Jacksons at their ease about Bertie, if they went into Bertie's room "to visit with him" the night they came. They never asked to, but Jane usually proposed it.

The Jackson evening turned out well. Everyone was in a good mood, and Jane didn't suggest during the pre-dinner drinks time, "saying hello to Bertie," and the Jacksons hadn't brought a toy for him, as they had a few times in the past — a small plastic beach ball, something inane, for a baby. Jane had made an excellent Hungarian goulash.

Then around ten o'clock, Jane said brightly, "I'll bring Bertie out to join us for a few minutes. It'll do him good."

"Do that," said Margerie Jackson automatically, politely.

Roland saw Margerie glance at her husband who was standing with his small coffee by a bookcase. Roland had just poured brandies all round into the snifters on the coffee table. Bertie could easily sweep a couple of snifters off the low table with a swing of his hand, Roland was thinking, and he realized that he had grown stiff with apprehension or annoyance.

Bertie was carried in, in Jane's usual manner, held by the waist, face forward, and rather bumped along against her thighs as she walked. Bertie weighed a lot for a five-year-old, though he wasn't as tall as a normal child of that age.

"Aaaaagh-wah!" Bertie's small slant eyes looked the same as they might if he were in his own room, which was to say they showed no interest in or awareness of the change of scene to the living-room or of the people in it.

"*There* you are!" Jane announced to Bertie, dumping him down on his diapered rump on the living-room carpet.

Bertie wore the top of his pyjama suit with its cuffs

34

turned up a couple of times because his arms were so short.

Roland found himself frowning slightly, averting his eyes in a miserable way from the unsightly — or rather, frightening — flatness of Bertie's undersized head, just as he had always done, but especially in the presence of other people, as if he wished to illustrate his sympathy with people who might be seeing Bertie for the first time. Then Margerie laughed at something Bertie had done. She had given Bertie one of the cheese stick canapés that were still on the coffee table, and he had crushed it into one ear.

Margerie glanced at Roland, still smiling, and Roland found himself smiling back, even grinning. Roland took a sip of his brandy. Bertie was a little clown, after all, and maybe he enjoyed these get-togethers in the living-room. Bertie did seem to be smiling now. Occasionally he *did* smile. Little *monster*! But he'd killed a man in return, Roland thought, and stood a bit taller, feeling all his muscles tense. He, Roland, wasn't entirely helpless in the situation, wasn't just a puppet of fate to be pushed around by — *everything* — a victim of a wildly odd chance, doomed to eternal shame. Far from it.

Roland found himself joining in a great burst of laughter, not knowing what it was about, till he saw Bertie rolling on his back like a helpless beetle.

"Trying to stand on his *head*!" cried Jane. "Ha-ha! Did you see that, Rollie, dear?"

"Yes," said Roland. He topped up the brandies for those who wanted it.

When the Jacksons departed around eleven, Jane asked Roland if he didn't think it had been a successful evening, because she thought it had been. Jane stood proudly in the living-room, and opened her arms, smiling.

"Yes, my love. It was." Roland put his arms around her waist, held her close for a moment, without passion, without any sexual pleasure whatsoever, but with the pleasure of companionship. His embrace was like saying,

"Thanks for cooking the dinner and making it a nice evening."

Bertie was stowed away in his room, in his low bed, Roland was sure, though he hadn't accompanied Jane when she was trying to settle him for the night. Jane was doing things in the kitchen now. Roland went to a corner of the bedroom where he and Jane stacked old newspapers. Because of Roland's work, he kept newspapers a long while, in case he had to look for a new tax law, or bond issue, or any of a dozen such bits of news that he or his colleagues might not have cut out. What he was looking for was not old and was rather specific: an item about a man found dead on a sidewalk during the night of April 26–27. In about four minutes, Roland found an item not two inches long in a newspaper one day later than he had thought it might be. MAN FOUND STRANGLED was the little heading. Francisco Baltar, 46, said the report, had been found strangled on East 47th Street. Robbery had evidently been the motive. Mr Baltar had been a consulting engineer of Vito, a Spanish agricultural firm, and had been in New York for a short stay on business. Police were questioning suspects, the item concluded.

Robbery, Roland thought with astonishment. Not the same man, surely, unless someone had robbed the corpse. Roland realized that this was pretty likely, in New York. A robber might suppose the man was drunk or drugged, and seize the opportunity to relieve him of wallet and wristwatch and whatever. The street fitted, Roland thought, and the date. And the man's age. But Spanish, with that brownish hair? Well, Roland had heard of blond Spaniards.

But they hadn't mentioned a missing button.

On the other hand, why should they mention a missing button in an item as short as this? As clues went, a greyish-brown button was infinitesimal. For the police to find the button in Roland's right-hand pocket (he kept the button in that pocket no matter which trousers he wore) would be like finding a needle in a haystack. And noticing the absence of a button on the man's jacket, why should the police assume the murderer had taken it?

Nevertheless, the finding of the corpse — or *a* corpse — gave the button a greater significance. The button became more dangerous. Roland thought of putting it in Jane's little tin box which held an assortment of buttons, but when he opened the box and saw the hundred or more innocent buttons of all sizes there, Roland simply could not.

Throw it away, Roland thought. Down the garbage chute in the hall. Better yet and easier, straight into the big plastic bag in the kitchen. Who'd ever notice or find it? Roland realized that he wanted to keep the button.

And as the weeks went by, the button took on varying meanings to Roland. Sometimes it seemed a token of guilt, proof of what he had done, and he felt frightened. Or on days when Roland happened to be in a cheery mood, the button became a joke, a prop in a story that he had told to himself: that he had strangled a stranger and snatched a button off the stranger's jacket to prove it.

"Absurd," Roland murmured to himself one sunny day in his office as he stood by his window, turning the button over in his fingers, scrutinizing its greyish-brown horn, its four empty holes. "Just a nutty fantasy!" Well, no need ever to *tell* anyone about it, he thought, and chuckled. He dropped the button into his right-hand pocket and returned to his desk.

He and Jane were going to a resort hotel in the Adirondacks for the last two weeks of June, Roland's vacation time, and of course they were taking Bertie with them. Bertie was walking better lately, but oddly this achievement came and went: he'd been walking better at three, for instance, than he was at the moment. One never knew. Jane had bought a suit of pale blue cotton —jacket and short trousers — and had patiently let out the waist by sewing in extra material, and had shortened the sleeves, "So he'll look nice at the dinner table at the St Marcy Lodge," Jane said.

Roland had winced, then rapidly recovered. He had always hated taking Bertie out in public, even for walks in Central Park on Sundays, and the Lodge was going to be worse, he thought, because they'd be stuck with the same people, other guests, or under their eyes, for almost two weeks. He would have to pass through that period of curious and darting glances, unheard murmurs as people confirmed to one another, "Mongoloid idiot," then the period of studied eyes-averted-no-staring that such a group always progressed to.

The St Marcy Lodge was a handsomely proportioned colonial mansion set on a vast lawn, backgrounded by thick forests of pine and fir. The lobby had a homey atmosphere, the brass items were polished, the carpet thick. There was croquet on the lawn, tennis courts, horses could be rented, and there was a golf course half a mile away to which a Lodge car could take guests at any hour of the day. The dining room had about twenty tables of varying sizes, so that couples or parties could dine alone if they preferred, or join larger tables. The manager had told the Markows that the guests were never assigned tables, but had freedom of choice.

Roland and Jane preferred to take a smaller table meant for four when the dinner hour came. A pillow was brought for Bertie by a pleasant waitress, who at once changed her mind and suggested a highchair. It was easy, she said, bustling off somewhere. Roland had not protested: a highchair was safer for Bertie, because the tray part pinned him in, whereas he could topple off a cushion before anyone could right him. Bertie wore his blue suit. His ridged tongue hung out, and his eyes though open, showed no interest in his new surroundings which he did not even turn his head to look at.

"Isn't it nice," Jane said, resting her chin on her folded fingers, "that the Lodge put that crib in the room this afternoon? Just the right thing for Bertie, isn't it?"

Roland nodded, and studied the menu. He was enduring those moments he had foreseen, when the eyes of several people in the dining room had fixed on Bertie, and for a few seconds it was worse as the waitress returned with the highchair. Roland sprang up to lift Bertie into it. *Slap!* The tray part was swung over Bertie's head to rest on the arms of the chair. Roland tugged Bertie's broad hands up and plopped them on the wooden tray where his food would be set, but the hands slid back and dropped again at Bertie's sides.

Jane wiped some drool from Bertie's chin with her napkin.

The food was delicious. The eyes around them now looked at other things. Jane had edged her chair closer to Bertie's, and she patiently fed him his mashed potatoes and tiny bits of tender roast beef. The lemon meringue pie arrived hot with beautifully browned egg white on top. Bertie brought his heavy little hand down on the right side of his plate, and his half-portion of lemon pie catapulted towards Roland. Roland caught it adroitly with his left hand and laughed, dumped it back on to Bertie's plate, and soaked an end of his napkin in his glass of water to wash the stickiness off his palm and fingers.

So did Jane laugh, as if they were alone at home.

They finished a bottle of wine between them.

As they were walking towards the stairway in the lobby, with an idea of getting Bertie to bed, because it was nearly ten, Roland heard voices behind him.

". . . a pity, you know? Young couple like that."

". . . could frighten other kids too. Did you notice that dog today, mom? That poodle?" This voice was young, female, with a giggle in it.

Roland remembered the dog, a black miniature poodle on a leash. The dog had stiffened and backed away from Bertie, growling, when Roland and Jane had been signing the register. Roland's hand reached into his right side pocket and squeezed the button, felt its reassuring reality, its hardness. He turned by the stairway to the two women behind him, one young and one older.

"Yes, Bertie," he said to them. "He's not much trouble, you know. Quite harmless. Sorry if he bothers you. He's quite a clown really. Gives us a lot of fun." Smiling, Roland nodded for emphasis.

Jane was smiling too. "Good evening," she said in a friendly tone to the two women.

Both the older and younger woman nodded with awkward politeness, plainly embarrassed that they had been overheard. "'Evening," said the older.

Roland and Jane held Bertie by the hands in their usual manner, hoisting him up one step at a time, sometimes two steps. They performed this chore without thinking about it. Bertie sometimes moved his blunt little feet in their blunt shoes to touch a step, but mostly he dragged them, and his legs went limp. Roland's right hand was still in his trousers pocket.

A pretty girl moved at a faster pace up the stairs on Roland's right. His eyes were drawn to her. She had soft, light brown hair, a lovely profile which instantly vanished, but she glanced back at him at the landing, and their eyes met: bluish eyes, then she disappeared. Roland had been aware of a sudden attraction towards her, like a leap within him, the first such feeling he had had in years. Funny. He was not going to approach the girl, he knew. Maybe best if he avoided looking at her if he saw her again, as he probably would. Still, it was nice to know he was capable of such an emotion, even if the emotion had completely gone in regard to Jane. He squeezed the button harder than ever as they heaved Bertie up the last step to the floor level. He had killed a man in revenge for Bertie. He had superiority, in a sense, one-upmanship. He must never forget that. He could face the years ahead with that.

Where the Action is

(First published in *Company*, London, 1984)

Here it was, some action finally — an armed hold-up of a town bus — and Craig Rollins was in urgent need of a toilet! Nevertheless, Craig raised his camera once again and snapped, just as a scared-looking man was hopping down the steps of the halted bus. Then Craig ran, heading for Eats and Take-Away, where he knew there was a men's room by the telephones.

Craig was back in something under a minute, but by then the action seemed to be over. He hadn't heard any gunshots. A cop was blowing a whistle. An ambulance had pulled up, but Craig didn't see anybody who was wounded.

"Take it easy, folks!" yelled a cop whose face Craig knew. "We've got everything in hand!"

"*I* haven't! They got my *handbag*!" cried a woman's voice, shrill and clear.

A June sun boiled down. It was mid-morning.

"There were *three* of 'em!" yelled a man in an assertive way. "You just got two here!"

Craig saw some shirt-sleeved police hustling two young men towards a Black Maria. *Click!*

The passengers from the bus, thirty or more, milled about the street as if dazed, chatting with one another.

"Hi, Craig! Get anything good?" It was Tom Buckley, another freelance photographer a couple of years older than Craig, and friendly, though Craig considered him competition.

Craig didn't want to ask if Tom had got a shot of the guy with the gun, because Craig had missed this shot,

43

which might have been possible at exactly the time he had had to dash to a men's room. "Dunno till they come out!" Craig replied cheerfully. He moved closer to the police wagon, and took a picture of the two young men, who looked about twenty, as they were urged into the back of the wagon. Tom Buckley was also snapping. One or maybe even two of Tom's photos would make it in the afternoon edition of the *Evening Star*, Craig was thinking. Craig shot up the rest of his roll, aiming at any place — at a cop reassuring an elderly woman, at a girl rushing from a narrow passageway into Main Street where the bus was, and being greeted by a man and woman who might have been her parents.

Then Craig went home to develop his roll. He lived with his parents in the home where he had been born, a two-storey frame house in a modest residential area. Craig had turned his bathroom — itself an adjunct to the house when he had been fifteen — into his darkroom. All his pictures looked dull as could be, worse than he had expected. No action in them, apart from a cluttered street scene of people looking bewildered. Still, Craig presented them at the office of Kyanduck's *Evening Star* about half past noon, imagining that Tom Buckley had got there a few minutes earlier and with better photos.

Ed Simmons bent his balding head over Craig's ten photographs. The big messy room held seven people at their desks, and there was the usual clatter of type-writers.

"Got there a little late," Craig murmured apologetically, not caring if Ed heard him or not.

"Hey! You got Lizzie Davis? With her *folks*! — Hey, Craig, this one is great!" Ed Simmons looked up at Craig through horn-rimmed glasses. "We'll use this one. Just the moment *after* — running out of that alley! Beautiful!"

"Didn't know her name," Craig said, and wondered why Ed was so excited.

Ed showed the photo to a man at another desk. Others

gathered to look at the picture, which was of a girl of twenty or younger, with long dark hair, her white blouse partly pulled out of her skirt top, looking anxious as she rushed forward towards a man and woman approaching her from Main Street.

"This is the girl who was nearly raped. Or maybe she even was," Ed Simmons said to Craig. "Didn't you know that?"

Craig certainly hadn't heard. Raped by whom, he wondered, then the snatches of conversation that he heard enlightened him. The third hold-up boy, who was still at large, had dragged Lizzie Davis off the bus and into an alley and threatened to stick a knife in her throat, or to rape her, unless she kept her mouth shut when the police came up the alley. The police hadn't come up that alley. In the picture, Lizzie's father, in a pale business suit and straw hat, was just about to touch his daughter's shoulder, while her mother on the right in the picture rushed towards the girl with both arms spread.

Now he saw, in the upside-down photo on Ed's desk, that the girl's eyes were squeezed shut with horror or fear, and her mouth open as if she were crying or gasping for breath.

"Was she raped?" Craig asked.

The reply he got was vague, the implication being that the girl wasn't telling. So Craig's photo appeared on page two of the Kyanduck *Evening Star* that day, and one by Tom Buckley of a local cop with two of the hold-up boys on the front page. Both photographs had a two-column spread.

Craig pointed out the photo to his parents that night at the supper table. Craig didn't make it every day, or even every week, a photo in the *Evening Star* or the Kyanduck *Morning News*. His father knew Ernest Davis, the girl's father, who was an old customer at Dullop's Hardware, where Craig's father was manager.

Craig received thirty dollars for his picture, which was

the going rate for local photographs, no matter what they were, and Craig mentioned this, with modest pride, to his girlfriend Constance O'Leary who was called Clancy. Craig, twenty-two and ruggedly handsome, had three or four girlfriends, but Clancy was his current favourite. She had curly reddish-blond hair, a marvellous figure, a sense of humour, and she loved to dance.

"You're the greatest," Clancy said, at that moment diving into her first hamburger at the Plainsman Café, just outside of town, where the juke box boomed.

Craig smiled, pleased, "Human interest. That's what Ed Simmons said my photo had."

And Craig didn't think any more about that picture of Lizzie Davis until ten days later, when on one of his visits to the *Evening Star* office with a batch of new photographs, Ed Simmons told Craig that the *New York Times* had telexed, wanting to use Craig's photograph in a series of articles about crime in America.

'You'd better be pleased, Craig."

"With a credit?" Craig was nearly speechless with surprise.

'Well, natch. — Now let's see what you've got here." Ed looked over Craig's offerings: three photos of the Kyanduck Boy Scouts' annual picnic at Kyanduck Park, and three of current weddings. Ed showed no visible interest. Tom Buckley had probably topped him on these events, Craig was thinking. "I'll look 'em over again. Thanks, Craig."

That was Ed's phrase when he wasn't going to buy anything.

Still, Craig's dazed smile at the news about the *New York Times* lingered on his face as he left the office. He'd never yet had a photo in the *New York Times*! What was so great about that picture?

Craig found out some five days later. His photograph was one of three in the first of a three-part series of articles in the *New York Times* called "Crime in America's Streets". His photograph had been cleverly cut to show it to better advantage, Craig noticed. The text beneath said:

> A young woman in a small town in Wyoming rushes towards her parents, seconds after being held hostage under threat of rape by one of a three-man armed hold-up team who robbed bus passengers in mid-morning.

And there was his name in tiny letters at one side of the picture: Craig Rollins.

When Craig showed the article to his parents that evening, he saw real joy and surprise in their faces. Their son with his work in the *New York Times*!

"That girl Lizzie's a changed girl, you know, Mart?" Craig's father addressed his mother.

"Yes, I've heard," said his mother. "Edna Schwartz was talking about Lizzie just yesterday. Told me Lizzie's broken off her engagement. You know, she was supposed to get married in late June, Craig."

Craig hadn't known. "Was she really raped?" he asked, as if his parents might know the truth, as indeed they might, because his mother worked behind the counter of Odds and Ends, a shop that sold dry goods and buttons, and his mother chatted with nearly every woman of the town, and his father certainly saw a lot of people in the hardware store.

"She's saying so," his mother replied in a whisper. "At least she's hinting at it. And nobody knows if she broke off her engagement or her boyfriend did. What's his name, dear? Peter Walsh?"

"*Paul* Walsh," corrected his father. "You know, the Walshes up on Rockland Heights," his father added to Craig.

Craig didn't know the Walshes, but he knew Rockland Heights, a neighbourhood famous for fine houses and the well-to-do minority of the populace of Kyanduck. Snobs, he thought, to break an engagement these days because a girl's virginity might have been lost. Like prehistoric times!

Craig looked with interest at the two following articles in the *New York Times*, which he was able to see daily at the office of the *Evening Star*. The series was about car thefts, robberies of apartments, muggings, plus the efforts of the police in big cities to control such crime, of course, but also about the danger of its increasing, now that unemployment was spreading among the under twenty-fives. A couple of photographs Craig admired very much: one a night-shot of a teenager picking the lock of a Chinese laundry; another of a mugging in the South Bronx, in which an elderly man had been flung to the ground, his grocery bag spilled beside him, while a boy in shorts and sneakers was diving into the inside pocket of the man's jacket. Now these were damned good photographs! Why had they liked his so much, Craig wondered. Because Lizzie Davis's face was pretty? Or because she really had been raped?

"You know any more details about this Lizzie Davis thing?" Craig asked Clancy on one of their dates.

"What do you mean, details? I know she broke her engagement with the Walsh boy. And she *says* she was raped."

"That's what I mean," said Craig. "Amazing."

"What is?"

"That a guy running away from a hold-up pushes a girl into an alley and rapes her — in maybe five minutes or less. I just don't believe it."

"Oh, you don't."

"No."

"Well, she says so. I heard through somebody — yes, Josie MacDougal, that a journalist came to Lizzie's house to interview her about it."

Craig frowned. "Journalist from here? Why didn't you tell me?"

"From Chicago, I think. And anyway, I only heard about it when it was all over. Couple of weeks ago, after the *New York Times* thing. Anyway, Lizzie doesn't go out much any more, so I've heard. Stays at home. She's like a psycho."

"Wha-at?" said Craig. "You mean she's gone nuts — at *home?*" At the same time, Craig was thinking that another photo or two of Lizzie Davis might be a good idea, saleable.

"I don't mean *nuts*," Clancy said, her freckled face sobering with thought for a moment. "Just that she's not interested in any kind of social life any more. She's become sort of a *reck*-loose."

That was a bit of a puzzle to Craig Rollins, but then he didn't understand girls completely and didn't really want to. He didn't believe Lizzie Davis had been raped, though she might well have been threatened with it. Maybe she was putting on an act, breaking her engagement with the Walsh fellow because she didn't really want to marry him.

The day after that evening, part of which Clancy had spent with him in his room at home, Craig received a letter that had been forwarded to him by the *Evening Star*. His 'excellent photograph' of June 10th, reprinted in the *New York Times*, had won the year's Pulitzer Prize for newspaper photography.

Craig, with lips parted in disbelief, looked at the letterhead again. It looked authentic with the committee's name, New York address and all that, but was somebody pulling his leg? The signature at the bottom was that of Jerome A. Weidmuller, Chairman of Selections Committee. The last paragraph expressed the pleasure and congratulations of the Committee, and stated that they would be in touch in regard to bestowing an award of a thousand dollars plus a citation.

Craig was afraid to mention the Pulitzer letter to his parents. It might be a joke.

But the next day, a man who said he was the secretary of Mr Weidmuller telephoned Craig at home. He said he had got Craig's telephone number from the *Evening Star*'s office. Craig was cordially invited to a dinner to be given in New York in a few days, and he would receive an invitation by post. His return air fare would be paid, plus hotel expenses in New York for one or two nights, as he preferred. "Congratulations, Mr Rollins," said the voice as it signed off.

If this was a joke, it was pretty convincing, Craig thought. A bit dazed, he crumpled up the wet photograph he had been developing in his darkroom, and went to the fridge for a beer to celebrate.

When an express letter arrived that same day at 6 pm, Craig knew that the Pulitzer Prize affair was real. The air ticket was in the envelope, with the proviso that if he could not keep the date six days thence, he would notify the Committee and return the ticket. His hotel was booked, with dates, and the letter assured him that all expenses would be paid by the Committee.

"What was that?" asked his mother, who was preparing supper in the kitchen.

Craig had walked into the kitchen with the letter in his hand. "Well, Ma — I wasn't sure it was true till now. I won the Pulitzer for my photo of Lizzie Davis."

"The Pulitzer?" said his father. "The Pulitzer Prize? Didn't know there was one for photography."

Craig attended the dinner in New York. For a few seconds Craig was visible on the TV screen, his parents told him, among other Pulitzer Prize winners for the novel, journalism, drama and so on.

After that, Craig's telephone began to ring. The Kyanduck *Evening Star* passed on callers and messages to Craig. Journalists wanted to interview him. A boy of nineteen wrote to him care of the *Evening Star*, asking if he gave photography lessons. This letter made Craig smile, because he had never had any lessons himself, apart from a course in high school, a course he had dropped after a month, because the work had become too complicated. A university in California that Craig had never heard of wanted him to come and give a lecture, travel expenses paid, plus fee of $300. A Philadelphia school of journalism invited him to make a speech of about forty-five minutes, and offered a fee of $500. Craig intended to write both schools a polite letter of refusal, on the grounds that he had never made a speech in his life and that the idea terrified him. But after a good dinner at home, and mentioning these invitations to his parents, and his parents' saying in their old-fashioned way, "Sure you can, Craig, if you just put your mind to it. Be friendly! People just want to see you and meet you now," Craig decided to accept the California offer.

This affair went off amazingly well. One of the audience asked a question, after that, Craig went rolling along, talking in his own free style about hanging around the office of the Kyanduck *Evening Star* and the town police station, hoping for a good photogenic story to break, hoping even for a fire, though it wasn't maybe very nice to hope for a fire that might hurt people. And then — *this* had happened, the great day when the bus had been held up in his home town, a minor tragedy by world standards, but upsetting for some thirty or forty ordinary citizens, disastrous for the young girl called Lizzie Davis, who had intended to marry in a few days, but whose life had been shattered, maybe ruined, by *crime in the streets*. Craig hammered the crime angle, because the articles on crime in the streets had launched his photograph. Never in the speeches that followed, or in his maiden speech in California, did he say that he had given up on that famous day, that he had thought the action was over when he had taken that photograph. Never would he say, though he tried to make his speeches as amusing as possible, that he had missed the action, because he had had to run to a toilet at the crucial instant when the hold-up man had been disarmed.

After four speeches, Craig had got the hang of it. And the fees were great. He began to insist on $1,000 plus expenses. He flew to Atlanta, Tucson, Houston and Chicago. Meanwhile, he had job offers. Would he care to join the staff of the Philadelphia *Monitor* at $40,000 a year? Craig wrote a stalling, polite answer to this job offer. He sensed that the lecture circuit could dry up. A tiny town in Atlanta wanted him, but for $100, and Craig had no intention of accepting that. He would take the highest salary offer, he thought, when he had exhausted the lecture invitations.

With the extra money from his speeches, Craig Rollins was a changed young man. He was able to buy more clothes, and discovered that he had a taste for quality in clothes and also in food. He acquired a new Japanese camera that could do more things than his old ones, which were second-hand anyway. He still had Clancy as his main girlfriend, but he had met a girl called Sue in Houston who seemed to like him a lot, and who had the money to fly to meet him sometimes in a town where he was making a speech. A pretty girl beside him enhanced his image, Craig had noticed.

Craig also went to a good barber now, his hair was not so short, and the barber fluffed it out in a style that Craig might have called sissy a few months ago, though no one could possibly have called Craig or his face sissy. He had the head and neck of a line-hitter, a tackle, which he had been on the high school football team and in his first year at Greeves College, Wyoming. Craig's grades would have got him kicked out of almost any college, he knew, but Greeves had been willing to keep him on, because of his football prowess. The coach had thought he might make All-American, but Craig had quit college after a month in sophomore year, out of sheer boredom with the scholastic part of it. Now, however, still in top physical form, Craig felt pleased with himself. He wrote to the *Monitor* saying that he had had a better offer from a California paper, but if the *Monitor* could raise their offer to $50,000, Craig would accept, because he preferred the east coast.

"Have you been to see Lizzie at all?" Clancy asked Craig.

"Lizzie — Davis? No, why should I?"

"Just thought it might be nice. She did bring you a lot of luck, and it seems she's so sad."

Craig knew Lizzie was sad, because a couple of newspapers had interviewed her. Kyanduck's *Evening Star* had, of course, in a discreet little piece with a picture of Lizzie in her family's house.

So Craig telephoned the Davis residence one day around 5 pm. A woman answered, sounding as if she might be Lizzie's mother. Craig identified himself and asked if he could speak with Lizzie.

"Well, I don't know. I'll have to ask her. She's just back from a little trip. Hold on a minute. — *Lizzie?*"

While he waited, Craig reflected that he might, with Lizzie's agreement, take a few more pictures of her.

Lizzie came on, with a sad voice. But she agreed to see him, when Craig proposed to come over in half an hour and stay just a few minutes.

Craig got into his car and picked up a bouquet of flowers at a shop on the way. He wore his camera on a strap around his neck, as if — today, anyway — his camera were as much a part of his dress as his woollen muffler.

Lizzie opened the door for him. She still had long dark hair that hung in gentle waves to below her shoulders. "Oh, thank you. That's very sweet of you," she said, accepting his gladioli. "I'll get a vase for these. Sit down."

Craig sat down in the rather swank living room. The Davises had a lot more money than his family. Lizzie came back, and set the vase in the centre of the coffee table between them.

Then she proceeded to tell him about her broken engagement, five months ago now, and how quiet her life had been since.

"In a way, I've lost my self-confidence — my self-respect. No use trying to gain it back," Lizzie said. "That was shattering — that day."

53

How had they got here so quickly, Craig wondered. Lizzie was talking to him as if he were interviewing her, though he hadn't asked her a single question.

"Just this afternoon — you won't believe it — I was being photographed in Cheyenne — for a perfume ad. I've become a photographer's model — maybe because I want to get the phobia of photographs out of my soul. Maybe I'm succeeding, I don't know."

Craig was wordless for a moment. "You mean — my picture embarrassed you so much? I'm sorry."

"Not the picture so much. What *happened*," Lizzie replied, lifting her round, dark eyes to his. "Well, it wasn't *your* fault, and the picture brought you a huge success, I know. It ruined my engagement, but — Well, in a way, I'm lucky too, because there's a market for a sad-dog face like mine. I can see that. The other day I even posed for an ad for men's clothing, you won't believe it, but I was supposed to be the girl with the knowing eyes — for clothing, that is — whose face would brighten up, if the fellow I liked just wore good-looking clothes, see? Very complicated, but it really came off. If I had the photo I'd show you, but the ad isn't even out yet."

Craig saw Lizzie's face brighten briefly, when she described the way the girl's face would brighten, if her boyfriend only wore good clothes. Then an instant later, Lizzie's glum expression was back, as if it were a garment she wore for the public. Craig moistened his lips. "And — your fiancé? I mean — I know you broke it off a few months back. I was thinking maybe you'd both get together again."

Lizzie's sadness deepened. "No. No, indeed. I felt as if — I'd never want to live with a man as long as I live. Still do feel that way."

But Lizzie was hardly nineteen as yet, Craig was thinking, though he kept silent. The funny idea came just then: he didn't believe Lizzie. What if she were faking this whole thing? Lying even about having been raped? What if she hadn't liked her boyfriend much anyway, and hadn't minded breaking off their engagement? "I'm sure your fiancé is sad too," Craig said solemnly.

"Oh, seems to be. That's true," Lizzie replied. "But I can't help that." She sighed.

"Would you mind if I took a couple of shots of you now?"

Lizzie lifted her eyes to his again. Her eyes were alert, wary, yet interested. "Whatever for? — Well, not while I'm in these shoes, I hope," she added with a quick smile. She was in house-shoes, but otherwise very smartly dressed in a hand-knitted beige sweater and dark blue skirt, with a gold chain around her neck.

"Don't have to take the feet," Craig said, standing now, aiming his camera. He could sell three or four photos to New York and Philadelphia newspapers, he was sure, if he suggested that a staff writer write a few lines about her quiet life five months after the rape. *Click!* A rape that Craig was more and more sure never took place. *Click! — Click!* "Look a bit to your left. — That's good! Hold it!" *Click!*

Five minutes later, as he was taking his leave, Craig said, "I sure appreciate your letting me snap you again, Lizzie. And would you mind if I found a writer to do a little piece on you? N-not for the local paper," Craig hastened to add. "For the big papers east. Maybe west too. Might help your fashion modelwork, mightn't it?"

"That's true." She was plainly reflecting on this, blinking her sad eyes. "It's funny, you know, that *day* bringing you all that success and prizes and everything, and *me* — just ruining my life. Nearly."

Craig nodded. "That's a great angle for the writer." He smiled. "'Bye, Lizzie. I'll be in touch soon."

"Let me see the photos first, would you? I want to make the choice."

That very evening, Craig telephoned Richard Prescott, a journalist of the *Monitor*, and gave him his ideas, which had developed a bit since he had seen Lizzie. He would be the puzzled, guilt-ridden, small town photographer

55

who had contributed to, even caused the upset of a young woman's life.

"She really was raped?" asked Prescott. "I remember the story and your photo, of course, but I thought she'd just been scared. The boy they caught always denied it, you know."

Never mind, Craig started to say, but instead he replied, "She certainly implied she was. Girls never want to say it flat out, y'know. But you get my angle, that *I'm* the one upset now, because I —" Craig squeezed his eyes shut, thinking hard. "Because I captured in a split second that expression of a girl who's just been — assaulted. You know?"

"Assaulted. Yeah, might work fine."

"In fact, the article should be as much about me as her."

Prescott said he would get in touch soon, because he had another assignment on the west coast, and might be able to squeeze Wyoming in.

Craig then rang up Tom Buckley, who agreed at once to take some pictures of Craig. Craig reminded Tom that Tom would get credit lines in some big newspapers, if he did the job. Tom was still friendly with Craig, and had never shown the least jealousy of Craig's success.

Tom Buckley came over the next morning to photograph Craig in his modest darkroom at home, and at his worktable, brooding over a print of the now famous "Crime in America's Streets" photo of Lizzie Davis. In this shot, Craig held the photograph at an angle at which it was recognizable, and in his other hand he held his head in the manner of a man with a terrible headache, or tortured by guilt. Tom chuckled a little as he snapped this one. "Good angle, yeah, your feeling sorry for the girl. She's doing fine, I heard, with her modelling work."

Craig straightened up. "But I do feel sorry for her. Sorry about her shame and all that stuff. She sure called her marriage off."

"She wasn't mad about that guy. And he wasn't about

her. One of these things the parents were keen on, y'know? — Everybody in town knows that. You haven't been paying much attention to town gossip, Craig old boy. Too busy with your big-town newspapers lately." Tom smiled good-naturedly.

In a curious way, Craig realized that he had to hold on to his conviction that Lizzie Davis's life had been altered, ruined — or he couldn't make a success of the article-plus-photos that he had in mind. "You think she's a phoney?" Craig asked in a soft, almost frightened voice.

"Phoney?" Tom was putting away his camera. "Sure. Little bit. Not worth much thought, is it? All the public wants is a sensational photo — someone killing themselves jumping off a building, somebody else getting shot. The hell with who's to blame for it, just give the public the action. The sex angle in your Lizzie picture gave it its kick, y'know? Who cares if she's telling the truth or not? — I don't believe for a minute she was raped."

That conversation gave Craig something to chew on after Tom Buckley had departed. Craig was sure Tom was right. Tom was a bright fellow. The public wanted pictures of buildings bombed high in the air, a wrecked car with a body in it, or bodies lying on pavements. *Action*. Even the story wasn't terribly important, if the picture was eye-catching. Now Craig struggled like a drowning person to hang on to the Lizzie story, that she *had* been raped and had broken her engagement because of the rape. Craig knew he would have to talk to Richard Prescott as if he believed what he was saying.

Craig did. He prepared himself as if he were an actor. He emoted. He struck his forehead a couple of times, grimaced, and a genuine tear came to support him, though Prescott had a tape-recorder and not a camera, unfortunately.

". . . and then the awful moment — moments — when I realized that in my last-minute shot that day, I'd caught the nineteen-year-old girl and her anxious parents

at maybe the most dramatic moment of their lives." Craig was giving this monologue in his parents' living room, both his parents being out at their respective jobs. Prescott had a few questions jotted down in his notebook, but Craig was going along well enough on his own. "And just after that," Craig continued, "the terrific, unbelievable acclaim that my photo got! Reproduced in the *New York Times*, and then winning the Pulitzer Prize! It really didn't seem fair. It made me rethink my whole life. I thought about fate, money, fame. I even thought about God," Craig said with earnestness, and a thrill passed over him. He believed, he knew now, that he was being sincere, and he wanted to look Prescott straight in the eyes. "I began to ask myself — "

Prescott at that moment stuck a cigarette in his mouth, reached for his lighter, and stared at the little black machine that was recording all this.

"— what I'd done to deserve all this, when the young girl — Well, she didn't get anything from it except suffering and shame. I began to ask myself if there was a God, and if so was he a just God? Did I have to do something in return for my good luck either to him or to —I mean — maybe to the human race? I began —"

"End of tape, sorry," Prescott interrupted. "In fact, this might be enough. You've talked through two tapes."

For a moment, Craig felt cut off, then glad it was over.

Prescott gave a laugh. "That bit about religion at the end. You thinking of writing a book, maybe? Might sell."

Craig didn't reply. He had decided in the last seconds that he didn't like Prescott. He had met Prescott only once before, in the *Monitor*'s office, knew he was highly thought of, but now Craig didn't like him.

However, the article that Prescott wrote which appeared ten days later in the *Monitor* was top-notch. Craig's words came out hardly changed, and they rang true, in Craig's opinion. In Tom Buckley's photos, Craig looked serious in one, agonized in the other. An excellent,

if only one, picture of Lizzie Davis showed her seated in an armchair in her house, holding what the caption stated was a print of the photograph that had changed her life. Lizzie looked hopeful, modest and pretty, as she stared the camera straight in its eye.

The article brought Craig a few more invitations to lecture, one from a prestigious university in the east, which he accepted. He wrote to the *Monitor* saying that for the next few months he expected to be busy on his own, and so could not at once say yes to the staff photographer's job they had offered, even with the augmented salary to which they had agreed. Craig had higher aspirations: he was going to write a book about it all. When he thought of Fate's part in it, God's part, his brain seemed to expand and to take wings of fancy. He might call his book *Fate Took the Picture*, or maybe *The Lens and the Soul*. The word *conscience* in the title might be a bit heavy. Craig gave a few more talks, and managed easily to bring his religious thoughts and pangs of conscience into his text. "Life is not fair sometimes — and it troubles me," he would say to an awed or at least respectfully listening audience. "Here *I* am, lauded by so many, recipient of honours — whereas the poor girl victim, Lizzie, languishes . . ."

Craig's book *Two Battles: The Story of a Photographer and a Girl* appeared four months later, after a rushed printing. The book was ghosted by a bright twenty-two-year-old journalist from Houston named Phil Spark, who was not given credit on the title page. *Two Battles* sold about twenty thousand copies in its first six months, thanks to aggressive publicity by its New York publisher and to a good photo of Lizzie Davis on the back of the jacket. This meant that the sales more than covered Craig's advance, so Craig was going to have more money in his pocket due to royalties. He and Clancy got married, and moved into a house with a mortgage.

He had sent half a dozen copies of *Two Battles* to Lizzie Davis, of course, and in due time she had replied with a formal note of thanks for his having told "her story". But she showed no sign of wanting to see Craig again, and he didn't particularly want to see her again, either. She and Craig had met briefly with the ghost writer to get some background in regard to Lizzie's schooldays in Kyanduck.

Craig appeared on a few religious programmes on TV, which did his book a world of good, and he dutifully answered almost all his fan mail — though some of it was pretty stupid, from teen-agers asking how they could start out "being a newspaper photographer". Still, contact with the public gave Craig the feeling that he was making new friends everywhere, that America was not merely a big playground, but a friendly and receptive one, which conflicted a bit with his playing the reflective and publicity-shy cameraman. Craig eased himself over this little bump in the road by convincing himself that he had discovered another métier: exploring God and his own conscience. This seemed to Craig an endless path to greater things. Craig decided to tour America with Clancy in his new compact station wagon, and to photograph poor families in Detroit and Boston, maybe some in Texas too; and fires, of course, in case he encountered any; rape and mugging victims the same; street urchins of wherever; sad-faced animals in zoos. He would make himself famous as the photographer compelled to photograph the seamier side of life.

He envisaged a book with a few lines under each photograph which would reflect his personal conflict in regard to God and justice. Craig Rollins was convinced of his own conviction, and that was what counted. Plus the belief, of course, that such a book would sell. Hadn't he proved by *Two Battles* that such a book would sell?

Chris's Last Party

Among the six or eight letters waiting for Simon Hatton in his hotel suite, he noticed a telegram and opened that first. The sender was Carl, a name that didn't ring a definite bell.

CHRIS NEAR THE END! WE ARE ALL HERE EXCEPT YOU. ELEVEN OF US. PLEASE COME DONT HESITATE. KNOW YOU ARE WORKING BUT THIS IS IMPORTANT. PHONE 01–984–9322 AND CONFIRM. CHRIS WONT BUDGE WITHOUT YOU! YOUR OLD PAL CARL.

Carl Parker, of course, and not an old pal, rather an acquaintance, even a rival once. But Christopher Wells on the brink of dying? It seemed incredible, but the old boy was ninety at least — no, ninety-four. And it was emphysema, of course. Chris had been living with an oxygen gadget in his bedroom for the last decade, Simon knew, inhaling from it when he needed it, trying not to inhale the mild cigars the doctor had yielded to and the occasional cigarette that Chris had never totally abandoned. The telegram had come from Zurich. Chris had a chalet with generous grounds near Zurich, and Simon had been there once, the last time he'd seen Chris, perhaps four years ago. Chris had spent half the time in a wheelchair, and what must he be like now? But Simon could imagine: Chris would be throwing a party, keeping his butler busy with champagne, his cook with gourmet dishes at all hours. Chris loved his protégés, and he wouldn't die without saying goodbye to all of them in person, including Simon, the twelfth (what a coincidence) of the disciples.

Simon felt suddenly afraid, and it occurred to him that he could ring Zurich and say he ought not to come, because as long as he didn't show up, Chris might go on living, not to mention that Simon was giving eight performances a week now in *William* in New York.

Simon jumped at a knock on his door. "Yes? Come in." He knew it was his champagne arriving.

"Good evening, sir," said the white-jacketed waiter. He bore a tray with a quarter-bottle of champagne and a few English biscuits of a non-sweet variety. "Am I too early, sir?"

"No, no, just right." Simon knew it was six or five past, but he glanced at his wristwatch anyway (it was four past six), then removed his overcoat and noticed that a drop of moisture fell from it. It was snowing today. His fair, rather crinkly hair was damp too.

Johnny took his coat before Simon realized it, and hung it in a wardrobe. "You'd like to be called as usual, sir, seven-twenty?"

"Y-yes." Seven-twenty for a curtain rise at eight-forty. Simon always took a nap at this hour until the hotel switchboard awakened him, though he had his own travel clock's alarm set too. Yesterday being Monday, he'd had the day off and gone to Connecticut to visit friends. He'd been fetched late Sunday night after the show and driven up to Connecticut in his host's car with a driver. Now Simon felt tired, though it hadn't been a strenuous holiday. Was he starting to feel old at forty-nine? Awful age, forty-nine, because the next number was fifty. No longer middle-aged, that number, but elderly, definitely.

He slipped out of his shoes and walked back to the sitting-room table for the rest of his letters. He took off his jacket, trousers and shirt and got into bed. Two letters were fan mail, he saw from the strange names on the return addresses, and one letter had a red EXPRES–EIL-

SENDUNG stamp on its front. He didn't recognize this hand either, but it was from Zurich. He opened this, bracing himself for further grim information about Chris. The letter was in longhand and signed Carl again.

Dec. 7, 19—

Dear Simon,

Chris took a turn for the worse about a week ago, and it really seems it is going to be the end. For one thing, he has summoned all his old what shall I call us — students? — to him. He wrote you to California, where he later realized you weren't, because of the N.Y. show. (Must congratulate you on *William*, by the way.) There are nine of us now at High-Ho, two due tomorrow, Freddy Detweiler and Richard Cook. Plenty of room here and you mustn't think it's a wake. Chris looks pretty well for a few hours a day when he's up entertaining us. The rest of the time he's in bed, but loves us to come in and talk with him round the clock!

So please come because for Chris there's something strange about your not being here. Use your understudy for a couple of days, but hurry, please.

Chris phoned me nearly a month ago and said he was sure he would die in December, end of year and a life and so on. So he said come on the first of December or as soon after as pos. and "I won't hold you up long." Isn't that typical of Chris? . . .

Yes, Simon understood, but his mind as he laid the letter aside and sank into his pillow was disturbed and undecided. He couldn't have found a word or words to describe how he felt. Shocked, and on guard too. It was as if Chris had given him a sharp poke in the ribs to remind Simon that Chris still existed. Chris hadn't always been kind or even fair. Or was that true? No, the kindness, the concern of Chris did outweigh the rest. Chris had been selfish, demanding of attention, but

Simon couldn't honestly tell himself that Chris had ever been heartless, or had ever let him down. And he had told Simon that he would be a fine actor, if he did this and that, if he disciplined himself, if he studied the technique of so-and-so. Chris was a director, if he could be called anything, and had three or four famous productions to his credit, but he had always had money from his family, and he dabbled, didn't have to work all the time.

But it was the word of praise in the ears of twenty-year-old Simon Hatton that had inspired him, coming as it had from a man over sixty, who had troubled to come backstage to meet him, when he had been acting with a summer theatre group in Stockbridge, Massachusetts. When Simon recalled this, his heart seemed to tumble. It was Christopher Wells' enthusiasm that had lighted his own fire. Could he ever have made it without Chris? Christopher Wells had been a silly, ageing dandy, in a way, wearing odd clothes to attract eyes in New York or London restaurants and theatres. Chris had taken Simon on his first trip to Europe.

For a few seconds, Simon felt a mixture of resentment, pride, and independence. Then came the memory of his happiness in those first weeks with Chris. He had felt bewildered, flattered, and as if he were walking on air, different from being in love, because the feeling was so much bound up with his work, yet like it too. Chris had cracked the whip at him, as if he were a circus dog, Simon remembered quite well.

At this recollection, Simon got up and walked around his bedroom, deliberately relaxed his shoulders, and did not take a cigarette that he was tempted to take. He went back to his bed and lay face down and closed his eyes. In forty-five minutes he had to be ready for his taxi downstairs, and he must do his job tonight. He must entertain. The audience would be silent and sad at the end. It was a serious and sad play, *William*.

And he knew he would get a ticket to fly to Zurich,

maybe not tonight but tomorrow, after he had arranged
for his understudy Russell Johnson to take over for
him.

Fantasy! *William* was fantasy, so was acting — all
make-believe. After the others in the cast, Simon took
one curtain bow, and not two. He was smiling, but a few
women in the audience, and men too, pushed hand-
kerchiefs against their lids. Simon closed his own wet eyes,
and walked off with a straight back.

Simon took off for Zurich the next morning. He had
spoken with his understudy who had been visibly elated
by the chance to replace him for a few days, as Simon
had thought he might be. Simon had played well last
night. He had recalled Chris's words: "It's a craft, it's
not magic — but the audience helps to inspire you, of
course. You could say the audience makes the magic."
Simon could hear Chris's voice saying, under varying
circumstances, "Of *course*" which was reassuring when
you'd already resolved to do something, and reassuring
also when Chris was proposing something like jumping
off a cliff without a parachute. "Of *course* — you can
make it. What's talent for? You've got it. It's like money
in the bank. Use it, my boy." And there was a couplet
from William Blake that Chris used to say:

> If the Sun and Moon should doubt,
> They'd immediately go out.

He felt strange, as if he were going to meet his own
death. What nonsense! He was in good form, and at
Chris's house there was not only fresh air but mineral
water, paths to hike on, a tennis court that had been
there when Chris bought the land, but which Chris had
never used. It was going to be something, renewing old
acquaintances such as Carl Parker, Peter de Molnay,
some phoney and some not, some maybe balding and
plump. But all successful, like himself. Simon wasn't in
close touch with any. At Christmas, he'd receive an

unexpected card from one or two, just as he on some impulse would send a Christmas card to one or two. They all had one thing in common, Chris Wells who had discovered or befriended or encouraged them all, touched them when they were young with a magic finger, like God giving life to Adam. The image of Michaelangelo's ceiling fresco flashed for an instant into Simon's mind's eye, and he flinched at the triteness of it.

Simon had telephoned High-Ho and told someone, who had sounded like a servant, at what time he would be arriving in Zurich. He had expected Peter or Carl at the airport, but he saw no identifiable faces among the group of waiting people, and then a card with HATTON written on it caught his eye. It was held by a stranger, a sturdy, dark-haired man.

Simon nodded. "Hatton, yes. Good evening."

"Good evening, sir," said the man with a German accent. "Is this all your luggage?" The man took it from Simon's grasp. "The car is just this way, sir. Please."

The air was crisp, different. Simon sank into the back seat of a large car, and they moved off. "And how is — Mr Wells?"

"Y-yes, sir. He is doing quite well. But he must rest much of the time."

Simon gave up asking anything more. They rolled on into darkness, and after an hour's drive Simon sensed the black mountains rising around them, hiding the glints of the stars, though the car did not seem to be climbing. Finally they drove between tall iron gates and tree-shaded houselights came into view. Simon braced himself. A tall, slender figure came to meet the car.

"Simon! Is that you?"

This was Peter de Molnay, who opened the door before the driver could. Peter and Simon shook hands firmly — they had known each other very well indeed fifteen years or so ago, but it occurred to Simon that they might as well be strangers now, polite, with polite smiles.

"Chris is in bed now — but still awake," Peter said.

It was midnight, but the eleven guests or visitors were all up, spread between the spacious living-room where a fire blazed and the arch-doored kitchen which was now fully lighted and where no doubt a chef was still working.

"Hello, Simon! Richard — Richard Cook. Remember?" Awkwardly, Richard drew back his hand and gave Simon an embrace with one arm. Richard had quite a belly and was bald on top, grey at the sides — but of course there were roles for just such types, and Simon knew Richard kept busy.

"Simon! Welcome!"

"Hey! There's *Simon*! — We knew you'd make it!" Carl Parker, blondish and slender still, the eternal juvenile, clasped Simon's hand.

Several people spoke to him at the same time. Questions. Was he tired? How long could he stay? The atmosphere was party-like. Simon felt not tired but nervous. He wanted to see Chris, and said so.

"Oh, he wants to see *you*, Simon! Go up!"

Simon followed the dark-haired man who carried his suitcase up to his room.

"I hope this will be all right, sir. You have it to yourself. This room has not a private bath but . . ."

Simon half-listened as the man (whose name was Marcus, Simon had learned downstairs) explained that there was a bathroom three doors down the hall on the left. "May I see Chris — Mr Wells?"

"Just a minute, sir." He went out.

Simon unlatched his suitcase lid, but did not open it. Then he stood at attention facing the door, as if Marcus would appear at any second with a military order, summoning him into Chris's presence. This was exactly what happened.

"You may come in now, sir."

Simon marched forward, turned left, and was escorted down the hall to a room on the right on whose door Marcus rapped gently.

"Yes, Marcus. Come in."

Simon heard the age in Chris's voice and felt a painful ache, though he realized he wasn't young either, and what would Chris think of him? Simon tripped on the threshold — not being used to raised thresholds — and laughed.

So did Chris. "Ha-ha! Splendid entrance! Bless you, Simon — for coming. Give us a kiss! — Um-m!"

Blinded with tears, Simon bent and kissed a half-pale, half-pink cheek. He was aware of a mountainous form under a white sheet and a pink blanket. The room was overheated. Simon stood back and blinked. "You're —"

"I'm looking bloody awful, don't say it, but I'll be up in a few minutes — and looking a bit better." Chris's thin blonde hair was even thinner, and limp, the face beneath it broader and flabbier than Simon could have imagined. My God, thought Simon, this is really death! Was Chris taking cortisone too? His blue eyes, once so bright and quick, seemed to be faking a brightness by a deliberate tightening at the corners. "I've read your reviews, Simon — of *William*, I keep up, y'know. Must congratulate you. Where's your hand?"

Simon gave his right hand again. His hand was colder than Chris's just now. Simon glanced again at the shiny cylinder at the end of the bed, which suggested a fire extinguisher.

"All goes well, doesn't it, Simon? I'm proud of you. I saw your film *Barter* — last year. You were excellent all the way through. Supporting actor — who really carried the cast."

"Yes, well —" Simon had seldom heard such praise from Chris, not even when he had been twenty-four, with his first good part in a Bernard Shaw play. What was its name?

"Wash your hands and face, go and have a nice drink, and I'll be down in five minutes. We've got a round-the-clock party going — going to see me out. Ask August to come up, would you? He's maybe — near the kitchen."

70

Simon watched Chris stirring under all the covers, perhaps trying to get out of bed, and Simon felt tongue-tied about asking if Chris wanted any help.

"Right away, Chris!" Simon made for the door.

Less than five minutes later, Simon was standing with a heavy glass of scotch in his hand, his back to the fire-place, Peter and Richard on either side of him, all chattering about nothing. Simon felt, yet of course something, because each knew something about the careers of the others, that Peter had been working in Hollywood for a year or two, that Richard had with difficulty, being American, played in a musical two years ago in London. Peter was in his mid-forties. In his twenties, nearly to the present, Peter had danced and sung. Simon was aware that he had a place of honour in the house, because he was the oldest, he reckoned, and had known Chris probably before the others had.

The phone was ringing again. Nobody paid any attention, because a servant was going to answer it.

A trio of men, one of whom Simon recognized as Jonathan Truman, was attempting to sing in harmony in an armchaired corner of the living-room. They looked unshaven and rumpled. Simon glanced at his watch: nearly 1 a.m. local time and nearly 8 p.m. in New York. His understudy would be in his dressing room, making up before Simon's mirror, ageing himself, not trying to look younger, and perhaps nervously saying some lines to himself. Simon drank all his glass.

Someone banged him on the back.

"Chris is here!"

"Chris is coming!" shouted Freddy Detweiler, spreading his arms at the foot of the stairs.

Chris was wheeled down, step by step, by Marcus and August, a blondish man whom Simon had indeed found in the kitchen. August leaned back like a thin mast in a wind against the weight of the chair.

"*Chris!*" A scattered cheer went up, a patter of applause that seemed to Simon pitiable, as when an audience was scant. Simon had not joined in, he merely stared in wonder at the heavy man in a blue and white-striped dressing gown with long-fingered hands gripping the arms of his chair, with the fixed pink and white smile on closed lips. Safely down with his charge, August went to the sideboard and poured champagne, while at least four figures fluttered around Simon like bees.

"Chris, what do you fancy? Carl on the piano? Me — standing on my head? Or my impersonation of an English tourist in Uganda?" This question came from Freddy, forty-five if he was a day, and could he still stand on his head? The question might have been unheard by Chris whose blue eyes were roving as usual, taking in essentials.

"What kind of music tonight, Chris?"

"Indian," said Chris absently, like a man doped or talking in his sleep. "*Simon* is here!" Chris announced, as if the others didn't know it.

Fortunately, only a couple of smiling faces troubled to turn to Simon for an instant, and Simon looked away. Simon squeezed his eyes shut, not near tears again, but something like it. He remembered the pleasure, the terror even, of meeting Christopher Wells at twenty. Well, maybe some of the others had met him when they were at that age too, or near enough. Otherwise why would they be here? Freddy was in a London show now, Simon knew, yet he was here. "Can I see you in New York? Do you ever come to New York?" Chris has asked that first night backstage in Stockbridge. Simon in those days had travelled everywhere by bus or by hitchhiking, his worldly goods in a duffel bag. Twenty-nine years ago, and Chris Wells had been even then sixty-five! Had Chris's age ever crossed Simon's mind then? Amazingly, it hadn't. "You'll go to school with me for a few weeks," Chris had said, meaning that Simon was to move into his Park Avenue apartment. That huge, rambling apartment with at least six big rooms looked as large in Simon's memory as if he had been a small child then.

You must do this and you must not do that, Chris had said a dozen times a day, and though Chris had often had lunch or dinner with people in Manhattan (Simon sometimes accompanied him too), Chris had always set Simon some lines to learn out of Shakespeare, Pirandello, Shaw, Eugene O'Neill. Simon hadn't had to memorize them, but he had had to be able to read them, and Chris would play the other parts, male or female. He showed Simon how to get up from a chair without lurching, corrected his diction without insulting him (Simon was from Idaho), and Chris had paid all the bills, saying that he was taking Simon away from possible work then. And when Simon had been strangely in love with Chris, Simon had known that Chris knew it. Simon was not homosexual, and would not have known, at least not then, what to do with a man in bed. But it was not so simple as bed, what he had felt for Chris. It was more like hero worship, more like devotion and absolute confidence. Chris had once said, "Your work is more important than I am — than anybody. *People* come and go." Had Christopher meant girls then? Or friends? Even that bit of advice had sunk in. Simon had had at least four affairs, two of which he considered important, meaning that they had made him happy and that the ends of them had hurt, but he had never married, and though he had not willed it, or taken it on himself, he realized now that he had followed Chris's advice: keep yourself independent, your work is more important than personal relationships.

In the next couple of minutes, the drink took effect, the atmosphere, the realization that Russ Johnson was on the stage now, playing William in New York. There was music, a buffet-banquet laid out on a table in a grotto of the garden, down some lighted stone steps from Chris's house. Simon remembered a summer lunch here the one time he had been to High-Ho. August was tending a brazier, grilling beef, and a few figures stood near the fire for warmth. The cheerful voices carried to the black

73

curtain of fir trees all around: they were talking of former visits, telling old anecdotes, and Chris was among them, in his wheelchair. How much longer did he have to live, Simon wondered.

Simon glanced at several faces. Whom did he dare ask that question? Who would give him a straight answer, even a straight opinion? However, he was here, the last of the disciples that Chris had wanted. The rest was up to Chris. Was Chris going to die with a smile on his lips, like now, lifting a glass of champagne? Simon watched Chris tip his head back and laugh at a remark Peter had made, and Simon fancied he saw Chris's belly shake like jelly under the mohair coverlet that was pulled up to his waist. Death and decay — was indeed not funny. Simon went to the buffet table for some wine with which to finish his supper. He had decided not to ask anyone his opinion of when Chris might die.

Now it was nearly 3 a.m. At least four had drifted off to the house to retire. Detweiler was rather drunk.

"A toast to Simon!" Chris shouted. "One of my more brilliant children. Oh, you're all brilliant! To Simon!"

"Simon!" echoed a half-dozen voices and the name seemed to reach the mountains.

"And to those who never doubt," Chris added.

They chuckled and drank.

A few minutes later, Detweiler did attempt to stand on his head, and fell, got up to mocking laughs, rubbing the end of his spine, but he wasn't hurt. Plucky of him to have tried it, Simon thought, with no soft grass to land on here, just stone.

Simon turned towards the descending steps, and took a deep breath. He needed relief from the scene of Chris surrounded, oppressed even, by his former protégés. Somewhere ahead on the stone path another electric light glowed. Then Simon caught his heel on an uneven stone and plunged forward. He had not been walking fast, but he was going to land on his head, and he was aware that he did not put out his hands to protect himself. He was

74

going to die, now. This was the great plunge, and it was like a dream, after all, painless yet final.

He woke up to a soft roar of voices that sounded like a sea, blinked his eyes and recognized the faces bending over him, smelt the wood smoke of Chris's fireplace. He was lying on one of Chris's long leather sofas in the living-room.

"He's come to! He's okay!"

"Oh, good — good." That was Chris's tired and relieved voice in the background.

A man laughed. "Simon, you really took a header! We heard the plop!"

"But there's no bleeding! Not a scratch on him!"

"Take a sip of this hot tea."

"I'm going off to bed . . ."

Simon got up, and in a near daze said good night to Chris and walked up the stairs, even washed to some extent before he donned pyjamas. He felt even stranger than when he had arrived, not drunk though he must be a little drunk, but as if he had left this world and entered another. He pinched his forearm hard through his pyjama sleeve, and felt it.

He flopped into bed and at once fell asleep.

He had a very vivid dream of being about sixteen, on a bicycle, hampered by groceries which he was supposed to bring to his family's house. He knew the old way — in the dream it was along certain curving unpaved lanes, though in Simon's boyhood the streets near his home had been paved — but he kept getting lost. And Chris Wells was hovering somewhere above, like God, saying, "Come on, Simon, to the *left* here. You know the way. What's the matter with you?" And Simon awakened, unsuccessful in returning home.

What did that dream mean? Anxiety, insecurity. Even Chris had not been able to show him the way.

Simon lay on his back in the near darkness of his room, enjoying the slow coming of dawn at his windows which made black lumps of Chris's handsome furniture, of the high-backed chair on which Simon had put his jacket last night. The jacket looked like a bat hanging there. The house was silent, and only one bird's voice — it did not sound like a lark — cried once or twice beyond the windows.

And maybe Chris would be found dead this morning in his bed. Simon imagined August going in with a tea tray and finding him. Simon tensed, preparing himself for this, as if it were a truth to be announced in an hour or so.

Weren't some of the others thinking the same thing, since his own arrival last evening?

Simon showered and shaved in the bathroom down the hall, then dressed in old grey flannels, a shirt and heavy sweater. The bruise on his head throbbed a bit more painfully. It had awakened him last night, an ache and a rising lump that felt like the classic egg. He wasn't going to mention it to anyone, though it made some of his short hair stand straight out.

Simon went out the front door and retraced his steps of last evening, went past the old stone table that had held their supper, and was unable to identify exactly the spot where he had tripped. Wouldn't it be odd if he had died here a few hours ago, if the others had carried up his corpse instead of him merely unconscious? Simon looked quickly back at the big chalet, and heard a faint *ting* of metal striking metal, a sound from the kitchen. Two soft lights glowed behind curtains.

He ran back up the steps.

Detweiler was in the living-room, on his feet, looking tired but nervously alert, dressed as was Simon in trousers and sweater. "Up already! 'Morning, Simon!"

"Good morning! And how's Chris?"

"Chris? Same, I suppose."

"Well —" Simon hesitated. "Is he really going to die? Is he on the brink, I mean? Carl's telegram to me — said so."

"Yes," said Freddy, looking Simon straight in the eye.

76

Was Freddy Detweiler still drunk? Simon strolled towards the fireplace where embers still burned, then turned. "Last night — I didn't have a chance and I didn't really want to ask what the doctors said. Do you know?"

"Oh, to hell with the doctor or doctors. They're amazed he's still alive. A piece of a lung he's got, as they said of old Keats, or maybe Keats said it about himself. The rest is water. But with Chris it's mental, whether and when he dies. You know that. I could use a weak scotch, how about you?"

"No, thanks." He watched as Detweiler poured an inch into a glass and added water from a Perrier bottle. "But now that we're all here —"

Just then, August came in with a tray. "Good morning, sir. Good morning. Your tea, sirs." He arranged teacups and toast plates on the low table near the fireplace.

"What?" asked Detweiler.

Simon saw in Detweiler's nervous eyes the same question that he had asked. When was Chris going to decide to die? "I meant," Simon began as he poured tea, "how long do you think this will go on?" He handed Detweiler his cup. "Sugar?"

"Today, tomorrow. Who knows?"

"You're going to stay — till the end?"

"Yes," said Detweiler with the same firmness as before, though now he looked whipped by fatigue. "But Richard has to go back to London today, I think. He's been here four days, and I — three or four."

Simon felt uneasy, and tried to take comfort from the tea. Chris would be incomplete again with Richard gone. Then what? "Won't it be — "

"We haven't had our presents yet," Detweiler interrupted on a suddenly cheerful note. "He's giving us all little presents. Maybe big ones, I don't know. — What were you going to say?"

"I — I started to say, isn't it impossible to imagine Chris gone? Not with us any more. He — Not that I wrote to him so often in the past — lately. But I always knew he was there. He always spoke on the phone at Christmas or around Christmas. Somehow we each found out where the other was."

"What're you trying to say?" asked Detweiler.

Simon frowned and glanced at the fire. August had added wood to it. "I suppose I'm asking, do you think Chris is going to die — or not?"

"Are you in a hurry?" Detweiler asked with a smile, and sipped his scotch.

Simon knew Detweiler wanted an angry reaction, but Simon didn't feel angry. "I love Chris — and I'm upset. Also I know he's going to die. So I'm sorry I asked you."

"You should be." Detweiler reached for the bottle again.

The telephone rang in the room. "Is a servant supposed to answer this?" Simon asked, but Detweiler showed only indifference, and Simon picked the telephone up. "Hello. Christopher Wells' residence."

"Simon, it's *you*. What luck! I know it's early for you but I had to tell you — all goes well. Russ did a good job, really made it last night. The *Times* this morning even had an item about him. Russ must've done some fast phoning before he went on or somebody else did it for him. He's happy as a fool. Probably thinks he's become Laurence Olivier overnight." It was the voice of Stew Davis, the director of *William*.

"I'm glad, Stew. That's a relief to know." Simon was glad, for the sake of *William* and for Russell Johnson who was a serious and dedicated young man. Young, yes, not quite thirty, and William in the play was not quite forty, which Russ would be able to do well. William was not supposed to be nearly fifty, as was Simon Hatton.

"When're you coming back? — Any news?"

"I really can't say, Stew. Maybe in two days, three. As long as things are going so well there — Would you tell Russ I'm delighted? Is he with you now?"

Stew laughed richly. "I'm sure he's asleep, if he can get to sleep. But I'll tell him."

78

They exchanged goodbyes, and Simon turned to Detweiler who was now drinking his tea. "Just found out my understudy made a big hit last night. Russell Johnson. Maybe you'll hear of him — very soon."

"But you're going back to the part."

"Oh — certainly. When I go back to New York. I — "

August came in again, slender and quiet, and bowed a little. "Excuse me, gentlemen, Mr Wells is awake and would like to see you — and anyone else who is up," he added with a glance at the windows as if he might see a figure or two walking in the garden.

"Haven't seen anybody else," Detweiler said, instantly alert. "Let's go, Simon."

Simon saw something unusual in both August's and Detweiler's attitude. He followed them up the stairs to Chris's room whose door was ajar. Simon heard voices from inside. August knocked for them.

Chris lay propped up on pillows, but he turned, fairly rolled his heavy body towards the door as they entered. "Simon — and Freddy. Bless you, come in. Having a wake — very early one. Shocking hours for me, don't you think, but I didn't sleep a wink, I felt so happy. With all of you here. I don't know why — "

"Now take it easy, Chris dear," said Richard Cook who was in pyjamas and a dark blue dressing gown under which his abdomen bulged. So was Carl Parker in pyjamas, and stood at the foot of the bed. "Of course we're all here. Maybe just not all up yet."

"But we can start the presents. Like Christmas when we were all children, you know, and got up early to see what we had from Santa Claus — much to the annoyance of our parents, but I'm not annoyed one bit. August?" Chris's tired, reddish eyes wobbled uncontrollably as he leaned to his left to see August, if he could. August was there, but plainly Chris didn't see him for a few seconds. "August — no, first champagne for all of us, and then — you know. Call Marcus to help."

"Yes, sir." August hurried off.

Chris was not going to live the day out, Simon thought. He watched Richard Cook expertly unhitch the oxygen tank from the foot of the bed and bring it with its deathly-looking mask of limp rubber to Chris, who clamped the mask over his nose and mouth. Chris's eyes above the flabby grey mask showed a childlike fear, did not focus on anything, and their expression seemed to Simon that of a scared human being, acquinted with life for a very long while and yet now terrified of leaving it.

Then there was a glass of champagne in Simon's left hand, a small white tissue-wrapped package in the other. Someone had told him to sit in a chair, so Simon sat. Three or four others had come into the room, and all had champagne and were unwrapping, talking, laughing.

"Jonathan isn't up yet. Typical," said Chris.

Simon's present was Chris's silver cigarette case — for six cigarettes, Simon remembered from the first dinner he had ever had with Chris — which Simon had admired so much then. A slightly raised snake with tiny emerald eyes coiled its way across the lid of the case, smooth to the touch, yet dangerous looking. The corners of the case were rounded by Chris's fingers over the years, by being slipped in and out of jacket pockets.

"Thank you, Chris," Simon said, looking at the man on the bed, but Detweiler was bending over to kiss Chris's cheek just then, below the ugly mask. Detweiler had a wristwatch in his left hand.

Richard was holding up a gold chain with a medallion on it.

August made discreet but anxious signs. They were to leave. Mr Wells needed repose.

But Chris was not having it. He removed his mask to call for more champagne, and coffee and tea and toast. "And we're not all here yet." Chris coughed. "August, where're my cheroots?"

August knelt and produced a box from a lower compartment of Chris's bedtable.

Simon slipped away, went to his room and dropped the cigarette box and its tissue and its card in Chris's hand saying, "This wise little snake has seen a lot. Try and show him something new. My love always, Chris." Simon went to the bathroom down the hall, splashed cold water on his face, dried himself on the corner of a towel probably not his own, and vowed not to have a drink today, not even a glass of wine. He still felt strange, and it was not jetlag or even like lack of sleep. Someone rapped gently on the door.

"One minute," said Simon with false cheer, and opened the door to a sleepy-looking Jonathan, barefoot and in pyjamas.

"You're looking spruce," said Jonathan.

"Am I? Have a wash and go in and see Chris. The party's already launched."

"At eight o'clock in the *mo-orning*," Jonathan moaned, shuffling in. "How much more of this can I stand? Can we stand?"

"Lots more." Simon closed the door on him.

That wasn't true. Was he going to go on pretending or not? Go on acting with false cheer or not? Detweiler had been acting last night, when he had tried to stand on his head. He hadn't been acting this morning, when he had said, "Yes," he was going to stay to the end.

Simon wondered if he could face the end? That was what the trouble was about. The truth was, that Simon felt he might become nothing, with Chris gone. Chris had picked him up from nowhere, when he had been (Simon knew) a rotten actor with barely a dream in his head. Chris had even given him his dream. Chris had made him able to achieve it. Chris had introduced him to the people who had helped him. So what was he, really? Now pushing fifty, and a twenty-nine-year-old had taken over his part with great success in New York. Who needed Simon Hatton any longer? *I'd better die before Chris*. The words came as soon as the thought.

Simon was suddenly frightened, yet resolved. Did any of the other fellows feel the same? Well, certainly not Richard with a wife and a couple of children. Not even Detweiler, probably, who was a realist. Jonathan? Somehow he looked the softest of the lot with his puzzled eyes. But why make a pact with Jonathan? Simon didn't need a pact with anyone.

He drifted towards the window, but looked away from the pine forest beyond the lawn to the writing table in the corner, cinquecento, scarred and much polished, and he stared at a brass letter-opener curved like a little scimitar with a single red stone in its haft. Kill himself with that? Absurd. Yet the letter-opener fascinated him, because it was beautiful. Then Simon realized that he had bought the letter-opener in Gibraltar, decades ago, and given it to Chris. Simon had been about twenty-two then, lithe and agile, running through the narrow cobbled streets of Gibraltar, up earlier than Chris as usual, bringing back the letter-opener in a brown paper bag from an unpretentious little shop, sneaking back into the hotel room where Chris still lay asleep. Chris's June birthday had been near.

Simon made an effort, picked up the letter-opener, ran his thumb along the edge as if it were a knife, then laid it down exactly where it had been.

Before noon, Simon had taken a walk around Chris's property, looking for a place, a gorge deep enough to throw himself down, fatally. But wouldn't it be a mess, his corpse on the estate, discovered perhaps by police dogs? Better to jump into the Limmat in Zurich. Better yet to take sleeping pills in an hotel, leaving money for disposal or shipping corpse back to America, or whatever they did.

Lunch was in Chris's big room, which really was big enough to hold them all. August had pulled back the curtains of its two big windows, sunlight poured in (Chris said he had cut down forty pines to obtain this low-slanting winter sunshine), and August had laid out meats and salads on a long wooden commode.

"This is bliss," announced Chris, beatifically smiling on all his twelve, and in danger of tipping the champagne glass which he held in his right hand. In his left was a long cigarette in a black and gold holder.

Simon's eyes were drawn to Chris, and then he had to look away. He held a glass of red wine, otherwise it would have been remarked that he had nothing to drink, but Simon had hardly sipped it. He went to Jonathan and asked softly, "Do you want to die too?"

Jonathan put a forkful of smoked salmon into his mouth. "No," he said, apparently amused.

Detweiler looked more awake, like a different person from earlier this morning. Carl Parker was standing beside him.

"Where's your plate, Simon?" said Detweiler. "Have you tried the potato salad? Divine."

"How's the bump on your head?" asked Carl, looking at Simon's head where the hair stood out. "You had a shock last night. Are you really feeling okay?"

"Yes, thanks. Do I look funny? — Did Freddy tell you my understudy in New York had a big success last night? The theatre phoned me this morning."

"No. Well, that's a relief to you, I'm sure," said Carl with his mid-Atlantic accent. "Did you tell Chris?"

"N-not as yet." Jonathan and Richard were on either side of Chris's bed just then, Richard cutting something on Chris's plate which lay on a big tray spanning his body. Chris would not be interested, Simon thought. It was rather a negative piece of information, nothing particularly to Simon's good.

"Simon, you must come and visit us, since you're working in New York," said Carl, fishing in his wallet for a card. "Us being me and Jennifer. My girl friend," he added with a smile, as if he expected Simon not to believe him. "This is our L. A. place, but I'll write our present number on the back. — New Canaan. We've rented a house for a year."

Simon thanked him, and pocketed the card. The noise of conversation made it difficult to talk. "Do you think —How does Chris look to you today? You've been here longer than I have."

Carl looked at Simon as if he didn't understand. Or maybe Carl understood Simon to mean that he, Simon, was in a hurry to leave. Thinking of this, Simon said:

"I understand Richard's taking off today."

"Or maybe tonight. You're pressed, Simon?"

"I'm *not*," said Simon, realizing painfully that Carl had misunderstood. "No, it's just that I don't know how Chris usually looks, if this is an ordinary day — "

"You can't tell with Chris." Carl smiled serenely, indulgently, as if he had all the time in the world, and worse, as if it didn't matter if Chris died today, tomorrow or next week. Carl's eyes were bright with confidence, even happiness, because his life would keep on its same runners with Jennifer and his work, whatever it was just now.

Nor did Detweiler understand, looking at Simon levelly, almost challengingly, as if Simon had said something disrespectful in regard to Chris. It was more comforting to hear Richard's deep laugh from the direction of Chris's bed, but Simon knew the laugh was half-phoney too.

No one loves Chris as I do, Simon thought. He felt bitter and miserable. He put on a pleasant face, said, "See you," and moved away towards Chris.

The white splotches on Chris's face looked whiter, and did Simon see a faint blueness at the lips or was he imagining? Chris's breathing was audible. His blue eyes, still alert and striving, swam in water or tears held within bounds by the pink lids. Simon clasped two fingers of the unnaturally plump hand that Chris extended, the left hand which held still another cigarette.

"Chris, I love the cigarette case," said Simon. "You know I always loved it. Just the right present for me. Thank you."

84

"Simon, what's the matter? You're not yourself."
Chris's voice creaked like old furniture, old bones.

"Noth—*ing*," Simon replied, smiling.

A few seconds later, Simon was out of the room. Chris
had called for music now, and was there enough
champagne?

Simon ran down the garden steps. Wasn't there a
gorge, a small waterfall somewhere down here to the
right? He looked through trees and underbrush, then he
found it — like a promise come true, but how small it
was! Barely seven feet to jump down there and hit the
rocks, then hardly enough water to drown a baby or a
cat! Still if he smashed his skull, that would do. Simon
rubbed his palms together, breathed deeply, and felt
himself smiling. He was happy, in a quiet and important
way. This scene had momentum, a tempo that didn't
wish to be slowed or hastened. He looked at the stony,
half-grassy ground under his desert boots: nothing to trip
him or cause a bad take-off. He prepared to run.

Then a crackle made him stop. It had come from his
right, up the slope.

"Simon? — Hey, *Simon*! We're all looking for you!" It
was Carl Parker loping towards him.

"Could you leave me alone? Would you?"

"What do you mean? — *Freddy*!" Carl called loudly
up the slope. "Simon's here!"

"Coming," Detweiler's voice said, not far distant.

Carl clapped an arm around Simon's shoulder
suddenly. "Come back," he said in a serious tone,
swinging Simon towards the house.

Simon's strength exploded, he threw off Carl, and saw
Detweiler approaching. Simon ran towards the little
gorge, aware that Carl was just behind him. Carl
grabbed his arm, Carl's hand slipped down and took a
grip on Simon's left hand, swinging Simon around.

"What're you — "

Simon silenced him with a hard punch in the face.
Now he had Freddy to deal with, and Freddy was trying

to hold his arms. Simon kicked with his knee — ineffectively — got his right arm free and swung at Freddy's chin. Simon dashed again for the gorge.

He was aware of a sharp and long-drawn-out pain, on his head, against his ribs.

His next sensation came through his ears. He imagined that he heard a chorus, though the tune was not discernible. Simon knew he had just passed through a crisis. What kind of crisis? Death. He was dead. Vaguely he recalled that he had wished to die. Where? No matter. So there was a consciousness after death then, not pleasant or unpleasant, and very hazy now, but clarity would come, if he tried for it. Human voices. And what were they speaking? Maybe a strange language that he would have to learn. He imagined that his eyes saw something, and that the colour was grey with some pink in it.

"Hello, Simon . . ."

"Simon . . ." said another voice.

"The *second* time . . ."

Simon could not move his arms. His feet also refused to move, or his knees to bend. He thought he was lying flat on his back. Shadow turned into images of human figures. A voice murmured in German. A thin man with a black moustache and white shirt bent over him, thrust a needle into Simon's left thigh or hip, but Simon felt nothing. It was Chris's house again. Or was it another world that merely looked like Chris's house?

"You're okay, Simon. You'll be all right." This was Carl bending over Simon.

Simon realized that he was again on the big leather sofa which was at least three yards long. "And Chris?"

The number of voices reached a crescendo, then died down.

"Go ahead!" a man's voice said in a tone of impatience.

"Chris died around one o'clock. Very peacefully. He — " This was Carl again, speaking softly. "Now it's nearly midnight. You've got to stay put for a while, Simon. Best not to move you tonight, the doctor said."

"Wh — " Simon was growing increasingly sleepy. He tried without success to form the word "Why?"

"Tell him!" said Detweiler's voice.

"You've got two broken arms, Simon, no doubt a few cracked ribs, and a very swollen ankle. Now do you understand why you can't move?" Jonathan spoke gently, then moved back from the sofa and became a shadow that disappeared among the others.

When Simon next woke up, it was different. Dawn was coming through the tall curtains that were not totally closed. And Detweiler — yes, it was Detweiler's form, propped on a similar big sofa some three yards away and parallel to the one Simon was lying on. A dim light from a standing lamp flowed down on Freddy, who had fallen asleep over his book. Freddy was in pyjamas and bathrobe again.

And Chris was dead, Simon remembered, his body probably no longer in the house. They were all alone, Detweiler, Jonathan, Carl, and the others who had not left. And Simon was in a state in which he could not move, like someone dead, too. He gasped, but the sound did not awaken Detweiler. He was going to live. He was broken a bit, and he would remain broken, even when the bones mended.

An existence now with Chris gone. That was the fact. And Simon had to see himself in a different way, not exactly reborn — at his age — but as having died and come back to life. He felt he had really done this. Call himself fifty, yes. And give the *William* lead to Russell Johnson. Tell him today. And carry on in Chris's tradition. Chris wouldn't want to see him downcast. Chris wouldn't have wanted him to try to kill himself, and at exactly the same time that Chris himself had died, Simon realized. Chris would have said, "Absurd, Simon. For me? I'm not that important. The rest of your life is important."

Simon laughed a little, and pain hit his ribs on both sides. Simon kept on smiling.

"Awake?" said Detweiler, and his book fell with a thud to the floor. "Good morning, Simon. Need something? — Hey, you're looking a lot better!"

Simon made an effort, lifted his head, his heavy arms with their boards and bandages.

"Stop that!" Detweiler rushed to him.

"I want to walk. I can walk!" Simon wanted to make a bet that he could.

"Not today you can't. Do you have to pee?"

"Where're the others?"

"Asleep, I trust." Detweiler's lean face creased with his grin. He still hadn't shaved. "Jonathan took off. Carl's leaving at ten this morning. I can stay for a day or so, at least till you get a plane to somewhere. Three or four of us are still here."

And wasn't he the oldest now, Simon thought. Very likely. Carl Parker was certainly three years younger.

"Chris left you the house. Did you know that?" asked Detweiler.

A Clock Ticks at Christmas

"Have you got a spare franc, madame?"

That was how it began.

Michèle looked down over her armsful of boxes and plastic bags at a small boy in a loose tweed coat and tweed cap that hung over his ears. He had big dark eyes and an appealing smile. "Yes!" She managed to drop two francs which were still in her fingers after paying the taxi.

"*Merci*, madame!"

"And this," said Michèle, suddenly remembering that she had stuck a ten-franc note into her coat pocket a moment ago.

The boy's mouth fell open. "Oh, madame! *Merci!*"

One slippery shopping bag had fallen. The boy picked it up.

Michèle smiled, secured the bag handle with one finger, and pressed the door button with an elbow. The heavy door clicked open, and she stepped over a raised threshold. A shove of her shoulder closed the door, and she crossed the courtyard of her apartment house. Bamboo trees stood like slender sentinels on left and right, and laurels and ferns grew on either side of the cobbled path she took to Court E. Charles would be home, as it was nearly six. What would he say to all the packages, the more than three thousand francs she had spent today? Well, she had done most of their Christmas shopping, and one of the presents was for Charles to give his family — he could hardly complain about that — and the rest of the presents were for Charles himself and her parents, and only one thing was for her, a Hermes belt that she hadn't been able to resist.

"Father Christmas!" Charles said as Michèle came in. "Or Mother Christmas?"

She had let the packages fall to the floor in the hall. "Whew! Yes, a good day! A lot done, I mean. Really!"

"So it seems." Charles helped her to gather the boxes and bags.

Michèle had taken off her coat and slipped out of her shoes. They tossed the parcels on the big double bed in their bedroom, Michèle talking all the while. She told him about the pretty white tablecloth for his parents, and about the little boy downstairs who had asked her for a franc. "A franc — after all I bought today! Such a sweet little boy about ten years old. And so poor looking — his clothes. Just like the old stories about Christmas, I thought. You know? When someone with less asks for such a little bit." Michèle was smiling broadly, happily.

Charles nodded. Michèle's was a rich family. Charles Clement had worked his way up from apprentice mason at sixteen to become the head of his company, Athenas Construction, at twenty-eight. At thirty, he had met Michèle, the daughter of one of his clients, and married her. Sometimes Charles felt dazzled by his success in his work and in his marriage, because he adored Michèle and she was lovely. But he realized that he could more easily imagine himself as the small boy asking for a franc, which he would never have done, than he could imagine himself as Michèle's brother, for instance, dispensing largesse with her particular attitude, at once superior and kindly. He had seen that attitude before in Michèle.

"Only one franc?" Charles said finally, smiling.

Michèle laughed. "No, I gave him a ten-franc note. I had it loose in my pocket — and after all it's Christmas."

Charles chuckled. "That little boy will be back."

Michèle was facing her closet whose sliding doors she had opened. "What should I wear tonight? That light purple dress you like or — the yellow? The yellow one's newer."

Charles circled her waist with his arm. The row of dresses and blouses, long skirts, looked like a tangible rainbow: shimmering gold, velvety blue, beige and green, satin and silk. He could not even see the light purple in all of it, but he said, "The light purple, yes. Is that all right with you?"

"Of course, dear."

They were going out to dinner at the apartment of some friends. Charles went back into the living room and resumed his newspaper, while Michèle showered and changed her clothes. Charles wore his house-slippers — the habit of an old man, he thought, though he was only thirty-two. At any rate, it was a habit he had had since his teens, when he had been living with his parents in the Clichy area. Half the time he had come home with his shoes and socks damp from standing in mud or water on a construction lot, and woollen house-slippers had felt good. Otherwise Charles was dressed for the evening in a dark blue suit, a shirt with cufflinks, a silk tie knotted but not yet tightened at the collar. Charles lit his pipe — Michèle would be a long while yet — and surveyed his handsome living room, thinking of Christmas. Its first sign was the dark green wreath some thirty centimetres in diameter, which Michèle must have bought that morning, and which leaned against the fruit bowl on the dining table. Michèle would put it on the knocker of the apartment door, he knew. The brass fixtures by the fireplace gleamed as usual, poker and tongs, polished by Geneviève, their *femme de ménage*. Four of the six or seven oil paintings on the walls were of Michèle's ancestors, two of them in white ruffled lace collars. Charles poured himself a small Glenfiddich whisky, and sipped it straight. The best whisky in the world, in his opinion. Yes, fate had been good to him. He had luxury and comfort, everywhere he looked. He stepped out of his clumsy house-slippers and carried them into the bedroom, where he put on his shoes for the evening with the aid of a silver shoehorn. Michèle was still in the bathroom, humming, doing her make-up.

Two days later Michèle again encountered the small boy to whom she had given the ten-franc note. She was nearly at her house door before she saw him, because she had been concentrating on a white poodle that she had just bought. She had dismissed her taxi at the corner of the street, and was carefully leading the puppy on his new black and gold leash along the curb. The puppy did not know in which direction to go, unless Michèle tugged him. He turned in circles, scampered in the wrong direction until his collar checked him, then looked up smiling at Michèle and trotted after her. A man paused to look and admire.

"Not quite three months," Michèle replied to his question.

It was then that she noticed the small boy. He wore the same tweed coat with its collar turned up against the cold, and she realized that it was a man's suit jacket, much too big, with the cuffs rolled back and the buttons adjusted so it would fit more tightly around the child's body.

"*B'jour*, madame!" the boy said. "This is *your* dog?"

"Yes, I've just bought him," said Michèle.

"How much did he cost?"

Michèle laughed.

The boy whipped something out of his pocket. "I brought this for you."

It was a tiny bunch of holly with red berries. As Michèle took it with her free hand, she realized that it was plastic, that the berries were bent on their artificial stems, the tinsel cup crushed. "Thank — you," she said, amused. "Oh, and what do I owe you for this?"

"Nothing at all, madame!" He had an air of pride and looked her straight in the eyes, smiling. His nose was running.

She pressed the door button of her house. "Would you like to come up for a minute — play with the puppy?"

"*Oui, merci!*" he replied, pleased and surprised.

Michèle led the way across the court and into the lift. She unlocked her apartment door, and unfastened the puppy's leash. Then she handed the boy a paper tissue from her handbag, and he blew his nose. The boy and the puppy behaved in the same manner, Michèle thought, looking around, turning in circles, sniffing.

"What shall I name the puppy?" Michèle asked. "Any ideas? What's your name?"

"Paul, madame," the boy replied, and returned to gazing at the walls, the big sofa.

"Let's go in the kitchen. I'll give you — a Coca-cola."

The boy and the puppy followed her. Michèle set down a bowl of water for the puppy, and took a bottle of Coca-cola from the fridge.

The boy sipped his drink from a glass, while his eyes wandered over the big white kitchen, eyes that reminded Michèle of open windows, or of a camera's lens. "You give the puppy *biftek hâché*, madame?" asked the boy.

Michèle was spooning the red meat from the butcher's paper into a saucer. "Oh, today, yes. Maybe all the time, a little bit. Later he can eat from tins." The child's eyes had fixed on the meat she was wrapping up, and she said impulsively, "Would you like some? A hamburger?"

"Even uncooked! A little bit — yes." He extended a hand whose nails were filthy, and took what Michèle held out in the teaspoon. Paul shoved the meat into his mouth.

Michèle put the meat package back into the fridge, and nudged the door shut. The boy's hunger made her nervous, somehow. Of course if he were poor, his family wouldn't eat meat often. She didn't want to ask him about this. It was easier for her, a moment later, to offer Paul some cookies from a box that was nearly full. "Take several!" She handed the box to him.

Slowly and steadily, the boy ate them all, while he and Michèle watched the puppy licking the last morsels from his saucer. Then Paul picked up the saucer and carried it to the sink.

"Is this right, madame?"

Michèle nodded. She and Charles had a washing machine, and seldom used the sink for washing dishes. Now the boy was putting the empty cookie box into the yellow garbage bin. The bin was almost full, and the boy asked if he could empty it for her. Michèle shook her head a little, in wonderment, feeling as if a Christmas angel had wandered into her home. The boy and the white puppy! The boy so hungry, and he and the puppy so young! "It's this way — but you don't have to."

The boy wanted to be of help, so she showed him the grey plastic sack at the servants' entrance, where he could dump the contents of the garbage bin. Then they went back into the living room and played with the puppy on the carpet. Michèle had bought a blue rubber ball with a bell in it. Paul rolled the ball carefully for the puppy. He had politely declined to remove his coat or to sit down. Michèle noticed holes at the heels of both his socks. His shoes were in worse condition, cracked between soles and uppers. Even his blue jean cuffs were tattered. How could a child keep warm in blue jeans in this weather?

"Thank you, madame," said Paul. "I'll go now."

"Aw-*ruff!*" said the puppy, wanting the boy to roll the ball again.

Michèle found herself as awkward suddenly as if she were with an adult from a different country and culture. "Thank you for your visit, Paul. And I wish you a happy Christmas in case I don't see you again."

Paul looked equally ill at ease, twisted his neck, and said, "And to you, madame, happy Christmas. — And you!" He addressed the white puppy. Abruptly he turned towards the door.

"I'd like to give you a present, Paul," Michèle said, following him. "How about a pair of shoes? What size do you wear?"

"Ha!" Was the boy blushing? "Thirty-two. Thirty-three maybe, since I'm growing, my father says." He lifted one foot in a comical manner.

"What does your father do?" Michèle was delighted to ask him a down-to-earth question.

"Deliverer. He takes bottles down from trucks."

Michèle imagined a sturdy fellow hauling down boxes of mineral water, wine, beer from a huge truck and tossing up empty crates. She saw such work all over Paris, every day, and maybe she had even glimpsed Paul's father. "Have you brothers and sisters?"

"One brother. Two sisters."

"And where do you live?"

"Oh — we live in a basement."

Michèle didn't want to ask him about the basement, whether it was a semi- or total basement, or whether his mother worked too. She was cheered by the idea of a present for him, shoes. "Come back tomorrow around eleven, and I'll have a pair of shoes for you."

Paul looked unbelieving, and wriggled his hands nervously in the pockets of his coat. "Yes, okay. At eleven."

The boy wanted to go down in the lift by himself, so Michèle let him.

The next morning at a few minutes past eleven, Michèle was strolling along the pavement near her apartment with the puppy on his leash. She and Charles had decided to name him Ezekiel last evening, a name already shortened to Zeke. Michèle suddenly saw Paul and a smaller figure beside him.

"My sister, Marie-Jeanne," said Paul, looking up at Michèle with his big dark eyes, then at his sister, whose hand he pushed towards Michèle.

Michèle took the little hand and they greeted each other. The sister was a smaller version of Paul, with longer black hair. *The shoes.* Michèle had bought two pairs for Paul. She asked them both to come up. The lift again, the apartment door opening, and the same wonder in the eyes of the sister.

"Try them on, Paul. Both pairs," said Michèle.

97

Paul sat on the floor and did so, excited and happy. "They both fit! Both pairs!" For fun, he put on a left and a right shoe of different pairs.

Marie-Jeanne was taking more interest in the apartment than in the shoes.

Michèle fetched Coca-cola. One bottle each might be enough, she thought. Her heart went out to these children, but she was afraid of overdoing it, of losing control somehow. When she brought the cold drinks in, Zeke was starting to chew on one new shoe, and Paul was laughing. Quickly his sister rescued the shoe. Some Coca-cola got spilled on the carpet, Michèle brought a sponge, and Paul scrubbed away, then rinsed the sponge.

Then suddenly they were both gone, each with a box of shoes under an arm.

That evening Charles could not find his letter-opener. It lay always on his desk in a room off the living-room which was their library as well as Charles's study. He asked Michèle if she had possibly taken it.

"No. Maybe it fell on the floor?"

"I looked," said Charles.

But they both looked again. It was of silver, like a flat dagger with the hilt in the form of a coiled serpent.

"Genevieve will find it somewhere," said Michèle, but as soon as the words were out of her mouth, she suspected Paul — or even his sister. A throb went through her, akin to a sense of personal embarrassment, as if she were responsible for the theft, which was only a possibility, not yet a fact. But Michèle felt guilt as she glanced at her husband's slightly troubled face. He was opening a letter with his thumbnail.

"What did you do today, darling?" asked Charles, smiling once more, putting his letter away in a business folder.

Michèle told him she had argued with the telephone company about their last bill and won, this on Charles's behalf as he had queried a long-distance call, had looked in at the hairdresser's but only for an hour, and had aired Zeke three times, and she thought the puppy was learning fast. She did not tell Charles about buying two pairs of shoes for the boy called Paul, or about the visit of Paul and his sister to the apartment.

"And I hung the wreath on the door," said Michèle. "Not a lot of work, I know, but didn't you notice?"

"Of course. How could I have missed it?" He embraced her and kissed her cheek. "Very pretty, darling, the wreath."

That was Saturday. On Sunday Charles worked for a few hours in his office alone, as he often did. Michèle bought a small Christmas tree with an X-shaped base, and spent part of the afternoon decorating it, having put it on the dining table finally, instead of the floor, because the puppy refused to stop playing with the ornaments. Michèle did not look forward to the obligatory visit to Charles's parents — who never had a tree, and even Charles considered Christmas trees a silly import from England — on Christmas Eve Monday at 5 p.m. They lived in a big old walk-up apartment house in the 18th *arrondissement*. Here they would exchange presents and drink hot red wine that always made Michèle feel sickish. The rest of the evening would be jollier at her parents' apartment in Neuilly. They would have a cold midnight supper with champagne, and watch colour TV of Christmas breaking all over the world. She told this to Zeke.

"Your first Christmas, Zeke! And you'll have — a *turkey* leg!"

The puppy seemed to understand her, and galloped around the living room with a lolling tongue and mischievous black eyes. And Paul and Marie-Jeanne? Were they smiling now? Maybe Paul was, with his two pairs of shoes. And maybe there was time for her to buy a shirt, a blouse for Marie-Jeanne, a cake for the other brother and sister, before Christmas Day. She could do that Monday, and maybe she'd see Paul and be able to give him the presents. Christmas meant giving, sharing,

99

communicating with friends and neighbours and even with strangers. With Paul, she had begun.

"Oo-woo-woo," said the puppy, crouching.

"One second, Zeke, darling!" Michèle hurried to get his leash.

She flung on a fur jacket, and she and Zeke went out. Zeke at once made for the gutter, and Michèle gave him a word of praise. The fancy grocery store across the street was open, and Michèle bought a box of candy — a beautiful tin box costing over a hundred francs — because the red ribbon on it had caught her eye.

"Madame — *bonjour*!"

Once more Michèle looked down at Paul's upturned face. His nose was bright pink with cold.

"Happy Christmas again, madame!" Paul said, smiling, stamping his feet. He wore the brown pair of new shoes. His hands were rammed into his pockets.

"Would you like a hot chocolate?" Michèle asked. A *bar-tabac* was just a few metres distant.

"*Non, merci.*" Paul twisted his neck shyly.

"Or soup!" Michèle said with inspiration. "Come up with me!"

"My sister is with me." Paul turned quickly, stiff with cold, and at that moment Marie-Jeanne dashed out of the *bar-tabac*.

"Ah, *bonjour*, madame!" Marie-Jeanne was grinning, carrying a blue straw shopping bag which looked empty, but she opened it to show her brother. "Two packs. That's right? — Cigarettes for my father," she said to Michèle.

"Would you like to come up for a few minutes and see my Christmas tree?" Michèle's hospitality still glowed strongly. What was wrong with giving these two a bowl of hot soup and some candy?

They came. In the apartment, Michèle switched on the radio to London, which was giving out with carols. Just the thing! Marie-Jeanne squatted in front of the Christmas tree and chattered to her brother about the pretty packages amassed at the base, the decorations, the little presents perched in the branches. Michèle was heating a tin of split pea soup to which she had added an equal amount of milk. Good nourishing food! The English choirboys sang a French carol, and they all joined in:

> *Il est né le divin enfant . . .*
> *Chantez hautbois, résonnez musettes . . .*

Then as before they were gone all too suddenly — their laughter and chatter — Zeke barked as if to call them back, and Michèle was left with the empty soup bowls and crumpled chocolate papers to clear away. Impulsively Michèle had given them the pretty cookie box to take home. And Charles was due in a few minutes. Michèle had tidied the kitchen and was walking into the living-room, when she heard the click of the lift door and Charles's step in the hall, and at the same time noticed a gap on the mantel. The clock! Charles's ormolu clock! It couldn't be gone. But it *was* gone.

A key was fitted into the lock, and the door opened.

Michèle seized a box — yellow-wrapped, house-slippers for Charles — and set it where the clock had been.

"Hello, darling!" Charles said, kissing her.

Charles wanted a cup of tea: the temperature was dropping and he had nearly caught a chill waiting for a taxi just now. Michèle made tea for both of them, and tried to seat herself so that Charles would take a chair that put his back to the fireplace, but this didn't work, as Charles took a different armchair from the one Michèle had intended.

"What's the idea of a present up there?" Charles asked, meaning the yellow package.

Charles had an eye for order. Smiling, still in a good mood, he left his first cup of tea and went to the mantel. He took the package, turned towards the Christmas tree, then looked back at the mantel. "And where's the clock? You took it away?"

Michèle clenched her teeth, longing to lie, to say, yes, she'd put it in a cupboard in order to have room for Christmas decorations on the mantel, but would that make sense? "No, I — "

"Something the matter with the clock?" Charles's face had grown serious, as if he were inquiring about the health of a member of the family whom he loved.

"I don't know where it is," Michèle said.

Charles's brows came down and his body tensed. He tossed the lightweight package down on the table where the tree stood. "Did you see that boy again? — Did you invite him up?"

"Yes, Charles. Yes — I know I — "

"And today was perhaps the second time he was here?"

Michèle nodded. "Yes."

"For God's sake, Michèle! You know that's where my letter-opener went too, don't you? But the clock! My God, it's one hell of a lot more important! Where does this kid live?"

"I don't know."

Charles made a move towards the telephone and stopped. "When was he here? This afternoon?"

"Yes, less than an hour ago. Charles, I really am sorry!"

"He can't live far from here. — How *could* he have done it with you here with him?"

"His sister was here too." Michèle had showed her where the bathroom was. Of course Paul had taken the clock, then, put it in that blue shopping bag.

Charles understood, and nodded grimly. "Well, they'll have a nice Christmas, pawning that. And I'll bet we won't see either of them around here for the next many days — if ever. How could you bring such hoodlums into the *house?*"

Michèle hesitated, shocked by Charles's wrath. It was

102

wrath turned against her. "They were cold and they were hungry — and poor." She looked her husband in the eyes.

"So was my father," Charles said slowly, "when he acquired that clock."

Michèle knew. The ormolu clock had been the Clement family's pride and joy since Charles had been twelve or so. The clock had been the one handsome item in their working-class household. It had caught Michèle's eye the first time she had visited the Clements, because the rest of the furnishings were dreadful *style rustique*, all varnish and formica. And Charles's father had given the clock to them as a wedding present.

"Filthy swine," Charles murmured, drawing on a cigarette, looking at the gap on the mantel. "You don't know such people perhaps, my dear Michèle, but I do. I grew up with them."

"Then you might be more sympathetic! If we can't get the clock back, Charles, I'll buy another for us, as near like it as possible. I can remember exactly how that clock looked."

Charles shook his head, squeezed his eyes shut and turned away.

Michèle left the room, taking the tea things with her. It was the first time she had seen Charles near tears.

Charles did not want to go to the dinner party to which they were invited that evening. He suggested that Michèle go alone and make some excuse for him, and Michèle at first said she would stay at home too, then changed her mind and got dressed.

"I don't see what's the matter with my idea of buying another clock," Michèle said. "I don't see —"

"Maybe you'll never see," Charles said.

Michèle had known Bernard and Yvonne Petit a long time. Both had been friends of Michèle's before she and Charles were married. Michèle wanted very much to tell Yvonne the story about the clock, but it was not a story one could tell at a dinner table of eight, and by coffee

103

time Michèle had decided it was best not to tell it at all: Charles was seriously upset, and the mistake was her own. But Yvonne, as Michèle was leaving, asked her if something was on her mind, and Michèle was relieved to admit there was. She and Yvonne went into a library much like the one in Michèle's apartment, and Michèle told the story quickly.

"We've got just the clock you need *here*!" said Yvonne. "Bernard doesn't even much like it. Ha! That's a terrible thing to say, isn't it? But the clock's right here, darling Michèle. Look!" Yvonne pushed aside some invitation cards, so that the clock on the library mantel showed plainly on its splayed base: black hands, its round face crowned with a tiara of gilded knobs and curlycues.

The clock was indeed very like the one that had been stolen. While Michèle hesitated, Yvonne found newspaper and a plastic bag in the kitchen and wrapped the clock securely. She pressed it into Michèle's hands. "A Christmas present!"

"But it's the principle of the thing. I know Charles. So do you, Yvonne. If the clock that was stolen were from my family, if I'd known it all my life, even, I know it wouldn't matter to me so much."

"I know, I know."

"It's the fact that these kids were poor — and that it's Christmas. I asked them in, Paul first, by himself. Just to see their faces light up was so wonderful for me. They were so grateful for a bowl of soup. Paul told me they live in a basement somewhere."

Yvonne listened, though it was the second time Michèle had told her all this. "Just put the clock on the mantel where the clock was — and hope for the best." Yvonne spoke with a confident smile.

When Michèle got home by taxi, Charles was in bed reading. Michèle unwrapped the clock in the kitchen and set it on the mantel. Amazing how much it did look like the other clock! Charles, behind his newspaper, said that he had taken Zeke out for a walk half an hour ago.

Otherwise Charles was silent, and Michèle did not try to talk to him.

The next morning, Christmas Eve, Charles spotted the new clock on the mantel as he walked into the living-room from the kitchen, where he and Michèle had just breakfasted. Charles turned to Michèle with a shocked look in his eyes. "All right, Michèle. That's enough."

"Yvonne gave it to me. To us. I thought — just for *Christmas* —" What had she thought? How had she meant to finish that sentence?

"You do *not* understand," he said firmly. "I gave the police a description of that clock last night. I went to the police station, and I intend to get that clock back! I also informed them of the boy aged 'about ten' and his sister who live somewhere in the neighbourhood in a basement."

Charles spoke as if he had declared war on a formidable enemy. To Michèle it was absurd. Then as Charles talked on in his tone of barely repressed fury about dishonesty, hand-outs to the irresponsible, to those who had not earned them or even tried to, about hooligans' disrespect for private property, Michèle began to understand. Charles felt that his castle had been invaded, that the enemy had been admitted by his own wife — and that she was on their side. Are you a Communist, Charles might have asked, but he didn't. Michèle didn't consider herself a Communist, never had.

"I simply think the rich ought to share," she interrupted.

"Since when are we rich, really rich, I mean?" Charles replied. "Well, I know. Your family, they *are* rich and you're used to it. You inherited it. That's not your fault."

Why on earth should it be her fault, Michèle wondered, and began to feel on surer ground. She had read often enough in newspapers and books that wealth had to be shared in this century, or else. "Well — and as for these kids, I'd do the same thing again," she said.

Charles's cheeks shook with exasperation. "They insulted us! This was thievery!"

Michèle's face grew warm. She left the room, as furious as Charles. But Michèle felt that she had a point. More than that, that she was right. She should put it into words, organize her argument. Her heart was beating fast. She glanced at the open bedroom door, expecting Charles's figure, expecting his voice, asking her to come back. There was silence.

Charles went off to his office half an hour later, and said he would probably not be back before three-thirty. They were to go to his parents' house between four and five. Michèle rang up Yvonne, and in the course of their conversation Michèle's thoughts became clearer, and her trickle of tears stopped.

"I think Charles's attitude is wrong," Michèle said.

"But you mustn't say that to a man, dear Michèle. You be careful."

That afternoon at four, Michèle began tactfully with Charles. She asked him if he liked the wrapping of the present for his mother. The package contained the white tablecloth, which she had shown Charles.

"I'm not going. I can't." He went on, over Michèle's protestations. "Do you think I can face my parents — admit to then that the clock's been stolen?"

Why mention the clock, unless he wanted to ruin Christmas, Michèle thought. She knew it was useless to try to persuade him to come, so she gave it up. "I'll go — and take their presents." So she did, and left Charles at home to sulk, and to wait for a possible telephone call from the police, he had said.

Michèle had gone out laden with Charles's parents' presents as well as those for her own parents. Charles had said he would turn up at her parents' Neuilly apartment at 8 p.m. or so. But he did not. Michèle's parents suggested that she telephone Charles: maybe he had fallen asleep, or was working and had lost track of time, but Michèle did not telephone him. Everything was so cheerful and beautiful at her parents' house — their tree, the champagne buckets, her nice presents, one a travel umbrella in a leather case. Charles and the clock story loomed like an ugly black shadow in the golden glow of her parents' living room, and Michèle again blurted out the events.

Her father chuckled. "I remember that clock — I think. Nothing so great about it. It wasn't made by Cellini after all."

"It's the sentiment, however, Edouard," said Michèle's mother. "A pity it had to happen just at Christmas. And it was careless of you, Michèle. But — I have to agreed with you, yes, they were simply little urchins of the *street*, and they were tempted."

Michèle felt further strengthened.

"Not the end of the world," Edouard murmured, pouring more champagne.

Michèle remembered her father's words the next day, Christmas Day, and on the day after. It was not the end of the world, but the end of something. The police had not found the clock, but Charles believed they would. He had spoken to them with some determination, he assured Michèle, and had brought them a coloured drawing of the clock which Charles had made at the age of fourteen.

"Naturally the thieves wouldn't pawn it so soon," Charles said to Michèle, "but they're not going to drop it in the Seine either. They'll try to get cash for it sooner or later, and then we'll nail them."

"Frankly, I find your attitude unchristian and even cruel," said Michèle.

"And I find your attitude — silly."

It was not the end of the world, but it was the end of their marriage. No later words, no embrace if it ever came, could compensate Michèle for that remark from her husband. And, just as vital, she felt a deep dislike, a real aversion to her within Charles's heart and mind. And she for him? Was it not a similar feeling? Charles had lost something that Michèle considered human — if he had ever had it. With his poorer, less privileged background, Charles should have had more compassion than she, Michèle thought. What was wrong? And what was right? She felt muddled, as she sometimes did when she tried to ponder the phrases of carols, or of some poems, which could be interpreted in a couple of ways, and yet the heart, or sentiment always seemed to seek and find a path of its own, as hers had done, and wasn't this right? Wasn't it right to be forgiving, especially at this time of year?

Their friends, their parents counselled patience. They should separate for a week or so. Christmas always made people nervous. Michèle could come and stay at Yvonne's and Bernard's apartment, which she did. Then she and Charles could talk again, which they did. But nothing really changed, not at all.

Michèle and Charles were divorced within four months. And the police never found the clock.

A Shot from Nowhere

The hotel room in which Andrew Spatz lay was yellowish and vaguely dusty, like the dry little plaza beyond his single window, like the town itself. The town was called Quetzalan. Three days ago, Andrew had taken a local bus from the city of Jalapa, not caring where the bus wandered to, and he had got off with his suitcase and box of oil paints, brushes and sketch pads in this town, because it had pleased him at his first glimpse through the bus window. It looked like a town that nobody knew of or cared about. It looked real. And on the plaza he had found the Hotel Corona, maybe the only hotel in the town.

Now, unfortunately, he was suffering from the usual intestinal cramps, and since yesterday he thought he had a fever, though in the heat it was hard to tell. In the early mornings, he set out and walked up in the hills around the town and made sketches to be used later, possibly, for paintings. He sketched everywhere, from an iron bench in the plaza, from a kerb, from a table in a bar. But when noon came, and after he had had a simple meal of tacos and beans and a beer, it was time to hide from the sun for a few hours, like everyone else. Quetzalan fell silent as a ghost town from half past twelve until nearly four every afternoon. And the yellow sun bore down with unnecessary force, as if to grind into the consciousness of man and beast and plant the fact that it had conquered, that rain and coolness were far away, maybe gone for ever. Andrew had strange dreams when he dozed in the afternoons.

On one afternoon he awakened from a dream of red snakes in a cave in a desert. The snakes did not notice him in the dream, he did not feel in any danger, but the dream was disturbing. Andrew threw off the sheet he had pulled over himself against the inevitable fly or two, and went to the basin in the corner of his room. He took off his drip-dry shirt, wet it again in cool water, and put it back on. His window was open about ten inches top and bottom, but no breeze came.

Andrew glanced at the window, and a movement outside caught his attention.

There was the boy again, with his milk pan for the kittens. The boy looked about thirteen, barefoot in soiled white trousers and white shirt with sleeves rolled up. He was only some six yards away from where Andrew stood in his room, so Andrew could see clearly the tin pie plate and the milk in it. Now as a skinny brindle kitten staggered from some bushes in the plaza, Andrew knew that the boy was going to draw the pan back, as he had done before.

A second kitten appeared, and as the two kittens hunched and lapped, the boy looked over his shoulder, grinning mischievously, as if to see if anyone were watching him. The plaza and the surrounding walks and streets were quite deserted. A grown cat, so thin its bones made shadows in its fur, galloped from the hotel side of the plaza towards the milk pan, and Andrew heard the boy giggle softly, and saw him scramble to his feet, spilling a little of the milk from the pan he was taking away. Why?

Andrew pulled on his jeans, shoved his feet into sneakers, and ran out of his room. Within seconds, he was outside the hotel door on the sidewalk. The boy was walking toward Andrew, but at an angle off to Andrew's right.

"*Porquè* —" Andrew stopped, hearing faint laughter from somewhere left of him.

The boy trotted away, dumping what remained of the milk on the street.

On his left, Andrew saw a group of three or four men, one with a hand camera of the kind that could make movies. Were they shooting a film? Was that why the boy had to repeat the cat-feeding scene? The men were middle-aged, and looked like ordinary Mexicans, though not peasants. Andrew saw one laugh, and wave a hand in a gesture that might mean "The hell with it" or "Muffed that one again". At any rate, they turned away, drifted out of Andrew's sight.

Back in his room, Andrew removed sneakers and jeans and again lay on his bed on his back. What was the meaning of it? Why were three or four men, one with a camera, out in the hot sun at 2 p.m.? Was the boy an actor or was he a little sadist? Strange.

Andrew felt that the whole past month had been strange. The girl he was in love with in New York, the girl he had thought would last, had met someone else a month ago. This had so thrown him, he hadn't been able to attend classes at the Art Students League for two or three days, and he had felt a bit suicidal or at least self-destructive. He had telephoned his married sister Esther in Houston, and she had invited him to come and stay for a few days. He had not talked much to his sister, but she had been cheering. And there was Mexico which he had never seen, so near when one was already in Houston, so he had taken a slow, cheap train south. Everything he had seen was different, fascinating. But as yet Andrew didn't know what to make of his life, or of his feelings now.

His nap was ended by the juke-box of the Bar Felipe starting up in a corner of the square, which meant it was around four. The juke-box would play nonstop till nearly midnight. Andrew washed at the basin, dressed again, and gathered his sketching equipment. The hotel lobby was deserted as usual when he walked out, though there were a couple of other guests in the hotel, Mexican men, both very quiet.

At the Bar Felipe, Andrew treated himself to an iced

tea, and kept an eye out for the men or any one of them whom he had seen watching the boy with the kittens. And for the boy himself. None of these came in through the open doors or walked past on the sidewalk. Other customers of Felipe, workmen with tattered sombreros, wearing tyre-soled sandals, came up to the bar to drink a bottle of beer or the brightly coloured orange drink that seemed very popular, and they all glanced at Andrew, but didn't stare at him as they had on his first day in town. A dog, thin as a whippet but of indeterminable breed, came up to Andrew's table hopefully, but Andrew hadn't ordered any potato chips or peanuts.

Andrew was pleased with his work of that afternoon. He had sketched two landscapes with colour pencils, introducing a lot of purple in the yellow and tan hills. One drawing showed the cluster of tan and pinkish houses that formed the town.

He dined at a tiny restaurant he had discovered in a side street off the plaza, a place hardly bigger than a kitchen, with only four tables. It catered to labourers, Andrew had observed, plus a couple of men of sixty or so who were unshaven and always slightly drunk. Andrew ordered *frijoles refritos*, *tortillas*, and a mug of boiled milk. The smell of peppery meat in the place sickened him.

The next day repeated the day before it. Sketching in the morning, a light lunch, an orange in his room afterwards. Fruit you had to peel was free of germs, Andrew remembered, and the sweet juice was wonderfully refreshing. Beads of sweat stood on his forehead and seemed to return as soon as he had wiped them away.

Gradually, then all at once, the silence of the siesta period fell outside his window. Not a footstep sounded, not the twitter of a bird. It was the sun's time, and the time lasted nearly four hours while life cowered in little rooms like his, in shade anywhere. Andrew was lying on his back with a wet towel across his forehead, when he heard the *tink* of metal on cement. With nervous energy, and out of curiosity, he got up to see what might be moving outside.

114

The boy was there, in the same clothing, in the same place, and with the same pie tin of milk. And here came one kitten shakier than yesterday. And there was the boy's smile over his shoulder, quick and furtive.

Andrew's sunbleached brows drew closer together as he stared. Now — yes, *now* the boy was sliding the pan back from the kitten who had been joined by the second kitten, and the boy set one foot under him, ready to rise with the pan.

There was a crack like a gunshot, not loud, but shocking in the silence.

The boy sagged at once, the pan made a little clatter and the milk spilled. The kittens lapped greedily. And here came the galloping older cat, the skinny brindle, as before.

A film, Andrew thought, still staring. Then he saw a red spot on the boy's shirt. It spread downward along the boy's right side. A plastic paint container that the boy had opened? Was the camera turning? The boy did not move.

Andrew got into his jeans and sneakers with crazy speed and left his room. He stopped on the sidewalk and looked left, expecting to see the camera crew again, but the corner there was deserted. No one was in sight, except the boy.

Andrew wet his lips, hesitated, then took a couple of steps in the direction of the boy, looked again to his left for the camera crew, then went on. The blood, or whatever it was, had reached the sidewalk and was flowing towards the street gutter. One of the kittens was in fact interested in it.

"Hey!" Andrew said. "*Hey*, boy!" Andrew stretched a hand out, but did not touch the boy's shoulder. The boy's eyes were half open. Andrew now saw the bullet hole in the white shirt.

He trotted towards the Bar Felipe, thinking that Felipe would be more easily aroused than the hotel proprietor, who seemed to close himself behind a couple of doors at the back of the hotel during siesta time.

"Hey! — *Felipe!*" Andrew knocked on the closed wooden doors of the bar. "Open! — *Por favor! Es importante!*" After a few seconds, Andrew tried again. He banged with his fist. He looked around the square. Not a shutter had opened, not a head showed at any window. Crazy!

"*Que quiere?*" asked Felipe, having opened his door a little. He wore only pyjama trousers and was barefoot.

"*Un niño — herido!*" Andrew gasped, pointing.

Felipe took two cautious steps on to the hot sidewalk, so he could see along the plaza's side, and at once jumped back into the shade of his doorway, waved a hand angrily and said something which Andrew took to mean "Don't bother me with that!"

"But — a doctor — or the police!" Andrew pushed against the doors which Felipe was trying rapidly to close, then heard a bolt being slid on the other side. Andrew trotted back to his hotel.

The hotel desk was deserted. Andrew banged his palm a couple of times on the little bell on the counter. "Señor *Diego!*"

There was nothing to stop him from using the telephone behind the counter, but he didn't know the police number and didn't see a directory.

"Señor *Diego!*" Andrew went to the closed door to the left of the counter and knocked vigorously.

He heard a grumbling shout from behind the door, then house-slippered footsteps.

Señor Diego, a middle-sized man with grey in his hair and moustache, looked at Andrew with surprise and annoyance. "What's the matter?" he asked, pulling his cotton bathrobe closer about him.

"A boy is dead! Out there!" Andrew pointed. "Didn't you hear the shot? A couple of minutes ago?"

Señor Diego frowned, walked a few paces across his lobby, and peered through the open doors of the hotel. The boy was quite visible from here. The three cats, the two kittens and the older cat, were still lapping at the

116

blood, but with less enthusiasm, as the blood was drying or not flowing any longer. "Bad boy," Señor Diego commented softly.

"But — we telephone the police?"

Señor Diego blinked and seemed to ponder. It was the first time Andrew had seen him without his glasses.

"The police or a doctor! — Or we carry him in?"

"No!" Señor Diego gave Andrew a scathing glance — as if he detested him, Andrew felt — and moved towards the door of his living quarters. Then he turned and looked at Andrew. "The police will find him."

"But maybe he's not *dead*!" Andrew felt torn between an impulse to carry the boy into the hotel, and to leave him as he was for police detectives to determine where the shot had come from. Andrew went behind the counter to the telephone, picked it up, and was looking at the disc of emergency numbers on the telephone's base, when Señor Diego yanked the telephone from his hands.

"All right, the police! *Then* you will see . . ."

Andrew could not understand the rest.

Señor Diego dialled a number. Then he mumbled several words into the telephone. "*Si-si*, Hotel Corona. Okay." He hung up, and shook his head nervously. "Do not move from this hotel!" he commanded, scowling at Andrew.

Anger flowed through Andrew, and his face felt as if it were going to explode. He went off down the hall to his room, whose door was slightly open still. *Do not move from this hotel!* Why should he? Andrew let cold water run in his basin. His face looked dark pink in the mirror. He took off his shirt again, wet it, and put it back on. At once he was too cool, even shivering. He had been listening for the sound of a car motor, and now it came. Andrew went to his window, but his eyes were drawn first to the boy in white who lay on the plaza's sidewalk, in sun and shadow. No cats now. A car door banged shut.

He heard voices in the lobby, then the creak of a couple of shutters in the plaza. A policeman in faded khaki and a visored cap bent over the boy, touched the boy's shoulder, then straightened and walked towards the hotel door.

Two policemen and Señor Diego came into Andrew's room. Suddenly all three seemed to be talking at once, but quite calmly, as in a dream, Andrew thought. The policemen questioned him calmly. Andrew kept saying, "I *heard* the shot, yes . . . I was *here* . . . Just ten minutes ago . . . No, no. Not me, *no!* I have no gun. I saw the boy fall! . . . Ask Señor Felipe!" Andrew pointed. "I went —"

"Señor Felipe!" said the oldest of the policemen, who now numbered three, and threw a smile at Señor Diego.

Andrew knew that he had not made his story clear. But why hadn't he? What he was saying was quite simple, even if his Spanish was primitive. He watched the policemen conferring. His ears started ringing, he wanted to sit down, but instead went to his window for some air. Three or four people now milled about the fallen boy, not touching him. Curious townspeople had at last emerged.

"You come with us," said a moustached policeman, reaching towards Andrew as if to take him by the wrist.

Andrew was suddenly conscious of the fact that each of the policemen carried a gun at his hip and a nightstick at his other hip.

"But I can tell you everything *here*," Andrew said. "I *saw* it, that's all."

"But if you shot?" said one cop.

Another policeman made a gesture as if to shut him up.

Señor Diego was smiling, murmuring something to the oldest policeman.

A handcuff snapped on one of Andrew's wrists as if by magic, and the policemen seemed to be arguing about whether to put the other wrist in the second handcuff or to attach that to a policeman's wrist, and they decided on Andrew. He was walked out between two policemen with his wrists together in front of him. The boy lay as

before, and the people around him now gave their attention to Andrew and the police, who were emerging from
the hotel door into the sunlight.

"My tourist card!" Andrew cried, jerking his arm away
from a policeman who had hold of him. In English he
said, "I demand to have my tourist card with me!"

"Hah!" But this same policeman, after a word with a
colleague, seemed to agree that they take Andrew back
to his room.

Andrew took his card from the pocket in the lid of his
suitcase, and a policeman took it from him, glanced at it
with the air of not reading a word, then stuck it in his
own back pocket.

The tan police wagon was a decrepit Black Maria with
metal benches inside. Cigarette butts littered the ridged
metal floor, along with stains that looked like blood and
what might have been dried vomit. The car had no
springs, and potholes jolted them up from the benches.
The vehicle, though open to the air with its heavy wire
mesh sides, seemed to hold heat like a closed oven. The
policemen's shirts became darker with sweat, they took
off their caps and wiped their foreheads, talking all the
while merrily.

Then suddenly Andrew was on the ridged floor. He
had almost fainted, had lost his balance, and now the
two policemen were hauling him back on to the bench.
Andrew had no strength, as in a dream in which he
couldn't escape from something. It's all a dream, he
thought, because of the fever he had. Wasn't he really
lying on his bed in his hotel room?

The wagon stopped. They all went up a couple of steps
into a yellowish stone building and into a large room
with a high ceiling, maybe formerly the anteroom of a
private dwelling, but which was now unmistakably a
police station. An officer in uniform approached an
unoccupied desk at the back of the room, beside which
hung a limp and faded flag on a tall staff.

Andrew asked for the toilet. He had to ask twice, had

119

to insist, and insist also that his handcuffs be undone. A police officer accompanied him and stood indifferently near the doorless toilet — a hole in a tiled square on the floor — while Andrew attended to his needs. There was no toilet paper, not even any newspaper scraps on the nail in the wall beside the hanging chain, which produced no water when Andrew tugged at it. It was during these unpleasant moments that Andrew became sure that he was not dreaming.

Now he was standing before the desk in the large room, with a policeman on either side of him. One policeman narrated something rapidly, and handed the man at the desk Andrew's tourist card. This was valid for a three-week stay in Mexico, and Andrew was so far well within that limit.

"Spatz — Andrew Franklin — born Orlando, Florida," the officer murmured, and continued with his birth date.

Suddenly Andrew had a vision of his blond sister Esther, happy and laughing, as she had looked just two weeks ago, when she had been trying to hold her two-year-old son still enough for Andrew to make a sketch. Andrew said in careful Spanish, "Sir, there is no reason why I am here. I saw a boy — shot."

"Hererra — Fernando," said a policeman at Andrew's elbow, as if performing a detail of duty. The name of the boy had already been uttered a few minutes earlier.

"*Si-si*," said the desk officer calmly, then to Andrew, "Who shot?"

"I did not see — from where the shot came."

"It was just outside your hotel window. Ground floor room you have. You could have shot," said the desk officer. Or was it, "You have shot?"

"But I have no gun!" Andrew turned to one policeman, then the other. "You have *seen* my room."

One policeman said something to the desk officer about the Bar Felipe.

"Ahah!" The desk officer listened to further narration.

Was the cop saying he'd got rid of a gun between his hotel room and the Bar Felipe? The shot must have come from a rifle, Andrew thought. What was 'rifle' in Spanish?

"The boy had robbed you," said the desk officer.

"No! I did not say that, never!"

"He was a very bad boy. A criminal," said the desk officer weightily, as if this altered the facts somehow.

"But I simply wanted to tell his death — to the Bar Felipe, to —" Andrew's hands were free, and he spread his arms to indicate a length. "With a gun so long — surely."

"You saw the gun?"

"*No!* I say — because of the *distance* — There was no one but the boy in the plaza when he — shot," Andrew finished lamely, exhausted now.

The desk officer beckoned, and the two policemen came closer to the desk. All three talked softly, and all at once, and Andrew hadn't a clue as to what they were saying. Then the two policemen returned to Andrew, and each took him by an arm. They were leading him towards a hall, towards a cell, probably. Andrew turned suddenly.

"I have the right to notify the American Consulate in Mexico City!" he shouted in English to the desk officer who was on his feet now.

"We shall notify the Consulate," he replied calmly in Spanish.

Andrew took a step towards the desk and said in Spanish, "I want to do it, please."

The desk officer shrugged. "Here is the number. Shall I dial it for you?"

"All right," said Andrew, because he didn't know the code for Mexico City. He didn't entirely trust the desk officer, but he was able to stand on the officer's left, and he saw that the number he dialled corresponded to the number in the officer's ledger beside EE UU Consulado.

"You see?" said the desk officer, after the telephone

had rung at the other end eight or nine times. "Closed until four."

Andrew's watch showed ten past three. "Then again at four — I try."

The officer nodded.

The two policemen took him in charge again. Down the hall they went, and stopped at a wooden door in which a square had been cut at eye level.

The cell had one barred window, a bed, and a bucket in a corner.

"At four!"Andrew said to his escort of two, pointing to his wristwatch. "To telephone."

They might not have heard him. They were chatting about something else, like old friends, and after turning of locks and sliding of a couple of bolts, Andrew heard them strolling down the hall, and their voices faded out and were replaced by a moaning and muttering much closer. Andrew looked around, half expecting to find another person in the cell with him, in a corner or under the bed, but the drunken or demented voice was coming from the other side of a brick wall that formed one side of the cell.

A crazy, boastful laugh came after a stream of angry-sounding Spanish.

The town drunk hauled in to sleep it off, Andrew supposed. Andrew sat on the bed. It felt like rock. There was one sheet on it, maybe to protect the blanket, a more valuable item, from being pressed too hard against the coarse wire that was the bed's surface. He felt thirsty.

"Ah—*waaaaah!*" said the non-stop voice in the next cell. "*Yo mi 'cuerdo—'cuerdo* — woooosh-la! *Oof!*"

Of all strange things to happen, Andrew thought. What if it were all a show, all pretence, as in a film? Why hadn't he told the officer at the desk about the three (or four?) men he had seen yesterday, apparently photographing the boy who had been shot today, laughing even, as the boy drew the pan of milk back from the kittens? Were those men of significance? Was someone filming a 'candid' movie, and could he even be part of it? Could

122

there be a hidden camera filming him now? Andrew glanced at the upper corners of his unlit cell, and became aware of the smell of old urine. He himself stank of nervous sweat. All he needed now was fleas or lice from the blanket. He snatched the blanket from the metal bed, and took it to the only source of light, the barred window opposite the brick wall. He didn't see any lice or fleas, but he shook the blanket anyway and a thin cockroach fell out. Andrew stepped on it, with a feeling of small triumph. The floor was of rather pretty gray stone slabs. This might have been a home once, he thought, because the floor was handsome, as was the stone floor in the big room in front. The red brick wall between him and the mumbling inmate had been recently put there. Reassured somewhat about the blanket, Andrew lay down on his back and tried to collect himself.

He could explain himself in one minute to an English-speaking person at the Consulate. If that didn't work, Mexico City was only about two hours away by car. A man from the Consulate could get here by six or so. And though Andrew had a New York address just now, his sister was next door in Houston, Texas. She could find a Spanish-speaking American lawyer. But surely things wouldn't get *that* bad!

Andrew gave a tremendous sigh and closed his eyes.

Hadn't he the right to a glass of water? Even a pitcher of it to wash with?

"Hey! — *Hey!*" he yelled, and banged on the door a couple of times. "*Agua — por favor!*"

No one came. Andrew tried the yelling and banging again, then gave it up. He had a response only from the drunk next door, who seemed to want to engage him in conversation. Andrew glanced at his watch, lay down again, and closed his eyes.

He saw the fallen boy, the spreading red on his white shirt, the dusty green of the plaza's trees. He saw it sharply, as if the scene were six yards in front of him, and he opened his eyes to rid himself of the vision.

At four, he shouted, then shouted and banged more loudly. After more than five minutes, a policeman said through the square aperture:

"*Que pasà?*"

"I want to telephone!"

The door was opened. They walked to the desk in front, where the desk officer sat, in shirtsleeves now, with his jacket over the back of his chair. The air seemed warmer than before. Andrew repeated his request to telephone the American Consulate. The officer dialled.

This time the Consulate answered, and the officer spoke in Spanish to a woman, Andrew judged from the voice he heard faintly, then to a man.

"I must speak to someone in English!" Andrew whispered urgently.

The officer continued in Spanish for a while, then passed the telephone to Andrew.

The man at the other end did speak English. Andrew gave his name, and said he was being held in a jail in Quetzalan for something he did not do.

"Do you have a tourist card?"

"Tourist card," Andrew said to the desk officer, not having memorized his number, and the officer pulled a manila envelope from a desk drawer and produced the card. Andrew read the number out.

"What are you being held for?" asked the American voice.

"I witnessed a shooting outside my hotel." Andrew described what had happened. "I reported it and — now I'm being accused of it. Or suspected of it." Andrew's throat was dry and hoarse. "I need a lawyer — someone who can speak for me."

"Your occupation, sir?" asked the cool voice.

"Painter. Well, I'm a student."

"Your age?"

"Twenty-two. Is there someone in this area who can help me?"

"Not today, I'm afraid."

The conversation dragged maddeningly on. The Consulate could not possibly send a representative until tomorrow noon. The slant of the man's questions gave Andrew the feeling that his interrogator was not sure whether to believe him or not. The man told Andrew that he was being held on suspicion, and that there was a limit to what the American Consulate could do at a moment's notice. Andrew was asked if he possessed a gun.

"No! — Can I give you the phone number of my sister in Houston? You can call her collect. She might be able to do something — faster."

The man patiently took her name and telephone number, repeated that he was sorry nothing could be done today, and as Andrew stammered, wanting to make sure the man would telephone his sister, the desk officer pulled the telephone from Andrew's grasp and came out with a spate of Spanish in a good-natured, even soothing tone, added a chuckle and hung up.

"Noon tomorrow," the desk officer said to Andrew, and turned his attention to some papers on his desk.

Had the desk officer told the Consulate that he had been drunk and disorderly? "Can you not ask Señor Diego of the Hotel Corona to come here?"

The desk officer did not bother replying, and gestured for the policemen to take Andrew away.

Andrew asked for water, and a glass was brought quickly. "More, please." Andrew held his hands apart to indicate the height of a pitcher.

The pitcher arrived a few minutes after Andrew was back in his cell. He washed his face and torso with his own wet shirt, letting the water fall on the stone floor. He was angry, and at the same time too weak to be angry. Absurd! He lay on the bed half awake and half asleep, and saw a series of visions, lots of people rushing (as he had never seen them) along the sidewalks of the plaza, and the grinning mouth, the big white fangs, the bulging eyes of the Aztec god he had sketched a few days

125

ago near Mexico City. The atmosphere was menacing in all these half-dreams.

Supper arrived around six, rice with a red pepper sauce in a metal bowl, another bowl of beans. The rice dish smelled as if the bits of meat in it were tainted, but he ate the rice and beans for the strength they would give.

Andrew spent a chilly night, curled in his blanket. He was still cold at ten in the morning. At a quarter to noon, he clamoured for the door to be opened. After several minutes, a different policeman from the ones Andrew knew arrived and asked what he wanted. Andrew said he was expecting a man from the American Consulate now, and said he wanted to speak to the "Capitano" at once, meaning the desk officer. All this was through the square in Andrew's door.

The policeman strolled away without a word, and Andrew didn't know whether he was going to be ignored or whether the policeman was going to return. The policeman returned with a second policeman, and they opened his cell door.

The desk officer had gone off to lunch, and Andrew was not allowed to use the telephone.

"I waited until twelve as I was told!" Andrew said, feeling that his Spanish was improving under his difficulties. "I demand —"

The two men took his arms. Andrew squirmed around to look at the wide open door again, hopefully, but it was empty save for the figures of two police guards standing facing each other, or rather leaning, in the doorway.

"You wait in your cell," said one policeman.

So Andrew was back in his cell. He had thrown up his breakfast of watery chocolate and bread hours ago, and now there was a smelly plate of something on the floor by his bed. He picked up the plate and tried to throw its contents through the barred window, but half of it fell on the floor.

"*Ah—tee-eee—ta—coraz—zon* ..." sang the idiot in the next cell. "*Adios, mujeres ... des al ...*"

Very likely he'd have to wait out the siesta period till four! Andrew uttered the worst curse he knew in English. The fact that he had the strength to curse cheered him. He would telephone his sister at four. He fell on his bed, not caring if he slept or not, wanting only the hours to pass until four.

Andrew was asleep when he heard the clink and scrape of various closures on his door being undone. Ten past four, he saw by his watch, and he got up from the bed, blinking.

"You come," said a policeman.

Andrew followed the one policeman to the front room again. The desk officer was on the telephone now. Andrew had to stand for several minutes while the officer made a few calls one after the other, one a personal call: the officer was asking about somebody's baby, and spoke about a dinner next Saturday night. At last the desk officer looked at Andrew.

"Spatz Andreo — you are to leave this building, leave your hotel, leave the United States of Mexico — for your safety," he said.

Andrew was puzzled, but leaving this building sounded pleasant. "I am free?"

The desk officer sighed, as if Andrew were not completely free of suspicion, or even guilt. "You have my orders," he murmured.

Andrew had nothing of his own in the cell, so he did not need to go back. "The *señor* from the American Consulate —"

"No one from the Consulate is coming."

Had the Consulate telephoned? Andrew thought it wise to ask no more questions.

"You will leave the country within twenty-four hours. Understood?" The desk officer handed Andrew his tourist card and a square of paper which he tore from a block and of which he had a carbon copy. "Please give this paper to the Mexican border police or the passport control at the airport before eighteen hours tomorrow."

Andrew looked at the form, which had his name, tourist card number and 18:00 written in with a pen. It was an order to leave, but in the list of 'reasons' nothing had been indicated.

"*Adios*," said the desk officer.

"*Adios*," Andrew replied.

Two policemen, one of whom drove the wagon, took Andrew to within two streets of the Hotel Corona, and asked him to get out and go straight to his hotel. Andrew started walking. He was aware that he looked filthy, and wavering from weakness he might appear drunk also, so he avoided the eyes of a couple of the townspeople — a woman with a basket of laundry on her head, an old man with a cane. They both stared at him. Had he imagined that the old man had nodded and smiled at him?

"*Señor!*" said a small boy on the sidewalk near the hotel door. This was a greeting, the boy had smiled shyly, and dashed on at a run.

Señor Diego was standing behind the counter in the hotel lobby when Andrew entered.

"*Tardes*," Andrew said in a weary voice, and waited for his key.

"*Buenos tardes, señor*," replied Señor Diego, laying Andrew's key on the counter. He nodded slightly, with the hint of a smile.

A contemptuous smile? Did Señor Diego know already, having been informed by a telephone call from the desk officer, that he had to leave the country in twenty-four hours? Probably. "Can I have a bath, please?"

He could. Señor Diego went at once to the bathroom, which was down the hall from Andrew's room. Andrew had had a couple of baths there; one paid a little extra, that was all. Andrew unlocked his room door. The bed was made. Nothing seemed changed. He looked into the top of his suitcase and saw that his folder of traveller's cheques was still there. His billfold was still in the inside pocket of his jacket in the closet, and he looked into it: several thousand pesos still, and maybe none at all had been removed.

Andrew took clean clothes with him into the bathroom. The humble but tidy bathroom looked luxurious. He soaped himself, washed his hair, cleaned the tub with a scrubbing-brush he found in a bucket, then soaked his jeans, shirt and underpants in more hot water, soap and cleaning powder, and rinsed his hair at the basin. Life had its sweet moments! And goddam the Consulate! A fat lot of help *they'd* been!

Or, Andrew thought a moment later as he pulled on clean levis, had the American Consulate rung up this morning, said or threatened something unless the police-station made itself clear? Andrew decided to keep his resentment or his gratitude to himself until he learned something definite.

He hung his damp clothes on hangers at the window in his room, and put some old newspapers on the tiled floor below them. Andrew did not know what attitude to take with Señor Diego, whether to consider him friend or foe or neutral, because certainly he hadn't been helpful yesterday when the police had come and taken him away. Andrew decided to be merely polite.

"Señor Diego," he began with a nod. "I leave tomorrow morning. On the first bus for Mexico City. So — I should like to pay you now."

Señor Diego reached for Andrew's note in a pigeon-hole behind him, and he added the item of the bath with a ball-point pen. "*Si, señor.* Here you are. — You are looking better now!"

Andrew smiled despite himself, as he pulled limp pesos out of his billfold. He watched Señor Diego count his money, then get some change for him from a locked drawer under the pigeon-holes. "*Gracias.* And — the boy out there —" He went on, "He is dead?" Andrew knew he was dead, but he had to say it, in the form of half-question, half-statement.

Señor Diego's eyes grew small and sharp under his greying brows, and he nodded. "A bad boy. *Muy malo.* Someone shot him," he finished softly, with a shrug.

"Who?"

"*Quién sabe?* Everyone hated him. Even his family. They threw him out of the house long ago. The boy stole. Worse!" Señor Diego pointed to his temple. "*Muy loco.*"

Señor Diego's tone was friendly now, man to man. Andrew began to understand, or he thought he did. Someone with a grievance against the boy had shot him, and maybe the whole town knew who, and maybe the police had had to find someone to take the blame or at least be suspected for a while, to keep up a show of justice. Or perhaps, he thought, if he hadn't been naive enough to insist on reporting the shooting, the body would have simply lain there for hours until somebody removed it. Now Andrew understood Felipe's pushing him out of his bar, not wanting to hear what he had to say. The town had had to shut him up.

"Yes," Andrew said, putting his pesos into his billfold. "A bad boy — with the little cats."

"The little *cats*! With people — shopkeepers! A thief! He was *all* bad!" Señor Diego spoke with fervour.

Andrew nodded, as if he agreed absolutely. He went back to his room, and slept for several hours.

When he woke up, it was dark. The Bar Felipe's juke-box played a *mariachi* song with xylophone, guitars, and an enthusiastic tenor. Andrew stretched and smiled. He smiled at his good luck. Twenty-four hours in a Mexican jail? He had read about dirtier jails, worse treatment in jails in books by Gogol, Koestler and Solzhenitsyn. He was ravenously hungry, and knew the little restaurant off the plaza would still be open, if Felipe's juke-box was playing. Andrew put on his cotton jacket against the evening cool. When he dropped his key on the counter, one of the men guests in the hotel said good evening to him, looked him in the eye, and gave him a friendly smile.

Andrew walked towards the little restaurant whose juke-box music he could hear before he reached the corner where he had to turn, the music overlapping for a few seconds with that from the Bar Felipe. There was no table free, but the young woman who served, who Andrew thought was the daughter of the woman who cooked, asked one man to move to a table with his friends, to whom he was talking anyway. Andrew was aware of more glances than on former evenings, but these glances seemed more friendly, as if the men knew him now, as if they were not merely curious about a *gringo* in the town.

"*Salud!*" A man of about fifty bent over Andrew's table, extending a hand. In his left hand he held a small, heavy tequila glass.

Andrew swallowed some of his first course of stuffed green peppers, put his fork down, and shook the man's thick hand.

"*Un tequila!*" said the man.

Andrew knew it would look rude to refuse. "Okay! — *Gracias.*"

"*Tequila!*" the man commanded.

"*Tequila!*" echoed the others. "*Andre-o!*"

It was "*Andre-o!*" again when the *tequila* arrived. In a discreet way, the dozen men in the restaurant toasted him. The young woman waitress suggested a special dish, which she said was ready in the kitchen. It turned out to be a substantial meal. When Andrew pulled out his billfold to pay, the waitress said:

"No, *señor.*" She wagged a finger and smiled. "You are invited tonight."

A few of the men laughed at Andrew's surprise.

At a quarter to eight the next morning, Andrew's bus, which had been half an hour late, rolled away from the plaza on the road to Jalapa, where he would board a larger bus. The town of Quetzalan looked sweet to him now, like a place he would like to return to one day. He smiled at his recollection of a man and woman, American

131

or English tourists he had seen getting off the bus one afternoon in the plaza: they had gazed around them, conferred, then got back on the bus. Andrew shied away from the memory of the dead boy, though the vision of his white-clad body came now and then, quick and brief as a camera flash.

In Mexico City he rang Houston. He could catch a plane and be in Houston at 6.15 that evening, he told his sister. Esther sounded delighted, but she asked why he was coming back so soon. He would tell her when he saw her, he said, but everything was fine, quite okay.

Esther's husband Bob picked Andrew up at the airport. Houston was another world: chrome and glass, Texas accents, the comforts of home at his sister's and Bob's house, containers of milk and ice cream in the fridge, a two-year-old tot who was learning to call him 'Uncle Andy'.

After dinner, Andrew told them about his last couple of days in Mexico. He had to tell them, before he showed them his drawing and painting efforts, which they were eager to see. Andrew had expected to narrate it smoothly, making it a bit funny, especially his time in the old jail-formerly-palace. But he found himself groping for the right words, particularly when trying to express what he had felt when he realized that the boy was dead.

Esther's face showed that he had made his story clear, however, in spite of his stammerings.

"How awful! Before your eyes!" she said, clasping her hands in her lap. "You should try to forget that sight, Andy. Otherwise it'll haunt you."

Andrew looked down at the living-room carpet. Forget it? Should he? Why? Or forget the jail also, just because he hadn't realized why he was there, because the jail happened to have no toilet paper? Andrew gave a laugh. He felt older than his sister, though he was a year younger.

"Any news from — the girl you liked up in New York?" asked Bob.

Andrew's heart jumped. "In Mexico? No," he replied casually, and exchanged a glance with his sister. He had told his sister that he had had a bad time with a girl he liked, and of course Esther had said something to Bob. *Lorrie* was what he had to forget. Could he? Any more than he could forget the instant when he had realized that the patch of red on the white shirt was blood?

In New York, Andrew returned to his friends' apartment in SoHo, where he had a room of his own. Someone had been sleeping in his room in his absence and had paid rent, so the main owner of the apartment, Phyllis, didn't charge Andrew for the three weeks he had been gone. Andrew got his part-time job back, as the arrangements were informal and he was paid by the evening. He checked in again at the Art Students League. He made several sketches of the boy lying on the sidewalk of the plaza, and tried a gouache in green, grey and red. He did an oil of it, two oils, then paintings based on the sketches he had made of the Mexican hills. He worked afternoons at his painting, and all day on the days when he did not go to the League in the morning.

One night in the SoHo restaurant where he worked, Lorrie was sitting at a table with a big fellow with dark hair. Andrew felt as if a rifle bullet had gone through him. He spoke to another waiter, who agreed to serve Lorrie's table, which was in Andrew's assigned area. Andrew continued working, but he felt disturbed and avoided glancing at Lorrie, though he was sure that she had spotted him carrying trays, moving back and forth past her table. He loved her as much as ever.

That night Andrew could not sleep, and got out of bed and started another painting of the dead boy. Death, sudden death at thirteen. The jagged and pointed leaves of the palm trees were dusty grey-green, outlined in black, as if in mourning. A curious pigeon flew into the picture, like a disappointed dove of peace, maybe soon to be converted to a bird of prey. A ghostly and skinny kitten stood amazed on stiff legs, confronted by the milk and the blood which had just reached the cement of the walk. One of the boy's puzzled eyes was open, as was his mouth, and there was the pie pan inches from his fingers. How would the colours look by daylight? Andrew disliked painting by electric light. No matter, he had felt like painting it once more.

The dawn was coming when he fell into bed.

The Stuff of Madness

When Christopher Waggoner, just out of law school, had married Penelope, he had known of her fondness for pets, and her family's fondness too. That was normal, to love a cat or dog that was part of the household. Christopher had not even thought much about the stuffed little Pixie, a white Pomeranian with shiny black artificial eyes, which stood in a corner of her father's study on a wooden base with her dates of birth and death, nor of the fluffy orange and white cat called Marmy, also preserved, which sat on the floor in another corner. A live cat and dog had lived in the Marshalls' house during his courting days, Christopher recalled, but long ago they had fallen into the taxidermist's hands, and now stood and sat respectively on an outcrop of rock in his and Penny's Suffolk garden. These were not the only animals that peopled, if the word could be used, the garden at Willow Close.

There was Smelty, a feisty little black Scotch terrier with one foot raised and an aggressive muzzle extended with bared teeth, and Jeff the Irish sheep dog, whose coat stood up the best against the elements. Some relics had been in the garden for twenty and more years. An Abyssinian cat called Riba, a name Penny had derived from some mystic experiment, stared with greenish-yellow eyes from a tree branch, crouched as if to pounce on anyone walking in the path below. Christopher had seen guests catch a glimpse of the cat and recoil in alarm.

All in all, there were seventeen or eighteen preserved

cats and dogs and one rabbit, Petekin, placed about the garden. The Waggoners' two children, Philip and Marjorie, long grown up and married, smiled indulgently at the garden, but Christopher could remember when they winced, when Marjorie didn't want her boyfriends to see the garden and there'd been fewer dead pets then, and when Philip at twelve had tried to burn Pixie on a bonfire, and had been caught by Penny and given the severest scolding of his life.

Now a crisis had come up, attentively listened to by their present dog and cat, Jupiter, an old red setter, and Flora, a docile black cat with white feet. These two were not used to a tense atmosphere in the calm of Willow Close. Little did they understand, Christopher thought, that he was taking a step to protect them from an eternal life after death in the form of being stuffed and made to stand outdoors in all weathers. Wouldn't any animal, if it were capable of choosing, prefer to be a few feet under the ground, dissolving like all flesh, when his time had come? Christopher had used this argument several times to no avail.

The present altercation, however, was over the possible visit of some journalists who would photograph the stuffed animals and write up Penelope's lifelong hobby.

"My old darlings in the newspaper," Penny said in a beseeching way. "I think it's a lovely tribute to them, Christopher, and the *Times* might reprint some of it with *one* photograph from the Ipswich paper anyway. And what's the harm in it?"

"The harm," Christopher began calmly but trying to make every word tell, "is that it's an invasion of privacy for me and for you too. I'm a respected solicitor — still going up to London once or twice a week. I don't want my private address to be bruited about. My clients and colleagues for the most part know my London where-abouts, only. Would you like the telephone ringing here twenty times a day?"

"Oh, Christopher! Anyone who wants your home address can get it, and you know that."

Christopher was standing in the brick-floored kitchen with some typewritten pages of a brief in his hand, wearing house-slippers, comfortable trousers and a coat sweater. He had come in from his study, because he had thought the last telephone call, which Penny had made a few moments ago, might have been to give the green light to the journalists. But Penny told him she had been ringing her hairdresser in Ipswich for an appointment on Wednesday.

Christopher tried again. "Two days ago, you seemed to see my point of view. Quite frankly, I don't want my London associates to think I dwell in a place so — so whimsical." He had sought for a word, abandoned the word 'macabre', but maybe macabre would have been better. "You see the garden a bit differently, dear. For most people, including me sometimes, it's a trifle depressing."

He saw he had hurt her. But he felt he had to take a stand now before it was too late. "I know you love all those memories in the garden, Penny, but to be honest Philip and Marjorie find our old pets a bit spooky. And Marjorie's two children, they giggle now, but — "

"You're saying it's only *my* pleasure."

He took a breath. "All I'm saying is that I don't want the garden publicized. If you think of Pixie and old Marmy," Christopher continued with a smile, "seeing themselves as they look now, in a newspaper, they might not like it either. It's an invasion of their privacy too."

Penny tugged her jumper down nervously over the top of her slacks. "I've already agreed to the journalists — just two, I think, the writer and the photographer — and they're coming Thursday morning."

Oh, my God, Christopher thought. He looked at his wife's round, innocent blue eyes. She really didn't understand. Since she had no occupation, her collection of taxidermy had become her chief interest, apart from knitting, at which she was quite skilled and in which she gave lessons at the Women's Institute. The journalists'

139

arrival meant a show of her own achievement, in a way, not that she did any taxidermy herself, the expert they engaged was in London. Christopher felt angry and speechless. How could he turn the journalists off without appearing to be at odds with his wife, or without both of them (if Penny acquiesced to him) seeming fullblown cranks to hold their defunct pets so sacred, they wouldn't allow photographs of them? "It's going to damage my career — most gravely."

"But your career is made, dear. You're not struggling. And you're in semi-retirement anyway, you often say that." Her high, clear voice pleaded pitiably, like that of a little girl wanting something.

"I'm only sixty-one." Christopher pulled his abdomen in. "Hawkins's doing the same thing I am, commuting from Kent at sixty-nine."

Christopher returned to his study, his favourite room and his bedroom for the last couple of years, as he preferred it to the upstairs bedroom and the spare room. He was aware that tears had come to his eyes, but he told himself that they were tears of frustration and rage. He loved the house, an old two-storey manse of red brick, the corners of its overhanging roof softened by Virginia creeper. They had an interesting catalpa in the back garden — on one of whose limbs unfortunately Riba the Abyssinian cat sat glowering — and a lovely design of well-worn paths whose every inch Christopher knew, along which he had strolled countless times, working out legal problems or relaxing from work by paying close attention to a rosebush or a hydrangea. He had acquired the habit of not noticing the macabre — yes, macabre — exteriors of pets he and Penny had known and loved in the past. Now all this was to be invaded, exposed to the public to wonder at, very likely to chuckle at too. In fact, had Penny a clue as to how the journalists intended to treat the article, which was probably going to be one of their full-page spreads, since the stuffed animals were in their way so photogenic? Who had put the idea into the heads of the *Chronicle* journalists?

One source of his anguish, Christopher knew, was that he hadn't put his foot down long ago, before Penny had turned the garden into a necropolis. Penny had always been a good wife, in the best sense of that term. She'd been a good mother to their children, she'd done nothing wrong, and she'd been quite pretty in her youth, and still took care of her appearance. It was he who had done something wrong, he had to admit. He didn't care to dwell on that period, which had been when Penny had been pregnant with Marjorie. Well, he had given Louise up, hadn't he? And Louise would have been with him now, if he had parted from Penny. How different his life would have been, how infinitely happier! Christopher imagined a more interesting, more richly fulfilled life, though he'd have gone on with his law career, of course. Louise had passion and imagination. She had been a graduate student of child psychiatry when Christopher met her. Now she had a high position in an institution for children in America, Christopher had read in a magazine, and years before that he had seen in a newspaper that she had married an American doctor.

Christopher suddenly saw Louise distinctly as she had looked when they'd had their first rendezvous at the Gare du Nord, she having been at the station to meet him, because she'd got to Paris a few hours before. He remembered her young, happy eyes of paler blue than Penny's, her soft, smiling lips, her voice, the round hat she wore with a beige crown and a black fur rim. He could recall the scent of her perfume. Penny had found out about that affair, and persuaded him to end it. How had she persuaded him? Christopher could not remember Penny's words, they certainly had not been threatening or blackmailing in any way. But he had agreed to give up Louise, and he had written as much to Louise, and then he had collapsed for two days in bed, exhausted as well as depressed, and so miserable, he had wanted to die. With the wisdom of years, Christopher realized that collapsing had been symbolic of a suicide, and that he was rather glad, after all, that he had merely spent two days in bed and not shot himself.

That evening at dinner, Penny remarked on his lack of appetite.

"Yes. Sorry," Christopher said, toying with his lamb chop. "I suppose old Jupiter may as well have this."

Christopher watched the dog carry the chop to his eating place in the corner of the kitchen, and Christopher thought: another year or so and Jupiter will be standing in the garden, perhaps on three legs, in a running position for ever. Christopher firmly hoped he wouldn't be alive to see it. He set his jaw and stared at the foot of his wine glass whose stem he twisted. Not even the wine cheered him.

"Christopher, I am sorry about the journalists. They looked *me* up, and begged me. I had no idea you'd be so upset."

Christopher had a feeling that what she said was not true. On the other hand, Penny wasn't malicious. He decided to chance it. "You could still cancel it, couldn't you? Tell them you've changed your mind. You won't have to mention me, I trust."

Penny hesitated, then shook her head. "I simply don't want to cancel it. I love my garden. This is a way of sharing it — with friends and with people I don't even know."

She probably envisaged letters from strangers saying they were going to take up the same method of preserving their pets in their houses or gardens — God forbid — and what was the name of their taxidermist? And so Christopher's will hardened. He would have to endure it, and endure it he would, like a man. He wouldn't even quit the house while the journalists were here, because that would be cowardly, but he was going to take care not to be in any photograph.

Wednesday, a pleasant and sunny day, he did not set foot in the garden. It was ruined for him. The blossoming roses, the softly bending willow, chartreuse-coloured in the sunlight, seemed a stage-set waiting for the accursed journalists. His work, a lot of it, making that garden so beautiful, and now the vulgarians were going to trample over the primroses, the pansies, backing up and stepping sideways for their silly photographs.

Something was building up inside Christopher, a desire to hit back at both the journalists and at Penny. He felt like bombing the garden, but that would destroy the growing things as well as part of the house, possibly. Absurd! But an insufferable wrath boiled in him. The white coat of Pixie showed left of the catalpa even from the kitchen window. A brown and white collie called Doggo was even more visible on a stone base near the garden wall. Christopher had been able to cut these out of his vision somehow — until today.

When Penny went to the hairdresser's on Wednesday afternoon, fetched by her friend Beatrice who went to the same hairdresser, Christopher took the car and drove rather aimlessly northward. He'd never done such a thing before. Waste of petrol, he'd have thought under usual circumstances, since he hadn't even a shopping list with him. His mind dwelt on Louise. *Louise* — a name he'd avoided saying to himself for years, because it pained him so. Now he relished the pain, as if it had a cleansing and clarifying power. *Louise* in the garden, that was what Penny needed to bring back to her what the past was all about. Louise, worthy of being preserved if any living creature ever had been. Penny had met her once at a cocktail party in London, while the affair was still going on, and had sensed something and later made a remark to Christopher. Months later, Penny had discovered his three photographs of Louise — though to give Penny credit, she had not been snooping, but looking for a cufflink that Christopher said he had lost in the chest of drawers. Penny had said, "Well, Christopher — this is the girl who was at that party, is it not?" and then it had come out, that he was still seeing her. With Penny preg-

143

nant, Christopher had not been able to fight for Louise. For that he reproached himself too.

Christopher turned the car towards Bury St Edmunds, to a large department store, and found a parking place nearby. He was full of an unusual confidence that he would have his way, that everything would be easy. He looked in the windows of the store as he walked towards the entrance: summer clothing on tall mannikins with flesh-coloured legs, wearing silly smiles or equally silly pouts, flamboyant with hands and arms flung out as if to say, "Look at me!" That wasn't quite what he wanted. Then he saw her — a blond girl seated at a little white round table, in a crisp navy blue blouse rather like a sailor's middy, navy blue skirt and black patent leather pumps. An empty stemmed glass stood on the table before her, and around her dummy men reared back barefoot in white dungarees, either topless or wearing striped blue and white jumpers.

"Where might I find the manager?" Christopher asked, but received such a vague answer from a salesgirl, he decided to push on more directly. He barged into a stockroom near the window where the girl was.

Five minutes later, he had what he wanted, and a young window-dresser called Jeremy something was even carrying her to his car, the girl in the navy blue outfit, without a hat and with very dead-looking strawy straight yellow hair. Christopher had offered a deposit of a hundred pounds for an overnight rental, half to be paid back on return of the dummy and clothing in good condition, and he had added encouragement by pushing a ten-pound note into the young man's hand.

With the dummy installed in the back seat, Christopher returned to shop for a hat. He found more or less what he was looking for, a round hat trimmed with black velour instead of fur, and the crown was white and not beige, but the resemblance to Louise's hat in the photograph, which he was sure Penny remembered, was sufficient and striking enough. When he returned to the car, a small child was staring curiously at the mannikin. Christopher smiled amiably, pulled a blanket (used to keep Jupiter's paws off the back seat when he went to the vet for arthritis shots) gently over the figure, and drove off. He felt a bit pressed for time, and hoped that Penny had decided to have tea at Beatrice's house instead of theirs.

He was in luck. Penny was not home yet. Having ascertained this, Christopher carried the dummy from the car into the house via the back door. He set the figure in his chair in front of his desk and indulged in a few seconds of amusement and imagination — imagining that it *was* Louise, young and round-cheeked, that he could say something to her, and she would reply. But the girl's eyes, though large and blue, were quite blank. Only her lips smiled in a rather absent but definite curve. This reminded Christopher of something, and he went quickly up the stairs and got the brightest red lipstick he could find among several on Penny's dressing table. Then down again, and carefully, trying his best to steady his hand which was trembling as it never had before, Christopher enlarged the upper lip, and lowered the under lip exactly in the centre. The upturned red corners of the lips were superb.

Just then, he heard the sound of a car motor, and seconds later a car door slamming, voices, and he could tell from the tone that Penny was saying goodbye to Beatrice. Christopher at once set the dummy in a back corner of his study, and concealed the figure completely with a coverlet from his couch. At any rate, Penny almost never looked into his study, except when she knocked on the door to call him to tea or a meal. Christopher put the bag with the hat under the coverlet also.

Penny looked especially well coifed, and was in good spirits the rest of the afternoon and evening. Christopher behaved politely, merely, but in his way, he felt in good spirits too. He debated putting the effigy of Louise out in

145

the garden tonight versus early tomorrow morning. Tonight, Jupiter might bark, as he slept outdoors in this season in his doghouse near the back door. Christopher could take a stroll in the garden, if he happened to be sleepless at midnight, tell Jupiter to hush, and the dog would, but if he were carrying a large object and fussing around getting it placed correctly, the silly dog just might keep on barking because he was tied up at night. Christopher decided on early tomorrow morning.

Penny retired just after ten, assuring Christopher cheerfully that "It'll all be over so quickly tomorrow," he wouldn't know it had happened. "I'll tell them to be very careful and not step on the flowerbeds." She added that she thought he was being very patient about it all.

In his study, Christopher hardly slept. He was aware of the village clock striking faintly at quite a distance every hour until four, when the window showed signs of dawn. Christopher got up and dressed. He sat Louise again in his desk chair, and practised setting the hat on correctly at a jaunty angle. The extended forearm, without the glass stem in the fingers of the hand, looked able to hold a cigarette, and Christopher would have put one there unlighted, except that he and Penny didn't smoke, and there were no cigarettes in the house just now. Just as well, because the hand looked also as if Louise might be beckoning to someone, having just called out someone's name. Christopher reached for a black felt pen, and outlined both her blue eyes.

There! Now her eyes really stood out and the outer corners turned up just a little, imitating the upturn of her lips.

Christopher carried the figure out the back door with the coverlet still over it. He knew where it should be, on a short stone bench on the left side of the garden which was rather hidden by laurels. Jupiter's eyes had met Christopher's for an instant, the dog had been sleeping with forepaws and muzzle on the threshold of his wooden house, but Jupiter did not bother to lift his

146

head. Christopher flicked the bench clean with the coverlet, then seated Louise gently, and put a stone under one black pump, since the shoe did not quite touch the ground. Her legs were crossed. She looked charming — much more charming than the long-haired Pekinese called Mao-Mao who peeked from the foliage to the left of the bench, facing the little clearing as if he were guarding it. Mao-Mao's tongue, which protruded nearly two inches and had been made by the taxidermist out of God knew what, had lost all its pink and was now a sickening flesh colour. For some reason, Mao-Mao had always been a favourite target of his and Penny's dogs, so his coat looked miserable.

But Louise! She was fantastically smart with her round hat on, in her crisp new navy outfit, her happy eyes directed towards the approach to the nook in which she sat. Christopher smiled with satisfaction, and went back to his study, where he fell sound asleep until Penny awakened him with tea at eight.

The journalist and the photographer were due at 9.30, and they were punctual, in a dirty grey Volkswagen. Penny went down the front steps to greet them. The two young men, Christopher observed from the sitting-room window, looked even scruffier than he had foreseen, one in a T-shirt and the other in a polo-neck sweater, and both in blue jeans. Gentlemen of the press, indeed!

Christopher had two reasons, his legal mind assured him, for joining the company in the garden: he didn't want to appear huffy or possibly physically handicapped, since the journalists knew that Penny was married and to whom, and also he wanted to witness the discovery of Louise. So Christopher stood in the garden near the house, after the men had introduced themselves to him.

"Jonathan, look!" said the man without the camera, marvelling at big Jeff the Irish sheep dog who stood on the right side of the garden. "We must get this!" But his exclamations became more excited as he espied old Pixie, whose effigy made him laugh with delight.

The cameraman snapped here and there with a compact little machine that made a whir and a click. Stuffed animals were really everywhere, standing out more than the roses and peonies.

"Where do you have this expert work done, Mrs Waggoner? Have you any objection to telling us? Some of our readers might like to start the same hobby."

"Oh, it's more than a hobby," Penny began. "It's my way of keeping my dear pets with me. I feel that with their forms around me — I don't suffer as much as other people do who bury their pets in their gardens.'

"That's the kind of comment we want," said the journalist, writing in his tablet.

Jonathan was exploring the foot of the garden now. There was a beagle named Jonathan back to the right behind the barberry bush, Christopher recalled, but either Jonathan didn't see him or preferred the more attractive animals. The photographer drifted closer to Louise, but still did not notice her. Then, focusing on Riba, the cat in the catalpa, he stepped backward, nearly fell, and in recovering glanced behind him, and glanced again.

Penny was just then saying to the journalist, "Mr Taylor puts a special weatherproofing on their coats with a spray . . ."

"Hey Mike! — *Mike*, look!" The second Mike had a shrill note of astonishment.

"What now?" asked Mike smiling, approaching.

"Mao-Mao," said Penny, following them in her medium-high heels. "I'm afraid he's not in the best — "

"No, no, the figure. Who is this?" asked the photographer with a polite smile.

Penny's gaze sought and found what the photographer was pointing at. "Oh! — Oh, *goodness*!" Then she took a long breath and screamed, like a siren, and covered her face with her hands.

Jonathan caught her arm as she swayed. "Mrs Waggoner! Something the matter? We didn't damage anything. — It's a friend of yours — I suppose?"

"Someone you liked very much?" asked Mike in a tactful tone.

Penny looked crushed, and for brief seconds Christopher relished it. Here was Louise in all her glory, young and pretty, sure of herself, sure of him, smack in their garden. "Penny, a cup of tea?" asked Christopher.

They escorted Penny through the back door and into the kitchen. Christopher put the kettle on.

"It's Louise!" Penny moaned in an eerie voice, and leaned back in the bamboo chair, her face white.

"Someone she didn't want us to photograph?" asked Jonathan. "We certainly won't."

Before Christopher could pour the first cup of tea, Mike said, "I think we'd better call for a doctor, don't you, Mr Waggoner?"

"Y-yes, perhaps." Christopher could have said something comforting to Penny, he realized — that he had meant it as a joke. But he hadn't. And Penny was in a state beyond hearing anything anybody said.

"Why was she so surprised?" asked Jonathan.

Christopher didn't answer. He was on his way to the telephone, and Mike was coming with him, because Mike had the number of a doctor in Ipswich, in case the local doctor was not available. But this got interrupted by a shout from Jonathan. He wanted some help to get Penny to a sofa, or anywhere where she could lie down. The three of them carried her into the sitting room. The touch of rouge on her cheeks stood out garishly on her pale face.

"I think it's a heart attack," said Jonathan.

The local doctor was available, because his nurse knew whom he was visiting just now, and she thought he could arrive in about five minutes. Meanwhile Christopher covered Penny with a blanket he brought from upstairs, and started the kettle again for a hot water bottle. Penny was now breathing through parted lips.

"We'll stay till the doctor gets here, unless you want us to take her directly to Ipswich Hospital," said Jonathan.

149

"No — thank you. Since the doctor's on his way, it may be wisest to wait for him."

Dr Dowes arrived soon after, took Penny's pulse, and at once gave her an injection. "It's a heart attack, yes, and she'd best go to hospital." He went to the telephone.

"If we possibly could, Mr Waggoner," said Jonathan, "we'd like to come back tomorrow morning, because today I didn't get all the pictures I need to choose from, and the rest of today is so booked up, we're due somewhere in a few minutes. — If you could let us in around nine-thirty again, we'd need just another half hour."

Christopher thought at once of Louise. They hadn't got a picture of her as yet, and he wanted them to photograph her and was sure they would. "Yes, certainly. Nine-thirty tomorrow. If I happen not to be here, you can use the side passage into the garden. The gate's never locked."

As soon as they had driven off, the ambulance arrived. Dr Dowes had not asked if anything had happened to give Penny a shock, but he had gathered the journalists' purpose — he knew of the stuffed animals in the garden, of course — and he said something to the effect that the excitement of showing her old pets to the public must have been a strain on her heart.

"Shall I go with her?" Christopher asked the doctor, not wanting at all to go.

"No, no, Mr Waggoner, really no use in it. I'll ring the hospital in an hour or so, and then I'll ring you."

"But how dangerous is her state?"

"Can't tell as yet, but I think she has a good chance of pulling through. No former attacks like this."

The ambulance went away, and then Dr Dowes. Christopher realized that he wouldn't have minded if the shock of seeing Louise had killed Penny. He felt strangely numb about the fact that at this minute, she was hovering between life and death. Tomorrow, Penny alive or not, the journalist and the photographer would be back, and they would take a picture of Louise. How would Penny, if she lived, explain the effigy of a young woman in her garden? Christopher smiled nervously. If Penny died, or if she didn't, he could still ring up the Ipswich *Chronicle* and say that under the circumstances, because his wife had suffered such emotional strain because of the publicity, he would be grateful if they cancelled the article. But Christopher didn't want that. He wanted Louise's picture in the newspaper. Would his children Philip and Marjorie suspect Louise's identity, or role? Christopher couldn't imagine how, as they had never heard Louise's name spoken, he thought, never seen that that photograph which Christopher had so cherished until Penny asked him to destroy it. As for what their friends and neighbours thought, let them draw their own conclusions.

Christopher poured more tea for himself, removed Penny's unfinished cup from the living room, and carried his tea into his study. He had work to do for the London office, and was supposed to telephone them before five this afternoon.

At two o'clock, the telephone rang. It was Dr Dowes.

"Good news," said the doctor. "She's going to pull through nicely. An infarction, and she'll have to lie still in hospital for at least ten days, but by tomorrow you can visit . . ."

Christopher felt depressed at the news, though he said the right things. When he hung up, in an awful limbo between fantasy and reality, he told himself that he must let Marjorie know about her mother right away, and ask her to ring Philip. Christopher did this.

"You sound awfully down, Dad," said Marjorie. "It could have been worse after all."

Again he said the proper things. Marjorie said she would ring her brother, and maybe both of them could come down on Sunday.

By four o'clock, Christopher was able to ring his office and speak with Hawkins about a strategy he had worked out for a company client. Hawkins gave him a word of praise for his suggestions, and didn't remark that Christopher sounded depressed, nor did Christopher mention his wife.

Christopher did not ring the hospital or Dr Dowes the rest of that evening. Penny was coming back, that was the fact and the main thing. How would he endure it? How could he return the dummy — Louise — to the department store, as he had promised? He couldn't return Louise, he simply couldn't. And Penny might tear her apart, once she regained the strength. Christopher poured a scotch, sipped it neat, and felt that it did him a power of good. It helped him pull his thoughts together. He went into his study and wrote a short letter to Jeremy Rogers, the window-dresser who had given him his card in the Bury St Edmunds store, saying that due to circumstances beyond his control, he would not be able to return the borrowed mannikin personally, but it could be fetched at his address, and for the extra trouble he would forfeit his deposit. He put this letter in the post box on the front gate.

Christopher's will was in order. As for his children, they would be quite surprised, and to what could they attribute it? Not to Penny's crisis, because she was on the mend. Let Penny explain it to them, Christopher thought, and had another drink.

Drink was part of his plan, and not being used to it, Christopher quickly felt its soothing power. He went upstairs to the medicine chest in the bathroom. Penny always had little sedatives, and maybe some big ones too. Christopher found four or five little glass jars that might suit his purpose, some of them overaged, perhaps, but no matter. He swallowed six or eight pills, washed down with scotch and water, mindful to think of something else — his appearance — while he did this, lest the thought of all the pills made him throw up.

In the downstairs hall looking-glass, Christopher combed his hair, and then he put on his best jacket, a rather new tweed, and went on taking pills with more scotch. He dropped the empty jars carelessly into the garbage. The cat Flora looked at him in surprise when he lurched against a sideboard and fell to one knee. Christopher got up again, and methodically fed the cat. As for Jupiter, he could afford to miss a meal.

"M'wow," said Flora, as she always did, as a kind of thank-you before she fell to.

Then Christopher made his way, touching doorjambs, fairly crawling down the steps, to the garden path. He fell only once, before he reached his goal, and then he smiled. Louise, though blurred at the edges, sat with the same air of dignity and confidence. She was alive! She smiled a welcome to him. "Louise," he said aloud, and with difficulty aimed himself and plopped on to the stone bench beside her. He touched her cool, firm hand, the one that was extended with fingers slightly parted. It was still a *hand*, he thought. Just cool from the evening air, perhaps.

The next morning the photographer and the journalist found him slumped sideways, stiff as the dummy, with his head in the navy-blue lap.

Not in This Life, Maybe the Next

(First published in *Ellery Queen's Mystery Magazine*, New York, 1970, under the title "The Nature of the Thing")

Eleanor had been sewing nearly all day, sewing after dinner, too, and it was getting on for eleven o'clock. She looked away from her machine, sideways towards the hall door, and saw something about two feet high, something greyish black, which after a second or two moved and was lost from view in the hall. Eleanor rubbed her eyes. Her eyes smarted, and it was delicious to rub them. But since she was sure she had not really seen something, she did not get up from her chair to go and investigate. She forgot about it.

She stood up after five minutes or so, after tidying her sewing table, putting away her scissors, and folding the yellow dress whose side seams she had just let out. The dress was ready for Mrs Burns tomorrow. Always letting out, Eleanor thought, never taking in. People seemed to grow sideways, not upward any more, and she smiled at this fuzzy little thought. She was tired, but she had had a good day. She gave her cat Bessie a saucer of milk — rather creamy milk, because Bessie liked the best of everything — heated some milk for herself and took it in a mug up to bed.

The second time she saw it, however, she was not tired, and the sun was shining brightly. This time, she was sitting in the armchair, putting a zipper in a skirt, and as she knotted her thread, she happened to glance at the door that went into what she called the side room, a room off the living-room at the front of the house. She saw a squarish figure about two feet high, an ugly little thing that at first suggested an upended sandbag. It took

157

a moment before she recognized a large square head, thick feet in heavy shoes, incredibly short arms with big hands that dangled.

Eleanor was half out of her chair, her slender body rigid.

The thing didn't move. But it was looking at her.

Get it out of the house, she thought at once. Shoo it out the door. What *was* it? The face was vaguely human. Eyes looked at her from under hair that was combed forward over the forehead. Had the children put some horrid toy in the house to frighten her? The Reynoldses next door had four children, the oldest eight. Children's toys these days — You never knew what to expect!

Then the thing moved, advanced slowly into the living-room, and Eleanor stepped quickly behind the armchair.

"Get out! Get away!" she said in a voice shrill with panic.

"Um-m," came the reply, soft and deep.

Had she really heard anything? Now it looked from the floor — where it had stared while entering the room — to her face. The look at her seemed direct, yet was somehow vague and unfocused. The creature went on, towards the electric bar heater, where it stopped and held out its hands casually to the warmth. It was masculine, Elanor thought, its legs — if those stumpy things could be called legs — were in trousers. Again the creature took a sidelong look at her, a little shyly, yet as if defying her to get it out of the room.

The cat, curled on a pillow in a chair, lifted her head and yawned, and the movement caught Eleanor's eye. She waited for Bessie to see the thing, straight before her and only four feet away, but Bessie put her head down again in a position for sleeping. That was curious!

Eleanor retreated quickly to the kitchen, opened the back door and went out, leaving the door open. She went round to the front door and opened that wide, too. Give the thing a chance to get out! Eleanor stayed on her front path, ready to run to the road if the creature emerged.

The thing came to the front door and said in a deep voice, the words more a rumble than articulated, "I'm not going to harm you, so why don't you come back in? It's your house." And there was the hint of a shrug in the chunky shoulders.

"I'd like you to get out, please!" Eleanor said.

"Um-m." He turned away, back into the living room.

Eleanor thought of going for Mr Reynolds next door, a practical man who probably had a gun in the house, as he was a captain in the Air Force. Then she remembered the Reynoldses had gone off before lunch and that their house was empty. Eleanor gathered her courage and advanced towards the front door.

Now she didn't see him in the living-room. She even looked behind the armchair. She went cautiously towards the side room. He was not in there, either, She looked quite thoroughly.

She stood in the hall and called up the stairs, really called to all the house, "If you're still in this house, I wish you would leave!"

Behind her a voice said, "I'm still here."

Eleanor turned and saw him standing in the living-room.

"I won't do you any harm. But I can disappear if you prefer. Like this."

She thought she saw a set of bared teeth, as if he were making an effort. As she stared, the creature became paler grey, more fuzzy at the edges. And after ten seconds, there was nothing. *Nothing!* Was she losing her mind? She must tell Dr Campbell, she thought. First thing tomorrow morning, go to his office at 9 a.m. and tell him honestly.

The rest of the day, and the evening, passed without incident. Mrs Burns came for her dress, and brought a coat to be shortened. Eleanor watched a television programme, and went to bed at half past ten. She had

159

thought she would be frightened, going to bed and turning all the lights out, but she wasn't. And before she had time to worry about whether she could get to sleep or not, she had fallen asleep.

But when she woke up, he was the second thing she saw, the first thing being her cat, who had slept on the foot of the bed for warmth. Bessie stretched, yawned and miaowed simultaneously, demanding breakfast. And hardly two yards away, he stood, staring at her. Eleanor's promise of immediate breakfast to Bessie was cut short by her seeing him.

"I could use some breakfast myself." Was there a faint smile on that square face? "Nothing much. A piece of bread."

Now Eleanor found her teeth tight together, found herself worldless. She got out of bed on the other side from him, quickly pulled on her old flannel robe, and went down the stairs. In the kitchen, she comforted herself with the usual routine: put the kettle on, feed Bessie while the kettle was heating, cut some bread. But she was waiting for the thing to appear in the kitchen doorway, and as she was slicing the bread, he did. Trembling, Eleanor held the piece of bread towards him.

"If I give you this, would you go away?" she asked.

The monstrous hand reached out and up, and took the bread. "Not necessarily," rumbled the bass voice. "I don't need to eat, you know. I thought I'd keep you company, that's all."

Eleanor was not sure, really not sure now if she had heard it. She was imagining telling Dr Campbell all this, imagining the point at which Dr Campbell would cut her short (politely, of course, because he was a nice man) and prescribe some kind of sedative.

Bessie, her breakfast finished, walked so close by the creature, her fur must have brushed his leg, but the cat showed no sign of seeing anything. That was proof enough that he didn't exist, Eleanor thought.

A strange rumbling. "Um-hm-hm", came from him.

He was laughing! "Not everyone — or everything — can see me," he said to Eleanor. "Very few people can see me, in fact." He had eaten the bread, apparently.

Eleanor steeled herself to carry on with her breakfast. She cut another piece of bread, got out the butter and jam, scalded the teapot. It was ten to eight. By nine she'd be at Dr Campbell's.

"Maybe there's something I can do for you today," he said. He had not moved from where he stood. "Odd jobs. I'm strong." The last word was like a nasal burr, like the horn of a large and distant ship.

At once, Eleanor thought of the rusty old lawn roller in her barn. She'd rung up Field's, the second-hand dealers, to come and take it away, but they were late as usual, two weeks late. "I have a roller out in the barn. After breakfast, you can take it to the edge of the road, if you will." That would be further proof, Eleanor thought, proof he wasn't real. The roller must weigh two or three hundred pounds.

He walked, in a slow, rolling gait, out of the kitchen and into the sitting room. He made no sound.

Eleanor ate her breakfast at the scrubbed wooden table in the kitchen, where she often preferred to eat instead of in the dining room. She propped a booklet on sewing tips before her, and after a few moments, she was able to concentrate on it.

At 8.30, dressed now, Eleanor went out to the barn behind her house. She had not looked for him in the house, didn't know where he was now, in fact, but somehow it did not surprise her to find him beside her when she reached the barn door.

"It's in the back corner. I'll show you." She removed the padlock which had not been fully closed.

He understood at once, rubbed his big yellowish hands together, and took a grip on the wooden stick of the roller. He pulled the thing towards him with apparently the greatest ease, then began to push it from behind, rolling it. But the stick was easier, so he took the stick again, and in less than five minutes, the roller was at the edge of the road, where Eleanor pointed.

Jane, the girl who delivered morning papers, was cycling along the road just then.

Eleanor tensed, thinking Jane would cry out at the sight of him, but Jane only said shyly (she was a very shy girl), "'Morning, Mrs Heathcote," and pedalled on.

"Good morning to you, Jane," Eleanor answered.

"Anything else?" he asked.

"I can't think of anything, thank you," Eleanor replied rather breathlessly.

"It won't do you any good to speak to your doctor about me," he said.

They were both walking back towards the house, up the carelessly flagged path that divided Eleanor's front garden.

"He won't be able to see me, and he'll just give you useless pills," he continued.

What made you think I was going to a doctor? Eleanor wanted to ask. But she knew. He could read her mind. *Is he some part of myself?* she asked herself, with a flash of intuition which went no further than the question. If no one *else* can see him —

"I am myself," he said, smiling at her over one shoulder. He was leading the way into the house. "Just me." And he laughed.

Eleanor did not go to Dr Campbell. She decided to try to ignore him, and to go about her usual affairs. Her affairs that morning consisted of walking a quarter of a mile to the butcher's for some liver for Bessie and a half-chicken for herself, and of buying several things at Mr White's, the grocer. But Eleanor was thinking of telling all this to Vance — Mrs Florence Vansittart — who was her best friend in the town. Vance and she had tea together, at one or the other's house, at least once a week, usually once every five days, in fact, and Eleanor rang up Vance as soon as she got home.

The creature was not in sight at that time.

Vance agreed to come over at four o'clock. "How *are* you, dear?" Vance asked as she always did.

"All right, thanks!" Eleanor replied, more heartily than usual. "And you? . . . I'll make some blueberry muffins if I get my work done in time . . ."

That afternoon, though he had kept out of sight since the morning, he lumbered silently into the room just as Eleanor and Vance were starting on their second cups of tea, and just as Eleanor was drawing breath for the first statement, the first introductory statement, of her strange story. She had been thinking, the roller at the edge of the road (she must ring Field's again first thing in the morning) would be proof that what she said was not a dream.

"What's the matter, Eleanor?" asked Vance, sitting up a little. She was a woman of Eleanor's age, about fifty-five, one of the many widows in the town, though unlike Eleanor, Vance had never worked at anything, and had been left a little more money. And Vance looked to her right, at the side room's door, where Eleanor had been looking. Now Eleanor took her eyes away from the creature who stood four feet within the room.

"Nothing," Eleanor said. Vance didn't see him, she thought. Vance can't see him.

"She can't see me," the creature rumbled to Eleanor.

"Swallow something the wrong way?" Vance asked, chuckling, helping herself to another blueberry muffin.

The creature was staring at the muffins, but came no closer.

"You know, Eleanor — " Vance chewed, " — if you're still charging only a dollar for putting a hem up, I think you need your head examined. People around here, all of them could afford to give you two dollars. It's criminal the way you cheat yourself."

Vance meant, Eleanor thought, that it was high time she had her house painted, or re-covered the armchair, which she could do herself if she had the time. "It's not easy to mention raising prices, and the people who come to me are used to mine by now."

"Other people manage to mention price-raising pretty easily," Vance said as Eleanor had known she would. "I hear of a new one every day!"

The creature took a muffin. For a few seconds, the muffin must have been visible in mid-air to Vance, even if she didn't see him. But suddenly the muffin was gone, being chewed by the massive, wooden-looking jaw.

"You look a bit absent today, my dear," Vance said. "Something worrying you?" Vance looked at her attentively, waiting for a confidence — such as another tooth extraction that Eleanor felt doomed to, or news that her brother George in Canada, who had never made a go of anything, was once more failing in business. Eleanor braced herself and said, "I've had a visitor for the last two days. He's standing right here by the table." She nodded her head in his direction.

The creature was looking at Eleanor.

Vance looked where Eleanor had nodded. "What do you mean?"

"You can't see him? — He's quite friendly," Eleanor added. "It's a creature two feet high. He's right there. He just took a muffin! I know you don't believe me," she rushed on, "but he moved the roller this morning from the barn to the edge of the road. You saw it at the edge of the road, didn't you? You *said* something about it."

Vance tipped her head to one side, and looked in a puzzled way at Eleanor. "You mean a handyman. Old Gufford?"

"No, he's — " But at this moment, he was walking out of the room, so Vance couldn't possibly have seen him, and before he disappeared into the side room, he gave Eleanor a look and pushed his great hands flat downward in the air, as if to say, "Give it up," or "Don't talk." "I mean what I said," Eleanor pursued, determined to share her experience, determined also to get some sympathy, even protection. "I am not joking, Vance. It's a little — creature two feet high, and he talks to me." Her voice had sunk to a whisper. She glanced at the side room doorway, which was empty. "You think I'm seeing things, but I'm not, I swear it."

Vance still looked puzzled, but quite in control of herself, and she even assumed a superior attitude. "How long have you — been seeing him, my dear?" she asked, and chuckled again.

"I saw him first two nights ago," Eleanor said, still in a whisper. "Then yesterday quite plainly, in broad daylight. He has a deep voice."

"If he just took a muffin, where is he now?" Vance asked, getting up. "Why can't I see him?"

"He went into the side room. All right, come along." Eleanor was suddenly aware that she didn't know his name, didn't know how to address him. She and Vance looked into an apparently empty room, empty of anything alive except some plants on the windowsill. Eleanor looked behind the sofa end. "Well — he has the faculty of disappearing."

Vance smiled, again superiorly. "Eleanor, your eyes are getting worse. Are you using your glasses? That sewing — "

"I don't need them for sewing. Only for distances. Matter of fact I did put them on when I looked at him yesterday across the room." She was wearing her glasses now. She was near-sighted.

Vance frowned slightly. "My dear, are you afraid of him? — It looks like it. Stay with me tonight. Come home with me now, if you like. I can come back with Hester and look the house over thoroughly." Hester was her cleaning woman.

"Oh, I'm sure you wouldn't see him. And I'm not afraid. He's rather friendly. But I *did* want you to believe me."

"How can I believe you, if I don't see him?"

"I don't know." Eleanor thought of describing him more accurately. But would this convince Vance, or anybody? "I think I could take a photograph of him. I don't think he'd mind," Eleanor said.

"A good idea! You've got a camera?"

"No. Well, I have, an old one of John's, but — "

"I'll bring mine. This afternoon. — I'm going to finish my tea."

Vance brought the camera just before six. "Good luck, Eleanor. This should be interesting!" Vance said as she departed.

Eleanor could tell that Vance had not believed a word of what she had told her. The camera said '4' on its indicator. There were eight more pictures on the roll, Vance had said. Eleanor thought two would be enough.

"I don't photograph, I'm sure," his deep voice said on her left, and Eleanor saw him standing in the doorway of the side room. "But I'll pose for you. Um-hm-hm." It was the deep laugh.

Eleanor felt only a mild start of surprise, or of fear. The sun was still shining. "Would you sit in a chair in the garden?"

"Certainly," the creature said, and he was clearly amused.

Eleanor picked up the straight chair which she usually sat on when she worked, but he took it from her and went out the front door with it. He set the chair in the garden, careful not to tread on flowers. Then with a little boost, he got himself on to the seat and folded his short arms.

The sunlight fell full on his face. Vance had showed Eleanor how to work the camera. It was a simple one compared to John's. She took the picture at the pre-scribed six-foot distance. Then she saw old Gufford, the town handyman, going by in his little truck, staring at her. They did not usually greet each other, and they did not now, but Eleanor could imagine how odd he must think she was to be taking a picture of an ordinary chair in the garden. But she had seen him clearly in the finder. There was no doubt at all about that.

"Could I take one more of you standing by the chair?" she asked.

"Um-m." That was not a laugh, but a sound of assent. He slid off the chair and stood beside it, one hand resting on the chair's back.

This was splendid, Eleanor thought, because it showed his height in proportion to the chair.

Click!

"Thank you."

"They won't turn out, as they say," he replied, and took the chair back into the house.

"If you'd like another muffin," Eleanor said, wanting to be polite and thinking also he might have resented her asking him to be photographed, "they're in the kitchen."

"I know. I don't need to eat. I just took one to see if your friend would notice. She didn't. She's not very observant."

Eleanor thought again of the muffin in mid-air for a few seconds — it must have been — but she said nothing. "I — I don't know what to call you. Have you got a name?"

A fuzzy, rather general expression of amusement came over his square face. "Lots of names. No one particular name. No one speaks to me, so there's no need of a name."

"I speak to you," Eleanor said.

He was standing by the stove now, not as high, not nearly as high as the gas burners. His skin looked dry, yellowish, and his face somehow sad. She felt sorry for him.

"Where have you been living?"

He laughed. "Um-hm-hm. I live anywhere, everywhere. It doesn't matter."

She wanted to ask some questions, such as, "Do you feel the cold?" but she did not want to be personal, or prying. "It occurred to me you might like a bed," she said more brightly. "You could sleep on the sofa in the side room. I mean, with a blanket."

Again a laugh. "I don't need to sleep. But it's a kind thought. You're very kind." His eyes moved to the door,

167

as Bessie walked in, making for her tablecloth of newspaper, on which stood her bowl of water and her unfinished bowl of creamy milk. His eyes followed the cat.

Eleanor felt a sudden apprehension. It was probably because Bessie had not seen him. That was certainly disturbing, when she could see him so well that even the wrinkles in his face were quite visible. He was clothed in strange material, grey-black, neither shiny nor dull.

"You must be lonely since your husband died," he said. "But I admit you do well. Considering he didn't leave you much."

Eleanor blushed. She could feel it. John hadn't been a big earner, certainly. But a decent man, a good husband, yes, he had been that. And their only child, a daughter, had been killed in a snow avalanche in Austria when she was twenty. Eleanor never thought of Penny. She had set herself never to think of Penny. She was disturbed, and felt awkward, because she thought of her now. And she hoped the creature would not mention Penny. Her death was one of life's tragedies. But other families had similar tragedies, only sons killed in useless wars.

"Now you have your cat," he said, as if he read her thoughts.

"Yes," Eleanor said, glad to change the subject. "Bessie is ten. She's had fifty-seven kittens. But three — no four years ago, I finally had her doctored. She's a dear companion."

Eleanor slipped away and got a big grey blanket, an army surplus blanket, from a closet and folded it in half on the sofa in the side room. He stood watching her. She put a pillow under the top part of the blanket. "That's a little cosier," she said.

"Thank you," came the deep voice.

In the next days, he cut the high grass around the barn with a scythe, and moved a huge rock that had always annoyed Eleanor, embedded as it was in the middle of a grassy square in front of the barn. It was August, but quite cool. They cleared out the attic, and he carried the heaviest things downstairs and to the edge of the road to be picked up by Field's. Some of these things were sold a few days later at auction, and fetched about thirty dollars. Eleanor still felt a slight tenseness when he was present, a fear that she might annoy him in some way, and yet in another way she was growing used to him. He certainly liked to be helpful. At night, he obligingly got on to his sofa bed, and she wanted to tuck him in, to bring him a cup of milk, but in fact he ate next to nothing, and then, as he said, only to keep her company. Eleanor could not understand where all his strength came from.

Vance rang up one day and said she had the pictures. Before Eleanor could ask about them, Vance had hung up. Vance was coming over at once.

"You took a picture of a chair, dear! Does he look like a chair?" Vance asked, laughing. She handed Eleanor the photographs.

There were twelve photographs in the batch, but Eleanor looked only at the top two, which showed him seated in the straight chair and standing by it. "Why, there he *is*!" she said triumphantly.

Vance hastily, but with a frown, looked at the pictures again, then smiled broadly. "Are you implying there's something wrong with *my* eyes? It's a chair, darling!"

Eleanor knew Vance was right, speaking for herself. Vance couldn't see him. For a moment, Eleanor couldn't say anything.

"I told you what would happen. Um-hm-hm."

He was behind her, in the doorway of the side room, Eleanor knew, though she did not turn to look at him.

"All right. Perhaps it's my eyes," Eleanor said. "But I *see* him there!" She couldn't give up. Should she tell Vance about his Herculean feats in the attic? Could she have got a big chest of drawers down the stairs by herself?

Vance stayed for a cup of tea. They talked of other things — everything to Eleanor was now 'other' and a bit uninteresting and unimportant compared to *him* — and then Vance left, saying, "Promise me you'll go to Dr Nimms next week. I'll drive you, if you don't want to drive. Maybe you shouldn't drive if your eyes are acting funny."

Eleanor had a car, but she seldom used it. She didn't care for driving. "Thanks, Vance, I'll go on my own." She meant it at that moment, but when Vance had gone, Eleanor knew she would not go to the eye doctor.

He sat with her while she ate her dinner. She now felt defensive and protective about him. She didn't want to share him with anyone.

"You shouldn't have bothered with those photographs," he said. "You see, what I told you is true. Whatever I say is true."

And yet he didn't look brilliant or even especially intelligent, Eleanor reflected.

He tore a piece of bread rather savagely in half, and stuffed a half into his mouth. "You're one of the very few people who can see me. Maybe only a dozen people in the world can see me. Maybe less than that. — Why should the others see me?" he continued, and shrugged his chunky shoulders. "They're just like me."

"What do you mean?" she asked.

He sighed. "Ugly." Then he laughed softly and deeply. "I am not nice. Not nice at all."

She was too confused to answer for a moment. A polite answer seemed absurd. She was trying to think what he really meant.

"You enjoyed taking care of your mother, didn't you? You didn't mind it," he said, as if being polite himself and filling in an awkward silence.

"No, of course not. I loved her," Eleanor said readily. How could he know? Her father had died when she was eighteen, and she hadn't been able to finish college because of a shortage of money. Then her mother had become ill with leukaemia, but she had lived on for ten years. Her treatment had taken all the money Eleanor

170

had been able to earn as a secretary, and a little more besides, so that everything of value they had possessed had finally been sold. Eleanor had married at twenty-nine, and gone with John to live in Boston. Oh, the gone and lovely days! John had been so kind, so understanding of the fact that she had been exhausted, in need of human company — or rather, the company of people her own age. Penny had been born when she was thirty.

"Yes, John was a good man, but not so good as you," he said, and sighed. "Hm-mm."

Now Eleanor laughed spontaneously. It was a relief from the thoughts she had been thinking. "How can one be good — or bad? Aren't we all a mixture? You're certainly not all bad."

This seemed to annoy him. "Don't tell me what I am."

Rebuffed, Eleanor said nothing more. She cleared the table.

She put him to bed, thanked him for his work in the garden that day — gouging up dandelions, no easy task. She was glad of his company in the house, even glad that no one else could see him. He was a funny doll that belonged to her. He made her feel odd, different, yet somehow special and privileged. She tried to put these thoughts from her mind, lest he disapprove of them, because he was looking, vaguely as usual, at her, with a resentment or a reproach, she felt. "Can I get you anything?" she asked.

"No," he answered shortly.

The next morning, she found Bessie in the middle of the kitchen floor with her neck wrung. Her head sat in the strangest way on her neck, facing backwards. Eleanor seized up the corpse impulsively and pressed the cat to her breast. The head lolled. She knew he had done it. But why?

"Yes, I did it," his deep voice said.

She looked at the doorway, but did not see him. "How could you? Why did you do it?" Eleanor began

171

to weep. The cat was not warm any longer, but she was not stiff.

"It's my nature." He did not laugh, but there was a smile in his voice. "You hate me now. You wonder if I'll be going. Yes, I'll be going." His voice was fading as he walked through the living room, but still she could not see him. "To prove it, I'll slam the door, but I don't need to use the door to get out." The door slammed.

She was looking at the front door. The door had not moved.

Eleanor buried Bessie in the back lawn by the barn, and the pitchfork was heavy in her hands, the earth heavier on her spade. She had waited until late afternoon, as if hoping that by some miracle the cat might come alive again. But Bessie's body had grown rigid. Eleanor wept again.

She declined Vance's next invitation to tea, and finally Vance came to see her, unexpectedly. Eleanor was sewing. She had quite a bit of work to do, but she was depressed and lonely, not knowing what she wanted, there being no person she especially wanted to see. She realized that she missed him, the strange creature. And she knew he would never come back.

Vance was disappointed because she had not been to see Dr Nimms. She told Eleanor that she was neglecting herself. Eleanor did not enjoy seeing her old friend Vance. Vance also remarked that she had lost weight.

"That — little monster isn't annoying you still, is he? Or is he?" Vance asked.

"He's gone," Eleanor said, and managed a smile, though what the smile meant, she didn't know.

"How's Bessie?"

"Bessie — was hit by a car a couple of weeks ago."

"Oh, Eleanor! I'm sorry. — Why didn't you — You should've *told* me! What bad luck! You'd better get another kitty. That's always the best thing to do. You're so fond of cats."

Eleanor shook her head a little.

172

"I'm going to find out where there's some nice kittens. The Carters' Siamese might've had another illegitimate batch." Vance smiled. "They're always nice, half-Siamese. Really!"

That evening, Eleanor ate no supper. She wandered through the empty-feeling rooms of her house, thinking not only of him, but of her lonely years here, and of the happier first three years here when John had been alive. He had tried to work in Millersville, ten miles away, but the job hadn't lasted. Or rather, the company hadn't lasted. That had been poor John's luck. No use thinking about it now, about what might have been if John had had a business of his own. Yes, once or twice, certainly, he had failed at that, too. But she thought more clearly of when *he* had been here, the funny little fellow who had turned against her. She wished he were back. She felt he would not do such a horrid thing again, if she spoke to him the right way. He had grown annoyed when she had said he was not entirely bad. But she knew he would not come back, not ever. She worked until ten o'clock. More letting out. More hems taken up. People were becoming square, she thought, but the thought did not make her smile that night. She tried to add three times eighty cents plus one dollar and twenty-five cents, and gave it up, perhaps because she was not interested. She looked at his photographs again, half expecting not to see him — like Vance — but he was still there, just as clear as ever, looking at her. That was some comfort to her, but pictures were so flat and lifeless.

The house had never seemed so silent. Her plants were doing beautifully. She had not long ago repotted most of them. Yet Eleanor sensed a negativity when she looked at them. It was very curious, a happy sight like blossoming plants causing sadness. She longed for something, and did not know what it was. That was strange also, the unidentifiable hunger, this loneliness that was worse and more profound than after John had died.

Tom Reynolds rang up one evening at 9 p.m. His wife

was ill and he had to go at once to an 'alert' at the Air Base. Could she come over and sit with his wife? He hoped to be home before midnight. Eleanor went over with a bowl of fresh strawberries sprinkled with powdered sugar. Mary Reynolds was not seriously ill, it was a day-long virus attack of some kind, but she was grateful for the strawberries. The bowl was put on the bed-table. It was a pretty colour to look at, though Mary could not eat anything just then. Eleanor felt herself, heard herself smiling and chatting as she always did, though in an odd way she felt she was not really present with Mary, not really even in the Reynolds' house. It wasn't a 'miles away' feeling, but a feeling that it was all not taking place. It was not even as real as a dream.

Eleanor went home at midnight, after Tom returned. Somehow she knew she was going to die that night. It was a calm and destined sensation. She might have died, she thought, if she had merely gone to bed and fallen asleep. But she wished to make sure of it, so she took a single-edged razorblade from her shelf of paints in the kitchen closet — the blade was rusty and dull, but no matter — and cut her two wrists at the bathroom basin. The blood ran and ran, and she washed it down with running cold water, still mindful, she thought with slight amusement, of conserving the hot water in the tank. Finally, she could see that the streams were lessening. She took her bath towel and wrapped it around both her wrists, winding her hands as if she were coiling wool. She was feeling weak, and she wanted to lie down and not soil the mattress, if possible. The blood did not come through the towel before she lay down on her bed. Then she closed her eyes and did not know if it came through or not. It really did not matter, she supposed. Nor did the finished and unfinished skirts and dresses downstairs. People would come and claim them.

Eleanor thought of him, small and strong, strange and yet so plain and simple. He had never told her his name. She realized that she loved him.

I am Not as Efficient as Other People

The shutters were the beginning of the crisis. Ralph's depression, his sense of failure, had been going on long before the shutters, of course, maybe since he had bought the house, if he thought about it, but the shutters seemed glaringly to illustrate his incompetence.

Ralph Marsh worked in Chicago, had an apartment there, but he had also a country house which he called sometimes his cottage, sometimes his shack, twenty miles outside of Chicago. He was a bachelor of twenty-nine, and a salesman of hi-fi equipment. He had had raises and promotions in his four years with Basic-Hi, he knew his job and was his company's best salesman, or so his superior had told him. Ralph knew the intricacies of a stereo set, and even considered himself reasonably good with his hands — not a genius do-it-yourself man, perhaps, but maybe better than average.

However, across Ralph's ten yards of lawn lived the Ralstons, Ed and Grace, who bustled about every weekend, doing not merely useful and necessary tasks such as lawn-cutting, fence-painting and hedge-trimming (their hedge was young and low, and Ed kept it cropped with the sharpest of corners), but more difficult jobs such as cement-mixing for bricklaying, which in the Ralstons' case had not meant simply piling one red brick on another: Ed had chipped into rectangles a number of large beige stones to create a low wall on the road side of his property. Part of the Ralstons' garage was a workshop, whence came the buzz of Ed's Black and Decker many hours every weekend. Ralph imagined Ed making furniture, repairing broken pipes, welding, doing things that Ralph would be afraid to attempt. Yet Ed Ralston, Ralph knew, was only a car salesman, probably hadn't finished university. Ralph was not chummy with the Ralstons, they only nodded greetings in a neighbourly way when they saw one another.

Ralph had realized, since his first weekend at his cottage, that he was going to be envious of Ed. For one thing, Ed had a wife, and a wife was certainly a help in a house. The Ralstons also had an apartment in Chicago, they had told Ralph on their first meeting, and they said they had bought their country place for next to nothing, because it had been an empty barn. Ed and Grace had chipped away at the stone facade of the barn to expose beautiful old masonry, had put in windows, and installed heating and electricity with the help of a couple of chums of Ed's. They had bought their barn six months before Ralph acquired his house, and they were still at it every weekend, improving and adding things. Grace Ralston was as active as Ed, forever shaking out a doormat, hanging a wash on their plastic four-sided clothes-line, or polishing windows.

Only when Ralph was tired around 7p.m., wishing that he had someone to call him to a dinner already prepared, did he feel a little sorry for himself. Most of the time, he preferred to consider himself lucky. Ralph was at least six years younger than Ed, he earned more, and for all Ed's expert stone-laying, Ed was stuck with a wife who was certainly a boring type, and stuck too with a tantrumy four-year-old daughter who didn't look quite bright, in Ralph's opinion, whereas Ralph was free as the breeze and had a mobile girlfriend of twenty-four who was fun and made no demands on him. She was a dark blonde named Jane Eberhart, married to an airline pilot. Most weekends she was able to come out to the country house and stay the night, perhaps three Saturday nights out of four. They could manage a few dates in Chicago, too.

But the shutters. Ralph had painted three shutters on three windows, meaning six panels in all, in matt black. Because of other chores, Ralph had had to take three swats at the shutters on various weekends, but finally they were done, and he meant to say casually to Jane, "How do you like my shutters? They look neater, no?" which he did say one Saturday morning around eleven, when Jane arrived. Then when he folded back the third pair, he saw that he had missed one upper third of what would be the inside of a shutter when it was closed. It was like a visual joke, the former sickly pale brown which he had not painted contrasting with the black, and Jane appropriately laughed.

"Ha-ha! — Ralphie, you're a doll! *Very* funny! Hope you've got some paint left. But otherwise — sure, they look great, darling." Then she strolled in her mustard-coloured slacks and clogs towards the house door.

Ralph felt a let-down, an embarrassment, as if he were on a stage and something had gone badly wrong. He folded the shutters back, so Ed Ralston wouldn't possibly see his blotch, but of course Ed would have his nose bent over some task of his own now, which he would complete perfectly. Absurd to feel like this, Ralph told himself, and deliberately smiled, though no one saw the smile. Ed Ralston would *not* have left an unpainted spot, or his wife would have noticed it in the course of Ed's painting, and called his attention to it.

Jane prepared lunch. She liked cooking for him more than for her husband, she said, because Ralph's taste was more catholic. Her husband was allergic to oysters, for instance, and disliked liver. That day, Jane made a delicious dish of fried shrimp with her own mayonnaise and tomato paste dressing, and Ralph had a bottle of cool white wine to accompany it. Usually after lunch he and Jane went to bed for an hour or so. After lunch and early morning, those were the times they both preferred.

Then Jane said during lunch: "So silly of you, that little unfinished spot on the shutters!" She laughed gaily again, as she bit into the last shrimp. "I bet old Ralston wouldn't've missed it! What's he up to today? — Remember the time he unplugged the kitchen sink with that electric gadget?" Jane shrieked with mirth at the memory.

Ralph remembered. Well, he hadn't a Rotoroot among his tools, and most people who were not professional plumbers didn't have one, in Ralph's opinion. "He's probably a health faddist, too," Ralph said. "Can't imagine him smoking or drinking a beer. Marches around with his back straight as if he's on parade somewhere. So does his wife."

Jane giggled, in a good mood, and lit a cigarette. 'I have to admit their place looks nice though — from the outside."

She'd never been in, though, and Ralph had. You could eat off the floor, as the saying went, but the furniture was not his style or Jane's, Ralph was sure. The Ralstons had an ugly, modern glass-top coffee table, and machine-made varnished furniture of rustic design or intention, suitable for the country, Ralph supposed the Ralstons thought. Grace Ralston had shown him with pride the brown and white tiles her husband had laid on the kitchen floor, and the cabinets with revolving corner sections which her husband had not made but had bought and sawed to measure and installed. Their rooms looked like sample rooms in a department store, not even a magazine out of place anywhere. Ralph had politely admired, but the Ralstons were not the kind of people he cared to cultivate, and he was sure Jane would feel the same way if she saw the inside of their house.

That afternoon, Ralph was not a success with Jane in bed. It was the first time in the four months they had known each other that this had happened, so Jane didn't take it seriously, and Ralph tried not to. One failure was unimportant, normal, Ralph told himself. But he knew otherwise. Jane's remarks comparing him with Ed Ralston had struck deep at his ego, even at his self-respect

180

and his manliness, somehow. Ralph pictured Ed Ralston in bed, doing just the right thing with his plump, dull wife, because Ralston would never doubt, never hesitate. He probably had a technique as unvarying as the manner in which he changed the oil in his car, but at least it worked, and in this department Ralston would be labelled efficient also.

As they smoked a cigarette after their unsatisfactory love-making, dread thoughts swept through Ralph's mind. They all concerned failures. He recalled the simple two shelves he had started to put up in an alcove in the kitchen (before he met Jane), a project which he had abandoned when his drill hit a water pipe and caused a small flood. This had necessitated a plumber to solder the pipe, then the replacement of a piece of wall there, followed by Ralph's repainting of the plastered spot, which in turn had caused him to repaint the entire kitchen. Then the fixing of the towel rack in the bathroom: one end of it was still not as steady or strong as it should be, because the damned plaster didn't hold well enough, despite the length of the screws he had put in. Nothing he did was perfect. Jane wasn't perfect, if he thought about it, or her, because she was married, and her main allegiance was of course to her husband, whose schedule varied, and a few times she'd had to cancel a date with him, because her husband was unexpectedly due home for the weekend. Her husband Jack must be more efficient, or more highly trained, than he, Ralph realized, because he was an airline pilot. Ralph up to now had enjoyed his relationship with Jane, just because it wasn't binding or heavy, but that afternoon it seemed second-rate, incomplete, inferior to other man's relationships with girls, whether they were married or not. Couldn't he do better than Jane if he tried?

Instantly, Ralph reproached himself for this thought. Jane had many good qualities, such as discretion, patience, poise. She was rather pretty, and she liked to cook. But he wasn't top dog, or man, because Jane's husband was. Politics and economics bored Jane, while Ralph found them constantly interesting. She wasn't as intelligent as he could have wished a girlfriend to be, but that wasn't it, Ralph knew. He could imagine himself quite happy with an even less intelligent girl than Jane, if he could only hold up his end of things by properly coping with the odd jobs around his house, the repairs that a house always needed. Ed Ralston even got on a ladder and straightened roof tiles! Ralph wasn't afraid of heights, but he didn't care to risk breaking an arm, since he had to drive, and he wasn't sure he knew how to put right a tile that was out of place. His one achievement, he remembered with a flash of pride, had been sneaking into Jane's and her husband's apartment, with Jane, and replacing a broken element in their stereo set. If her husband had come in, Jane had intended to say that Ralph was a repairman, but her husband hadn't come in. The replacement had been simple, but Jane had been most grateful and impressed. Could Ralston have done that? Ralph doubted it! Ralston wouldn't have known what was the matter, even after reading a brochure and an instruction book. Yet that triumph had been so long ago, three months or more now, and so brief.

"'You're getting bored with me. Well — that happens," Jane said the next morning, when they were lying in bed.

'No. Don't be silly, Jane.' Smiling, Ralph got out of bed, and put on his dressing gown.

But it was the end, and they both knew it, although they didn't mention it again that day. Jane left in her car before six in the evening, as her husband was due home before nine, and expected dinner. Ralph closed his house after Jane had gone, left a clean sink, and looked with bitter amusement at the vertical rafter or kingpin that extended from the middle of the living-room floor up to the ceiling, and farther up through the top floor to the roof. Symbol of substantiality? What a laugh! The shutter discrepancy was on the inside, now that the shutters were closed, but Ralph was still aware of it as he drove off for Chicago. He thought it wisest and best if he didn't ring Jane again, and he was pretty sure she was not going to ring him.

A gloom settled over him, so large, so many-sided, that Ralph didn't know how to analyse it, much less get rid of it. He had no pep, no confidence. It was as if he had taken a sleeping pill, which he seldom did, though at the same time his thoughts came in nervous stabs: should he tell the office he needed a week off? They'd grant him that. But what good would it do? Should he visit a singles bar and look for a new girlfriend? With his lack of zest now, would he get one? On Wednesday of that week, he failed on a sale to a three-store chain in Chicago for a Basic-Hi product, because of his own lack of enthusiasm. The sale should have been a cinch, almost to be taken for granted, but a rival company with the same innovation in their line of gadgets won it. The day after his visit to the chain store, Ralph learned of his defeat from his boss, Ferguson. These things sometimes happened, but Ralph knew that Ferguson had noticed his depression that week.

"What's the matter, Ralph? — Had a tough weekend?" The weekend was four days past, but Ralph had been drooping all week. "Want to take tomorrow off? Sleep it off?" Ferguson grinned, knowing Ralph wasn't a big drinker, but perhaps thinking that Ralph had exhausted himself with a harem of girls last weekend at his country place.

"No, no. Thanks," Ralph said. "I'll shake it off. Just a mental attitude."

"Mental attitudes are important."

That day Ralph had lunch with Pete Barnes, another salesman of Basic-Hi, with whom Ralph was on closer terms. Ralph didn't mention his state of mind, and didn't need to, he supposed, because it showed. Pete also asked him what was the matter, if he'd had bad news, and Ralph told him about breaking with a girlfriend.

"Certainly not a tragedy," Ralph said. "For one thing, she's married. And we weren't in love. But of course for a couple of days, it's a let-down." Then Ralph turned the conversation to something else, their work, but even as he listened to Pete's news about their advertising budget, Ralph realized that it was the Ralstons' eternal bustling and efficient presence and proximity in the country that was gnawing at him far more than the loss of Jane. The Ralstons had the strange power to make him feel like a worm.

By Thursday evening, Jane had not telephoned. She always phoned at least by Thursday in regard to the weekend. Ralph thought it not fitting for him to ring, so he didn't. Ralph was sure the information about a break-up with a girlfriend reached Ferguson's ears at once via Pete Barnes, because the next day Ferguson asked if Ralph could come for dinner Saturday night, and added, "A very nice girl's coming — Frances Johnson. She's a personnel director for a bank, I forget which. You might enjoy meeting her."

Enjoy meeting her. What a phrase! You could meet somebody in five seconds, but *enjoy* it? Nevertheless, Ralph accepted graciously, and forewent his usual excursion to his country house that Saturday. His shack would only have depressed him further.

Ralph was bowled over by Frances Johnson. She was nearly as tall as he, with longish blonde hair — more blond than Jane's — cool, slender, and long-legged, wearing a trouser suit that might have been made by the highest of *haute couture*, Ralph wasn't sure. Even the scent she wore was different and fascinating. Why was a girl like this free? And maybe she wasn't. Unless she had just broken with somebody too.

"Ralph's our number one representative," Stewart Ferguson said to Frances during dinner, and Ferguson's wife nodded agreement.

The evening went well. When Frances was taking her leave, Ralph asked if he could see her to a taxi. She acquiesced, and he rode with her, as they had to go in the same direction. Frances's apartment house came first, and Ralph got out and held the door for her. By then, he had a date with her on Tuesday evening for dinner. She smiled as she said, "Good night, Ralph."

Ralph watched a grey-liveried doorman touch his cap and open a big glass door for her. Now that girl was nice, and maybe she liked him. Maybe she was important. She was a Smith graduate, plus having a degree in a business school whose name had escaped Ralph, maybe because when Ferguson had mentioned it at the table, Ralph had been looking into Frances's eyes, and she into his.

Tuesday evening, Frances still remained cool and collected, though Ralph fancied he felt a warm glow from her. She inspired him to be gallant and masterful, and he liked that. He had gone to his country place the preceding Sunday, tidied it more than he usually troubled to, with an idea of asking Frances if she would like to come out the following Saturday and stay overnight, if she cared to.

"I have two bedrooms," Ralph said, which was true.

Frances accepted. She knew how to drive, she said, but hadn't a car now. Ralph said it would be a pleasure to pick her up Saturday morning around eleven, and they could drive out together.

However, Ralph spent Friday night at his country house, did the shopping early Saturday morning, then drove the twenty miles to fetch Frances. He was in good spirits, and his work had gone well that week. Maybe he was in love with Frances, in love as he had never been with Jane. Maybe he could win Frances. But he hardly dared think of that. Frances was not the type to say "yes" quickly to anybody, about anything. But for the moment, her nearness was exhilarating.

As soon as he drove with Frances into the lane that curved towards his and the Ralstons' properties, Ralph was aware of the Ralstons' prettier, better tended front

185

lawn, better clipped roses (it was already autumn), and he at once told himself to put such negative thoughts out of his head. Was Frances going to judge him as a man, as a possible lover, or even husband, by the way he clipped three rose bushes in front of his house?

In fact, Frances paid his shack a few compliments. She said the fireplace was just the right size. She liked his kitchen — yellow-walled, everything visible on shelves or pegs, and just now very clean and neat. Ralph put another log on the fire. They had a gin and Dubonnet. Frances did not want a refill before their lunch of cold lobster. They talked a little about their work, about their childhood and parents, and the minutes swam by. Ralph had forgotten his query to himself, was Frances free? She appeared free to him, she seemed to like him, but Ralph counselled himself not to move too fast, or he might lose all. As it was, that afternoon, he felt in a happy glow of expectation, as if the wine had gone to his head, though he had drunk less than he usually did.

"You did all this yourself?" Frances asked, as she stood with her coffee in the living-room. She had been looking at the pictures on his walls, the bookcases.

"This shack? Well, I furnish it. I can't say much more for myself. I — " He broke off, thinking that all he could say was that he had painted the kitchen. He had bought his bookcases. She had seen his two bedrooms and bath, and put her overnight case in the bedroom with the single bed.

"It's very nice and cosy," said Frances, smiling, tossing her long hair carelessly back with one hand. But she shivered.

Ralph's start of pleasure at her compliment at once gave way to concern about her comfort. "Just a sec, I'll turn up the heat." He went and did so, in the broom closet off the kitchen where the heating control was. Then he poked the fire into greater action. His next little chore was a final touch to his weatherstripping, which he had nearly completed that morning. This was to drive a small wedge of wood into a gap at the upper corner of a door in his living room, a door which opened on his small back garden in summertime. Ralph had just the piece of pine board that he needed, plus a hatchet in his lean-to shed, so he said, "Back in two minutes, Frances," and went out the front door.

He took the piece of wood, held it on end, and gave its edge a whack at its lower end. The point of the hatchet hit the cement threshold of the shed, but only a curled shaving came off the wood.

"What're you doing?" Frances asked.

Ralph had been aware of her approach. "Nothing serious," Ralph said with a smile, still stooped with his hatchet and wood. "I need a wedge for the door in the living room. The door never did fit at the top corner." Ralph struck again with the hatchet. This time a larger piece came off, but so large that it was not usable for his purpose. Ralph tried to laugh. Was he going to fail again? On a primitive little job like this?

"How big do you want it?" Frances asked, stooping nimbly beside him.

"Oh — like this." Ralph held his finger and thumb not half an inch apart. "That thick. Then tapering."

"I see," she said, and was ready to take the hatchet from him, but Ralph said:

"I'll try it again." He lifted the hatchet and tried to come down with direct aim and the right degree of strength, and once more his result was a useless shaving. He banged again more vigorously, which simply put an indentation in the side of the board.

Frances laughed a little. "Let me try. It's fun!"

"No." Quickly, as Frances drew her slender hand back, Ralph hacked again. He had it — but it was an oversized wedge, too long, and not worth the effort to shorten.

Frances was still smiling. "My turn." She succeeded with the first stroke. The hatchet had not even touched the cement threshold. She held up the wedge. "Something like this?"

"Perfect," said Ralph, rising. A faint sweat came over him.

In the house, he stood on a chair and banged the wedge into the top crack of the door with the hammer side of the hatchet. It went in perfectly, closed the door corner flush with the jamb, and didn't even stick out. "Makes a lot of difference with the draught," Ralph said.

"I'm sure." Frances was watching him. "Excellent. Good."

A hotter sweat came over Ralph, as if his banging in the wedge had caused him to expend a great deal of muscular effort. But he knew that was not the cause of his physical warmth. He was experiencing some kind of crisis. And Frances was smiling at him, casually but steadily. She liked him. Yet he felt at that moment like a wretch, worthless and inferior. What was it? He reminded himself, in a quick flash of reality, of his job, his 'position' — not bad at his age, and even enviable for a man ten years older. His self-congratulation vanished at once. *It was the Ralstons. It was the wedge.* If, with some tact and finesse tonight, he might persuade Frances into his bed (he had changed the sheets that morning), he knew he would not be able to make it. And was he going to impose that failure, yet another failure, upon himself?

"What's the matter?" Frances asked. "You're all pink in the face."

"Blushing maybe?" Ralph tried to smile, and laid the hatchet on the floor by the front door to remind himself to take it back to the shed. When he turned to Frances again, she was still looking at him. "I'm cracking up, that's all," Ralph said.

"What? — Why?"

Suddenly words came bubbling out of him. "Because I can't do anything efficiently! Really, it's true! I'm not sure I could change a washer on the kitchen sink! — I — The fellow next door, Ed Ralston, even his wife — "

Ralph gestured in the Ralstons' direction with a wave of

his arm. " — they can do *everything!* You'd be amazed! He's a mason, plumber, electrician, and she's a gardener and *super* housekeeper. They never stop working — and doing things efficiently. Whereas I can't. I don't." Here Ralph was aware that he was or might be boring Frances, because she was looking at him with a puzzled frown, even though she smiled a little, but he plunged on. "It's — I don't expect you to understand. Yôu've just met me. I've got to get out of this house or — " Or collapse under it, Ralph had been about to say.

Frances's calm, beautiful grey-blue eyes looked in the direction of the Ralston house, visible through the window.

She seemed lost in her own thoughts for a few seconds, and her gaze, to Ralph, seemed the gaze of a person who wished to escape (and who could blame her?). He had lost her. Ralph took a quick, deep breath. He could have collapsed with defeat, with unhappiness, and yet at the same time an insane energy boiled within him.

'I think you'd better leave," Ralph said in a hoarse but gentle tone.

"Leave? — Well — of course I will, if — " Now her eyes grew wider, with fear.

Because I'm going to destroy this house, Ralph thought. But he didn't want Frances to be crushed under it, just himself, perhaps.

"If you're so upset — "

"Yes," Ralph said. "I'm sorry. I can drive you — home." He stood rigid, boiling with heat and purpose again, ashamed of his behaviour, yet ashamed as if he saw himself from a distance, as if he weren't himself, standing here, looking at the girl.

"All right. I'll get my case."

"Oh, no, I'll do it!" Ralph dashed past her and up the stairs. Her overnight case was still closed on the floor near the single bed, and a glance into the bathroom. showed that she had not put out any toothbrush or cosmetics. Ralph went down with the case.

189

Now Frances had lit a cigarette, and she seemed calmer, standing where she had been before. "You know, it's absurd — thinking that you're inferior somehow — just because you're not a mason."

A mason was not what he meant. Ralph meant that he couldn't do *anything* properly. "I am not as efficient as other people," he said tensely, gasping. He could have leapt to the ceiling as easily as he had just run up the stairs. He twitched with repressed brute strength. "Can you — perhaps leave me alone for a minute or two? Could you take a little walk for five minutes?"

She had mentioned the woods across the road, said something about taking a walk there when they had arrived today. Now she said, "But of course."

When he saw that she had crossed the road, he took her suitcase and set it outside the house by his car. Then he fetched his large saw with the bow-shaped handle from his shed, and attacked the vertical rafter in the centre of his living room. This was a blissful outlet for his energy. The wood seemed to cut like butter, though after a moment the saw stuck with friction, so he attacked the post from the other side, which would result in a V-shaped incision a little lower than his waist as he stood.

Done! He could see through the V even, yet the damned house didn't fall. "Curse you!" Ralph said.

He took a few steps backwards, rubbed his palms together, bent and charged.

His right shoulder struck the top part of the severed rafter, and he pushed harder against it, aware of a crackling, deep yet sharp, over his head. He was aware of pain in his shoulder, then a brief roar as of an avalanche. Then he blacked out.

When Ralph was next aware of consciousness, or of thought, he seemed to be floating, weightless, horizontal perhaps, and on his back. Frances was beside him, the beautiful Frances, and she was sitting by his bed. Of course he was on a bed, or in a bed, in a hospital. He remembered. What he saw through drugged, half-open eyes was a grey-white. He tried to lift his hands, and couldn't. But there sat Frances, he saw when he groggily looked to his left.

"I've come to see you — but I think I shouldn't see you again, Ralph. You frighten me. I hope you'll understand."

Ralph opened his dry lips to reply, and nothing came. Of course he understood. He was a failure, and worse, he had lost his head. He remembered, he had tried to blow up his house. No, not bomb it, but wreck it. He had attacked it with a sledge-hammer. No, a *saw*. He remembered now. No wonder Frances had fled! He wondered if she were all right? And he hadn't the power to ask her. His eyes when he turned them to the left, whence came her voice, would not even bring Frances into focus. But there was her voice again:

"Ralph, I'm sorry. But I'm afraid of you. You must understand."

Ralph tried to nod in a pacific, polite and reconciled way. Could she see his nod? Ralph squeezed his eyes shut, wanting to weep, detesting himself, and feeling in agony at the loss, the predictable, inevitable loss of Frances. He wanted to die. And so he gave a groan.

"*O-oh-h!* A-ah-h!"

And Frances fled out the door. Who could blame her? And a nurse arrived quick as lightning, her figure a vague cloud at the left side of his bed, and she made a motion which Ralph knew was the injection of a needle into his arm, though he didn't feel anything.

Once more, consciousness stirred, he imagined that he saw things, such as the upper corners of his room, Frances somewhere on his left again, maybe sitting on a chair, leaning forward.

"You're going to be all right," said Frances in a soft voice. "Things — it's not so bad. Just a broken collarbone and a bang on the head."

"It is hopeless," Ralph murmured, mumbling like a

drunk, and sleepy unto death. Maybe he was already dead? "I'm — hopeless."

"No! — Ralph, I understand why you did it. It's just a house. So what?" Frances's voice said with more conviction.

Now Ralph felt a pressure on his left hand. Frances might have been holding his hand in both hers. "I can't — " Ralph stopped, wanting to make the statement that he was not efficient, *not* efficient. "I can't do *anything*."

"Who cares?" Frances's blond personage or aura bent and kissed him on the lips.

Ralph blinked. "Are you real?" His vision of her was still fuzzy at the edges, but he felt the pressure on his hand,

"I am *real*. And I love you, Ralph."

Ralph sighed, and relaxed in a mingling of pleasure and pain. It was real. Frances was really here, and his earlier vision had been a dream, an hallucination. "Stay with me," he whispered.

"I will! I can stay all night in the next room. It's already two in the morning now!" she said with a laugh. "Oh, Ralph, I'm not very efficient either, except a little bit in the kitchen. I mean, I can't change a washer. Does it matter?" She kissed him again on the lips.

This was real. Ralph smiled, felt like dying again, but in a different way. The nurse came in, shooing Frances away. Did that matter? She would be near him, all night, in the next room.

Ralph saw her wave, as she went out the door. Ralph tried to look firmly at the nurse, steadily, and as usual, he failed. It didn't matter any more.

The Cruellest Month

Odile Masarati was having a boring, ordinary day. That was the way she thought of it, meaning everything was "the same as always". She was sitting at her desk (really just a table with a drawer) on its low platform in front of a class of fifteen- and sixteen-year-olds, all with heads bent as they scribbled away at their English exam. Noticing a movement out of the corner of her eye, Odile looked up from her book.

"Philippe?" she said gently, her mind still on what she had been reading.

Philippe's head ducked back into line, and bent again over the paper.

The little rat had been trying to cheat again, peering at the paper of the girl next to him! Odile returned to Graham Greene. She had read the novel at least twice before, but she never tired of it. How she admired his writing! Such economy, such intellect! She recalled that she had written him two or three highly complimentary letters, care of his publishers, but he had never replied. Well, he wouldn't reply. He was one of the Pantheon. But no matter. She had a correspondence going now with three of her idols, two men and one woman, so her life was not exactly empty. In fact, what cheered her at that moment was the thought of hurrying home at three and dashing a letter off to Dennis Hollingwood of Essex, England, a writer of adventure novels.

On the dot of three, Odile stood up and said mechanically, "Very good, boys and girls. It's three o'clock. *Merci — et bon après-midi!*"

"Ou-u-u!" moaned one boy.

Others giggled in sudden release, called to friends, stood up, or threw their pens down like angry businessmen.

The students deposited their papers on a corner of Odile's desk, and these she gathered up, stuck into a folder and stuck the folder into her briefcase. Odile walked briskly to her locker down the hall, barely saying "*Bon soir*" to a couple of colleagues whom she passed, but then half the time the teachers were feuding with her or among one another, and some were jealous of her, Odile suspected. Why bother keeping track of it all? Provincials, Odile thought, stupid and mediocre. Odile knew she was a born linguist, Italian being her mother-tongue, French a close second, because of her family's moving to France when she was four, Spanish had been a piece of cake, and her German wasn't bad either, and as for English, she loved English literature so, that that language might as well have been another mother-tongue. She tugged on her raincoat. It was raining again. Odile unlocked her Deux Chevaux, and drove off down a street bordered with cropped plane trees that reminded her of freshly trimmed tails of poodles. She might write that to Dennis Hollingwood, though his prose wasn't inclined to similes, but rather to blunt narration and action. She passed the one butcher's shop of the town, not open till four, and reminded herself that she must buy some *viande hâchée* for her father either on her way to or coming from the ecology meeting at 4.30. Odile was almost a vegetarian, but her father liked his meat.

She turned left on to a smaller road at almost the edge of town, and now farm fields spread to right and left, and the few houses were stone farm dwellings and barns. Odile's house was a bit grander, formerly a small château, though one wing of it had suffered fire and collapsed long ago and had never been rebuilt. Her parents had bought the place for a song thirty years ago, when her father had fled from Italy because of a business scandal due to his brother, who had been a crook, whereas her father was merely naive. The Masarati house was a two-and-a-half storey, as Odile described it to her penpals and when she sent photos, which she often did to brighten up her letters, the half at the top being now their two attic rooms, but formerly the rooms of servants, Abominable ivy had been allowed to grow in ages past, and resisted Odile's vigorous efforts to oust it, though she cut through the thick stems at their base. She and her mother, a really energetic soul, might have conquered the ivy together, but her mother had been killed in a stupid car accident seven years ago, right here in Ezèvry-la-Montagne where the lane joined the main road into town. Her mother had been on foot.

Now Odile lived with her father alone, stuck with him, as she put it in many of her letters, though her feelings about the old man were mixed. Michel wasn't unintelligent, he had had a respectable career as hydraulic engineer, until Parkinson's syndrome had struck him about two years ago. Lately he had not been able to walk at all, and lived in a wheelchair, not an electrically propelled one, but one that he could manoeuvre all over the ground floor where he lived and slept. Bars beside the toilet and over the tub in the downstairs bathroom enabled him to use both these facilities without assistance. Michel read a lot, but the pills he took made him sleepy, and in Odile's opinion he slept more than their dog Trixie, which was fifteen hours in twenty-four according to the dog books.

"Hello, Papa!" Odile cried, having let herself in with her key.

Her father sat in the living-room in his wheelchair, reading under the yellowish light of the standing lamp, which always struck Odile as insufficient.

"Hello, my child. You had a nice day?" The old man always said this.

"Ye-es, thank you." Odile hung her raincoat on a peg in the dim hall, slipped out of her boots and went in stockinged feet up the stairs to her room, greeted Trixie who was asleep in her basket by the radiator, and opened her briefcase. "Ready for your walk, Trixie?" Odile asked, as she laid the folder of exam papers on a clear spot on her desk. She put on loafers. She wasn't going to walk any distance in this rain, just let the dog out on the back terrace to pee.

Trixie followed her, having yawned and groaned a little. The dog was eleven years old, a little plump, though Odile was strict about food and exercise when the weather permitted, taking walks of two miles with Trixie in the lanes and fields around. It was just that dogs who were part dachshund and part cocker (both these breeds being famous for overeating, Odile thought) needed discipline or they gained too much weight. Odile was back in her room with Trixie in five minutes, and sat down at her desk to spend a happy twenty minutes or so.

She addressed an envelope to Dennis Hollingwood at Five Oaks. She knew the rest of the long address and its postal zone by heart.

Dear Dennis,

What a day! Two English exams today, morning and afternoon for my little beasties, one of whom I caught cheating! If I find any amusing bloopers in the exams, which I have to start on later this afternoon after an ecology meeting of the locals, I shall regale you with same. Meanwhile it rains incessantly, reminding me of the old English soldiers' song, First World War: "Raining, raining, raining, always bloody well raining ..." I hope weather is nicer at Five Oaks.

Did you receive my last letter with photos of my ivy which I've told you so much about? It fairly obscures all sunlight, when we have any, in downstairs living room. Must cut again around the windows.

She paused, ballpoint pen's end against her upper lip. She had sent Dennis cufflinks at Christmas, for which he had written a note of thanks (they were a bit pricey), and he had added, "I hope you'll forgive me, but I haven't the time to answer every letter you write or in fact any of them just now." That had been Dennis's second and last letter, his first having been in response to a carefully wrought letter of praise from Odile in regard to *Devil's Bounty*, which Dennis Hollingwood had deigned to acknowledge with the remark, "I don't usually receive such intelligent fan mail, so yours was a pleasure — though I hardly fancy myself the equal of Conrad." This first letter had made Odile spin with joy (after all, Dennis Hollingwood was rather famous, and two of his eight novels had been made into films), and Odile had responded with a spate of letters to him, all of which she wrote in a light vein, but she had told him a lot about her own life, and about Stefan, a married man she had fallen in love with when she had been twenty-seven, and with whom she had had an affair for five years, until Stefan broke it off. Stefan Mockers was a doctor, a nose and throat specialist, dashing and handsome when she had met him, an Adonis to many women and girls, Odile had known, but she had also known that she had been his only mistress while their affair had lasted. The sad sequel to her five years of bliss with Stefan was that three months after Stefan had broken it off, he had been in a car accident (Stefan had been driving but it hadn't been his fault) on the Corniche near Marseille, had suffered broken legs and a head injury that had done him permanent brain damage. Stefan had had to abandon his practice, and was now not even a shadow of his old self, lived at home with his wife and their two teen-aged children, and occasionally Odile saw Stefan and his wife shopping in Ezèvry, Stefan creeping around with a cane as if he were ninety instead of fifty-five, and Odile always looked the other way and was sure Stefan never saw her. On her cluttered, ever-changing desk top, Odile still found room for a small photograph of Stefan, virile and smiling, with dark hair and moustache (now his hair was all grey), in a frame which stood up. Odile believed that Stefan had been the love of her life, that she might, just might, meet another man with whom she might fall in love, but no one would ever be able to hold a candle to the brilliant Stefan in his prime.

However, back to Dennis Hollingwood. She had told Dennis (whom she had started addressing as Dennis after his thank-you letter for the cufflinks) about her first meeting with Stefan, their discretion in making rendez-vous in the area, Stefan's fantastic wit and charm, the tragedy of his breaking it off, followed so soon by his accident — and all this flashed through her head again like a recorded tape, and she experienced it all again in a matter of seconds, as if indeed it were a tape that she couldn't switch off until it played itself out.

Odile had realized that Dennis's letter saying he hadn't time to answer her letters had been a brush-off, but she had felt that silence on her part after that would have looked as if she were hurt or sulking, so she had gone on writing to Dennis every two weeks or so, as if he had said nothing of this kind. Odile didn't see that an oc-casional cheerful letter could be annoying. She wasn't telephoning him, which she had once tried to do and discovered that he had an unlisted number which the English operator had refused to give out.

> I wonder what you're working on now? I hope another masterpiece like *Devil's Bounty*. I shall never forget the scene in which Ally learns the truth about his sister . . .

Odile went on for a few lines, glanced at her watch and saw that she still had time to inform Dennis that she was about to go off to the ecology meeting concerning tree care today, on which *she* would be expected, as town workhorse, to write a report of four or five hundred words, the report to be dropped into the post box of *La*

Voix d'Ezèvry before she went to bed tonight.

She attended the ecology meeting — ten people, nearly all women — in the rundown bourgeois house of Mme Gauthier of the village. Odile was bored, though she took notes on what was said. Ecology interested Odile, but the town was doing all right in the tree department, and Odile was more concerned about animal protection, the local rabbits and deer during the hunting season.

Soon she was back at her desk at home, and the letter to Dennis had to be put aside while she dashed off the ecology report on her French typewriter. Always best to get it done while it was fresh in her mind.

Then it was time to prepare dinner. She had picked up the mince. The kitchen was old like the house, but it had a modern gas stove and a refrigerator. Her father had set the table, as he always did, and he hovered in the hall in his chair, leaving her room to pass to carry things to the table.

"Anything new happen today?" asked her father.

"Ha! What's ever new? No, indeed! Nothing!" Odile replied cheerfully, stirring butter into her cooked fresh spinach.

She and her father spoke in French, though Odile had the habit of speaking Italian to Trixie, Italian being cosier than French, in Odile's opinion, and more suitable for children and animals. She gave Trixie her dinner of raw diced steak and a couple of dog biscuits, then she and her father sat down. Odile had a good appetite and ate more rapidly than her father, who of course dallied because it was his only social event of the day, and Odile always sat on as long as she could stand it.

'You ought to get out more, Odile," said her father.

"Oh? And where?" Odile replied, eyebrows raised, smiling. "And with whom? Do you know the people around here have never heard of *Céline* even? You expect me to have intellectual conversations with these hicks?" She laughed goodnaturedly, and so did her father. "You took all your pills today, Papa?"

"Ah, yes, I don't forget," he answered with resignation. As Odile was pouring her father's *décaféiné* at half past nine, the telephone rang.

"And there's Marie-Claire," said her father calmly, just to be saying something.

Odile, who had poured her cup of real coffee, good and strong, excused herself and took the cup to the telephone on the other side of the room.

Marie-Claire Lambert rang nearly every evening between 9.30 and 10. She was Odile's best friend, almost her only friend in Ezèvry. They had made acquaintance a couple of years ago at an ecology meeting. Marie-Claire was also unmarried, about thirty-two, raised in Paris, and she had inherited a large property on the south-east edge of town, including a château, part of which she rented to a married couple, plus two houses in which working-class families lived, paying Marie-Claire a rent that was rather low, because the families tended the garden and the grapevines and generally looked after things, not to mention that one of the wives was a full-time housekeeper in the part of the château where Marie-Claire lived. One thing Odile and Marie-Claire had in common was boredom with the town and its inhabitants. They could at least make each other laugh with their stories of tedium, stupidity, inefficiency, or whatever other local drawbacks they might have encountered in the course of the day.

That evening, after their usual chit-chat, Marie-Claire proposed a trip to England during Odile's Easter vacation in April. "Six days. I just happened to see this special rate in Hercule's window this morning." Hercule was the tiny travel agency of the town, based in a shop which sold electrical appliances.

Odile was interested. Her mind fixed at once on Dennis Hollingwood, whose face she knew from photographs on the jackets of his books. She wondered if she could somehow wangle a meeting with him, or at least see the outside of his house?

". . . Brighton, ha-ha," Marie-Claire went on, reading from the brochure. "Hotel's not included, you understand, this is just the *aller-retour*, but my God it's cheap!"

They both had to watch their pennies, Marie-Claire considerably less, but Odile appreciated her friend's sympathy for her smaller income and thought it rather noble of Marie-Claire to be concerned with economizing. Marie-Claire had a great-aunt in England, Odile knew, and Odile had gathered from Marie-Claire's description of her big country house that the great-aunt had money. Was Marie-Claire deriving some money from her? Odile had never asked and never would.

"Got time for a bite of lunch on Sunday?" asked Marie-Claire, switching to English as she often did.

"Dunno why not," Odile replied. "With pleasure. What time?"

Odile did not turn her light out that night until two in the morning, as usual. She had corrected and graded seven of the nearly one hundred English exam papers which she had to finish by Monday, and indulged in starting a letter to Wilma Knowles, an elderly writer of romance novels who lived in Canada, and who now and then answered a letter from Odile, which Odile admitted to herself was more gratifying than writing to a stone wall like Graham Greene. She and Wilma Knowles led rather the same kind of quiet lives in small towns, Odile thought. Wilma Knowles had written, at Odile's request, a description of her daily life, work in the mornings, maybe some shopping in the afternoons, she lived alone with two dogs in a country house a mile from town, and she still did her own housework and drove her car at the age of seventy-two.

The next morning when Odile stopped at the post office just after eight to collect her post and buy stamps, she received, besides an Eléctricité de France bill, a letter from Ralph Cowdray of Tucson, Arizona. This gave Odile a lift. She read it, sitting in her DC.

Dear Miss Masarati,

Can't write French but it's plain your English is great. Thanks for writing me. Glad you enjoyed *A Dead Man's Spurs* so much. Not my best in my opinion. Sorry I took so long to answer your letter but I've been busy doing research for my book-in-progress. You asked what color hair I've got? It's slightly red, not what we call carrot red here but still red.

Sorry your life is so boring in that little town which ought to have some pretty spots, if you look for them. Your story about your mother being hit by a car and about your lost love (if I may venture to call it that) touched me very much. Maybe you should write all this tragedy out some time, just for your own sake and kind of get it out of your system.

Meanwhile I'm pretty flattered that someone in a small town in France has discovered my books and likes them. My publishers still publish my stuff (paperback only of course) but I still can't make ends meet without the waiter's job I told you about in first letter, summers and Christmas in a hotel here.

> Best of luck, keep your chin up,
> Ralph Cowdray

This was Ralph Cowdray's second letter, and Odile answered it that very evening. Her letter was four foolscap pages long, written on both sides in her flowing, legible hand.

The Sunday lunch on Marie-Claire's handsome terrace (which faced in the right direction for sun, unlike Odile's) made Odile more excited about the coming trip to England. Marie-Claire had booked them at the Hotel Sherwood near the British Museum. And Easter holidays were just a few days off!

"Have some more oysters, dear," Marie-Claire said,

gesturing towards the well-filled platter garnished with parsley and lemon halves in the middle of the table.

Odile did. They were lunching on oysters only, thin bread and butter, a good chilled white white, to be followed by Marie-Claire's early *fraises des bois* now in a bowl on a silver tray of ice. Marie-Claire looked pretty and animated today, her light brown hair fluffy and fresh. Like Odile, she wore a sweater, slacks and flat shoes. After lunch, they were going for a walk across the fields. Odile had brought Trixie.

"Do you know, I saw Alain going into the bar with that blond whore this morning when I was buying bread?" Marie-Claire said during the *fraises*.

Odile knew the two she meant: Alain the recently married son of the grocery shop owner, and the blonde whose name Odile thought was Françoise. "Oh, she's not a whore. Is she?" They were talking in English, and Odile thought the word a bit strong.

"Well, everybody's girlfriend, shall we say? Alain's drinking more *pastis* than he can hold. He'll lose his wife and his job, if he doesn't watch out. And his wife's pregnant, did you know?"

Odile knew, and thought it all too boring, though she didn't say so. Her thoughts were of England, the huge city of London, the old buildings, its accents that she had to make an effort to understand sometimes, its theatres, lights.

Then the day came. Odile was up before dawn. One of the two women at Marie-Claire's, the one who was not Marie-Claire's housekeeper, had agreed to look in at the Masarati house twice a day, to see that Odile's father had everything he needed, to tidy the house, and to walk Trixie a little because all her father could do was let Trixie out on the terrace.

This same young woman, Jolaine, arrived in her car at six in the morning with Marie-Claire to drive them to Marseille for the train. Then the train from Marseille to Paris, very fast indeed and more thrilling than an aeroplane, then the train from Gare du Nord to Calais, and the Channel ferry on which they dozed on bench seats part of the time. Victoria Station at dusk in a light rain evoked Sherlock Holmes stories for Odile, hansom cabs, gas lights. The lovely, grimy English cruddiness! Was that the word? If so, Odile meant it affectionately.

They slept like logs in the high-ceilinged room at the Sherwood. Then a morning at Foyle's, which Marie-Claire loved too, but not with such passion as Odile, a walk to Trafalgar Square and to Piccadilly, where Odile fell in love with a tan raincoat at Simpson's, but the price really was sky-high, considering what she had just spent in orders from Foyle's, so she ended by buying a cheaper though much the same kind of raincoat at Lillywhites.

"Got to think of my aunt, you know?" said Marie-Claire that evening when they were in their hotel room. She frowned a little as if she suddenly had a stomach pain. "May as well ring her now."

"Want me to leave the room?" Odile asked, giggling.

"My great-aunt? Ha-ha."

Marie-Claire made the call while Odile looked at the *Evening Standard*. She heard Marie-Claire making a date for "tomorrow afternoon" and getting the times of trains out of Victoria. Marie-Claire chose an 11.20.

"No, no, Aunt Louise, thank you anyway. I'm with my friend Odile and we're in a hotel, so — Thanks, I'll ask her." She addressed Odile with her hand over the receiver. "Want to come for lunch?"

Odile screwed her eyes shut and shook her head. 'Tell her thanks."

"Odile says many thanks, but she has a date somewhere," said Marie-Claire.

By noon the next day, Odile was at Liverpool Street Station, having seen Marie-Claire off at Victoria. Odile had bought a hardcover copy of *Devil's Bounty* for Dennis Hollingwood to sign, if she were lucky enough to meet him. No matter, to glimpse his house would be enough!

She bought a day-return ticket to Chelmsford, and boarded a train.

At Chelmsford, she was told that there was no transportation to Little Starr, Dennis's village, except a bus at 4 p.m., but it was only five and a half miles away, Odile knew from a detailed map she had at home, so she took one of the taxis at the station. The driver asked where she wanted to go in Little Starr.

"The main square," she replied. "The centre, please."

They sped through a couple of communities that were towns, judging from their name-markers at the edge of the road, then the driver came to a halt in a village square bordered by two-storey houses and shops and graced by several elms. Odile paid and got out, realizing that she would have to ask someone for Five Oaks, otherwise she could go marching off in quite the wrong direction. She saw a plump and cheerful-looking man arranging apples in front of his fruit shop.

"Five Oaks," he repeated. "Mr Hollingwood's place." He looked at her with more attention and what might have been surprise. "That's — " He swung round, pointing. " — down that road about a mile. On the left."

"Thank you very much." The man probably thought she had a car, but Odile didn't look back to see if he were watching her. She had decided to walk.

Along the curving two-lane road, Odile passed a few houses which became ever fewer. She well knew how long a mile was, and when she saw on her left a two-storey house of whitish stone with two chimneys and a climbing rose at the doorway, set a hundred yards or more back from the road, she felt sure that it was Five Oaks. She saw four oaks. There was a garage to the left, nearly concealed by trees and bushes.

Was Dennis Hollingwood at this moment bent over his typewriter, composing first draft prose, his handsome face frowning? Or was he wandering into the kitchen for another cup of coffee or tea to take back to his desk? A window to the right of the door was half raised. Could that be the window of Dennis's study or workroom? Could he see *her* now if he looked out?

A pang of shame and excitement struck Odile. She would be visible, just, if Dennis looked out, even though a hedgerow would conceal half her figure. She knew Dennis was not married, and she presumed he lived alone.

But the minutes went by and nothing happened. The spring wind blew softly in Odile's ears, and seemed to whisper friendliness and courage. Odile advanced along the smooth gravel driveway that wound towards Dennis's garage. A flagstone path went off to the right and led to the house. Odile would of course not go to the door. But as a matter of fact she did have her brand-new hardcover of *Devil's Bounty* in her big handbag which she pressed hard against her side out of nervousness. Her steps grew smaller, slower. Couldn't she dare knock on his door — she saw a brass knocker — and ask him for an autograph? Since his telephone number was unlisted, she couldn't have rung him, and he would realize that. When she was some five yards from the house, the front door opened.

Dennis Hollingwood stood in the doorway, tall, blondish, frowning in the bright sunlight!

"Afternoon," he said. "Help you?"

"Good afternoon. I'm — " Odile's eyes devoured his figure, and she realized that she was trying to memorize every detail as if he might vanish in a split-second: he wore brown corduroys, a white shirt with sleeves rolled up, a dark green sleeveless sweater. "I'm Odile Masarati. I've written you once or — " She stopped, because he had thrust his fingers through his hair with an air of irritation. "I don't mean to disturb you. I have a book of yours with me and I'd — "

He nodded, and came down the two steps on to the path. He had a pen in his right hand. But suddenly he stopped and looked at her, still frowning. "How'd you find my house?"

208

"I asked. In the village." She was fumbling with the first pages of *Devil's Bounty*, looking for the title page, so Dennis could sign below his printed name. "I'm sorry if—"

He ruffled his hair again and tried to smile. "No, it's just that — Right here on my property, you know — " He signed his name rapidly with a hand that shook slightly.

His hand shook with repressed anger, Odile knew. She saw a muscle in his jaw tighten. "Thank you!" she said, taking the book back.

"I hope you'll understand — I can't answer those letters of yours. Too many, too often, you know?" He took a step back from her. "Goodbye, Miss — "

"Masarati," she said. She added in a feeble voice that was a ghost of her own, "Goodbye, Mr Hollingwood." Then she turned and walked towards the road.

He had turned away first, and she heard his door close firmly.

She walked back towards the town of Little Starr in a daze of shame and confusion. He had detested her! And she had nourished a fantasy of being invited in for a cup of tea, invited to take a look at the desk where he worked! Odile felt that she had just made the worst social gaffe of her life. She had intruded, like a piece of riff-raff off the street! She walked with her eyes on the ground, never looking up until she found herself in the square of Little Starr again, and she set about finding a taxi to take her to the station at Chelmsford.

In the taxi, her tears came, though she held her head high. It was as if Dennis Hollingwood had suddenly died, had suddenly been erased from — what? From her circle of friends and beloveds, anyway. No letter that she might write him could ever explain or excuse her advancing up the path to his house. Maybe he'd been having difficulties with his work today, but no matter, *she* had been the invader of his privacy, unannounced and uninvited.

Even after the train journey, Odile's mood was no

better and no different. She felt that her guilt must be visible, as if she wore a hair shirt.

She was supposed to meet Marie-Claire at their hotel around six. That didn't matter any more. Eschewing the taxis at Liverpool Street Station, Odile walked on towards the tube station called The Angel, where she could either look for a taxi or take the tube in the direction of her hotel, or even just keep on walking. Then at a corner near The Angel station, she deliberately stepped out in front of a taxi which was making a turn quite fast. Odile had wanted to injure herself, perhaps kill herself, though she had realized this only a few seconds before she leapt into the taxi's path.

Odile woke to find herself lying on her back in a bed, and she felt pain all along the right side of her head and face. She lifted her right hand, and her fingertips encountered thick bandages that extended under her chin. The light was dim, but she could make out beds on either side of her and more beds against an opposite wall. Palely clad nurses came and went. One nurse, noticing her arm movement, perhaps, turned with a tray to look at her.

"Waking up now? Want another pain-killer? — You speak English?"

"Oh, yes," said Odile in a faint voice.

She was given a pill. Odile learned that she had suffered a concussion and a 'laceration' down her right cheek. She was asked where she had been staying in London. The hospital had found her passport in her handbag. Odile told them the Hotel Sherwood, and they rang Marie-Claire Lambert, who came at once, even though it was nearly midnight by then. Marie-Claire was both shocked and relieved. She had thought Odile might have been kidnapped and maybe also murdered.

"*Me* kidnapped? For what?" Odile could still joke.

Odile had to remain in the hospital another five days at least, and Marie-Claire wanted to stay on in London and wait for her, but Odile insisted that she go back on her return ticket. Odile had some money with her, and could pay her hospital bill with a transfer of money from her father, which Marie-Claire promised to arrange. Marie-Claire pressed Odile's arm, and departed, promising to come again the next day.

Odile watched her friend tiptoe towards the door of the ward, then turn back.

"Odile, I can't go home without you. I'll stay till you can leave this place and we'll go back together." Tears rolled down her cheeks. "It's unbelievable!" she whispered in French. "What on earth has happened to your *face*, my darling?"

Odile said nothing. She was prepared for the worst and expected it, a broad, gravelly scar, perhaps, going from her temple down to her jaw.

She was still bandaged lightly and had not seen her wound when she and Marie-Claire made their way home six days later. Odile was rather weak, and Marie-Claire was sure it was from shock. She did not tell Marie-Claire that she had seen her literary idol Dennis Hollingwood that fateful day. That was Odile's secret and would always remain her secret.

In due time, two days after her return home, Odile's loose bandage was changed by the Masaratis' doctor, Dr Paul Resquin, who shook his head solemnly and murmured some words about the incapacity of English doctors. Odile, sitting in his office for this, nearly fainted even in that position, and she did not ask for a mirror. She imagined the wound bright pink, and rough, an inch and a half or four centimetres broad, slanting across her cheek to well under her jaw, horrid and repellent, making people wince and look away.

When she did have the courage to look at her scar on another day at the doctor's, when he removed the bandage for the last time, she saw that it was not as broad as she had feared, nor as rough (Dr Resquin had deplored its "unnecessary roughness"), but still it was shocking enough. The doctor gave her smelling salts, and made her lie down on his sofa for ten minutes. Then she got into her DC and drove straight home.

Marie-Claire was sympathetic and at the same time cheerful about it. "It won't always be pink, Odile. With a little make-up, you'll hardly see it!"

This of course wasn't true. Even with make-up, the roughness made shadows in most lights, no doubt even in candlelight, Odile thought with grim humour, and when would she ever have a romantic dinner by candlelight again? The days of stolen rendezvous with Stefan seemed now to have taken place in prehistoric time, the girl she had been then not even herself, not even related to the woman she was now. Her love life was finished, over, just as surely as Dennis Hollingwood was finished, any further correspondence with him or hope of meeting him again one day in happier circumstances. Oddly, the loss of Dennis Hollingwood, his profound exasperation with her, was to Odile almost as weighty a thing as the loss of her beauty. The word 'beauty' might not ever have applied to her, she realized, but she had had a freshness in her not-bad-looking face which now was gone for ever.

Odile had managed her return to school, the stares and questions and kind words from colleagues, with a quiet courage. But in those first days of facing the public with the big pink scar that lost itself under her jaw — Odile's mind churned.

Sometimes she felt almost glad that she had the scar, felt that it was a mark of honour, an announcement to the world that she had paid for her sins. But what sins? Wanting to meet a writer whom she admired? Then her thoughts would become lost, because for one thing, she would realize that Dennis Hollingwood *per se* hadn't been worth it, as a writer. There were other writers, Graham Greene for instance, whom she definitely admired more, and who hadn't replied at all to her letters. *Pride*, she thought, it was all nothing but pride on her part. True enough, but good writers, writers of great talent, were worth it all. In a sense, it was these good writers who had rebuffed her, not Dennis Hollingwood himself or *per se*. Odile felt that she had turned an important corner in her life, because of the brand she bore on her face, and that her ignominy, her abysmal shame of her appearance, now, had made her someone different, humbler, but maybe even stronger, who knew? Time would tell that.

At other moments, even when she was taking Trixie for a long walk in the fields, Odile would believe that her conspicuous blemish was due to the hand of fate striking her yet again, as it had with her mother's early death, with the loss of Stefan, and now excluding her from any future happiness with lover or husband. Then she would feel depressed, like a leper who couldn't ever be cured, like someone even doomed to die in a short time. Odile then saw herself, as she strode vigorously up a slope or leapt a ditch more gracefully than Trixie, growing old with this same scar, and the scar becoming part of her by the time she was forty, for instance, all her friends accustomed to it, accustomed to her solitary existence, for surely it would be by then, with her father likely to die within the next two or three years.

Odile continued to write to Wilma Knowles, the writer who lived in Canada. She wrote fan letters to two more writers with her old zest and her old genuine admiration — one an Australian, the other American, both novelists. Such correspondence, even if doomed to be one-sided, was Odile's real life and joy, she realized. And so be it.

In spring of the next year, her father was laid to rest, as the priest said, in the little cemetery in Ezèvry-la-Montagne, and after the funeral, Odile invited some twenty villagers including Marie-Claire, of course, to the house for food and wine, what the English called funeral meats. Odile was a cheerful and efficient hostess. She was not yet thinking about her father's absence, but rather that one day she would likely be lowered into the same ground here. Life was nothing but trying for something, followed by disappointment, and people kept on moving, doing what they had to do, serving — what? And whom? Odile felt wise and calm that day, and shed not a tear for her dear old father.

The Romantic

(First published in *Cosmopolitan*, London, 1983)

When Isabel Crane's mother died after an illness that had kept her in and out of hospitals for five years and finally at home, Isabel had thought that her life would change dramatically. Isabel was twenty-three, and since eighteen, when many young people embarked on four happy years at college, Isabel had stayed at home, with a job, of course, to help with finances. Boyfriends and parties had been minimal, and she had been in love only once, she thought, or maybe one and a half times, if she counted what she now considered a minor hang-up at twenty on a married man, who had been quite willing to start an affair, but Isabel had held back, thinking it would lead nowhere. The first young man hadn't liked her enough, but he had lingered longer, in Isabel's affections, more than a year.

Yet six weeks after her mother's funeral, Isabel found that her life had not changed much after all. She had imagined parties, liveliness in the apartment, young people. Well, that could come, of course. She had lost contact with a lot of her old high-school friends, because they had got married, moved, and now she didn't know where to reach most of them. But the world was full of people.

Even the apartment on West 55th Street had not changed much, though she remembered, while her mother had still been alive, imagining changing the boring dubonnet-and-cream coloured curtains, now limp with age, and getting rid of the nutty little "settles" as her mother had called them, which took up space and

217

looked like 1940 or worse. These were armless wooden seats without backs, which no one ever sat on, because they looked fragile, rather like little tables. Then there were the old books, not even classics, which filled more than half of the two bookcases (otherwise filled with better books or at least newer books), which Isabel imagined chucking, thereby leaving space for the occasional *objet d'art* or statuette or something, such as she had seen in magazine photographs of attractive living-room interiors. But after weeks and weeks, little of this had been done, certainly not the curtains, and Isabel found that she couldn't shed even one settle, because nobody she knew wanted one. She had given away her mother's clothes and handbags to the Salvation Army.

Isabel was a secretary–typist at Weiler and Diggs, an agency that handled office space in the Manhattan and Queens areas. She had learned typing and steno in her last year at high school. There were four other secretaries, but only Isabel and two others, Priscilla (Prissy) and Valerie, took turns as receptionist at the lobby desk for a week, because they were younger and prettier than the other two secretaries. It was Prissy, who was very out-spoken, who had said this one day, and Isabel thought it was true.

Prissy Kupperman was going to be married in a few months, and she had met her fiancé one day when she had been at the front desk, and he had walked in. "Re-ception" was a great place to meet people, men on the way up, all the girls said. Eighty per cent of Weiler and Diggs' clientele was male. A girl could put herself out a little, escort the man to the office he wanted, and when he left, ask him if his visit had been successful and say, "My name is Prissy (or whatever) and if you need to get a message through or any special service, I'll see that it's done." Prissy had done something along these lines the day her Jeff had walked in.

Valerie, only twenty and a more lightweight type than Prissy, had had several dates with men she had met at work, but she wasn't ready for marriage, she said, and besides had a steady boyfriend whom she preferred. Isabel had tried the same tactics, escorting young men to the office they wanted, but this so far had never led to a date. Isabel would dearly have loved 'a second encounter' as she termed it to herself, with some of those young men who might have phoned back and asked to speak with Isabel. She imagined being invited out to dinner, possibly at a place where they had dancing. Isabel loved to dance.

"You ought to look a little more peppy," Valerie said one day in the women's room of the office. "You look too serious sometimes, Isabel. Scares men off, you know?"

Prissy had been present, doing her lips in the mirror, and they had all laughed a little, even Isabel. Isabel took that remark, as she had taken others, seriously. She would try to look more lighthearted, like Valerie. Once the girls had remarked on a blouse Isabel had been wearing. This had been just after her mother's death. The blouse had been lavender and white with ruffles around the neck and down the front like a jabot. The girls had pronounced it "too old" for her, and maybe it had been, though Isabel had thought it perky. Anyway, Isabel had never worn it again. The girls meant well, Isabel knew, because they realized that she had spent the preceding five years in a sad way, nursing her mother practically single-handed. Isabel's father had died of a heart attack when Isabel had been nineteen, and fortunately he had left some life insurance, but that hadn't been enough for Isabel and her mother to engage a private nurse to come in now and then, even part-time.

Isabel missed her father. He had been a tailor and presser at a dry cleaning shop, and when Isabel's mother's illness had begun, her father had started working overtime, knowing that her cancer was going to be a long and expensive business. Isabel was sure that this was what had led to his heart attack. Her father, a short man with brown and grey hair and a modest manner that Isabel loved, had used to come home stooped with fatigue around ten at night, but always able to swing his arms forward and give Isabel a smile and ask, "How's my favourite girl tonight?" Sometimes he put his hands lightly on her shoulders and kissed her cheek, sometimes not, as if he were even too tired for that, or as if he thought she might not like it.

As for social life, Isabel realized that she hadn't progressed much since she had been seventeen and eighteen, dating now and then with boys she had met through her high-school acquaintances, and her high school had been an all-girls school. Isabel considered herself not a knockout, perhaps, but not bad looking either. She was five feet six with light brown hair that was inclined to wave, which made a short hair-do easy and soft looking. She had a clear skin, light brown eyes (though she wished her eyes were larger), good teeth, and a medium-sized nose which only slightly turned up. She had of course, checked herself as long as she could remember for the usual faults, body odour or bad breath, or hair on the legs. Very important, those little matters.

Shortly after Prissy's remark about her looking too serious, Isabel went to a party in Brooklyn given by one of her old high-school friends who was getting married, and Isabel tried deliberately to be merry and talkative. There had been a most attractive young man called Charles Gramm or maybe Graham, tall and fair-haired, with a friendly smile and a rather shy manner. Isabel chatted with him for several minutes, and would have been thrilled if he had asked when he might see her again, but he hadn't. Later, Isabel reproached herself for not having invited Charles to a drinks party or a Sunday brunch at her apartment.

This she did a week or so later, inviting Harriet, her Brooklyn hostess, and her fiancé, and asking Harriet to invite Charles, since Harriet must know how to reach him. Harriet did, Charles promised to come, Harriet said, and then didn't or couldn't. Isabel's brunch went quite well with the office girls (all except one who couldn't make it), but Isabel had no male partner in her efforts, and the brunch did not net her a boyfriend either.

Isabel read a great deal. She liked romance novels with happy endings. She had loved romances since she had been fourteen or so, and since her mother's death, when she had more time, she read three or four a week. most of them borrowed from the Public Library, a few bought in paperback. She preferred reading romance novels to watching TV dramas in the evening. Whole novels with descriptions of landscapes and details of houses put her into another world. The romances were rather like a drug, she realized as she felt herself drawn in the evenings towards the living-room sofa where lay her latest treasures, yet as drugs went, books were harmless, Isabel thought. They certainly weren't pot or cocaine, which Prissy said she indulged in at parties sometimes. Isabel loved the first meetings of girl and man in these novels, the magnetic attraction of each for each, the hurdles that had to be got over before they were united. The terrible handicaps made her tense in body and mind, yet in the end, all came out well.

One day in April, a tall and handsome young man with dark hair strode into the lobby of Weiler and Diggs, though Isabel was not at the reception desk that day. Valerie was. Isabel was just then carrying a stack of photostatted papers weighing nearly ten pounds across the lobby to Mr Diggs's office, and she saw Valerie's mascaraed lashes flutter, her smile widen as she looked up at the young man and said, "Good morning, sir. Can I help you?"

As it happened, the young man came into Mr Diggs's office a minute later, while Isabel was putting the photostats away. Then Mr Diggs said:

". . . in another office. Isabel? Can you get Area six six A file for me? Isn't that in Current?"

"Yes, sir, and it's right here. One of these." Isabel pulled out the folder that Mr Diggs wanted from near the bottom of the stack she had just brought in.

"Good girl, thanks," said Mr Diggs.

Isabel started for the door, and the eyes of the young man met hers for an instant, and Isabel felt a pang go through her. Did that mean something important? Isabel carefully opened the door, and closed it behind her.

In less than five minutes, Mr Diggs summoned her back. He wanted more photostats of two pages from the file. Isabel made the copies and brought them back. This time the young man did not glance at her, but Isabel was conscious of his broad shoulders under his neat dark blue jacket.

Isabel ate her coffee-shop lunch that day in a daze. Valerie and Linda (one of the not-so-pretty secretaries) were with her.

"Who was that Tarzan that came in this morning?" Linda asked with a mischievous smile, as if she really didn't care. She had addressed Valerie.

"Oh, wasn't he *ever*! He ought to be in movies instead of — whatever he's doing." Valerie giggled. "His name's Dudley Hall. *Dudley*. Imagine."

Dudley Hall. Suddenly the tall, dark man had an identity for Isabel. His name sounded like one of the characters in the novels she read. Isabel didn't say a word.

Around four that afternoon, Dudley Hall was back. Isabel didn't see him come in, but when she was summoned to Mr Diggs's office, there he was. Mr Diggs put her on to more details about the office space on Lexington Avenue that Mr Hall was interested in. This job took nearly an hour. Mr Hall came with her into another office (used by the secretaries, empty now), and Isabel had to make four telephone calls on Mr Hall's behalf, which she did with courtesy and patience, writing down neatly the information she gleaned about conditions of floors and walls, and the time space could be seen, and who had the keys now.

As Mr Hall pocketed her notes, he said, "That's very kind of you, Miss — "

"Isabel," she said with a smile. "Not kind. Just my job. Isabel Crane, my name is. If you need any extra information — quick service, just ask for Isabel."

He smiled back. "I'll do that. Could I phone my partner now?"

"Indeed, yes! Go ahead," said Isabel, indicating a telephone on the desk. "You can dial direct on this one."

Isabel lingered, straightening papers on the desk, awaiting a possible question or a request from Mr Hall to note down something. But he was only making a date with his partner whom he called Al to meet him in half an hour at the Lexington address. Then Mr Hall left.

Had he noticed her at all? Isabel wondered. Or was she just another face among the dozen or so girl secretaries he had seen lately? Isabel could almost believe she was in love with him, but to be in love was dangerous as well as being pleasant: she might never see Dudley Hall again.

By the middle of the next week, the picture had changed. There were a few legal matters that caused Mr Hall to come to Weiler and Diggs several times. Isabel was called in each time, because by now she was familiar with the file. She typed letters, and provided Dudley Hall and Albert Frenay with clear, concise memos.

"I think I owe you a drink — or a meal," said Dudley Hall with his handsome smile. "Can't make it tonight, but how is tomorrow? There's The Brewery right downstairs. Good steaks there, I've tried 'em. Want to make it around six or whenever you get off? Or is that too early?"

Isabel suggested half past six, if that was all right with him.

She felt in the clouds, really in another world, yet one in which she was a principal character. She didn't mention her date to Valerie or Prissy, both of whom had commented on her "devotion" to Dudley Hall in the last days. Isabel had made the date for 6.30 so she would have time to get home and change before appearing at The Brewery.

She did go home, and fussed so long over her make-up, that she had to take a taxi to The Brewery. She had rather expected to see Dudley Hall standing near the door inside, or maybe at the bar, but she didn't see him. At one of the tables? She looked around. No. After checking her light coat, Isabel moved towards the bar, and obtained a seat only because a man got up and gave her his, saying he didn't mind standing up. He was talking to a friend on an adjacent stool. Isabel told the barman she was waiting for someone, and would be only a minute. She kept glancing at the door whenever it opened, which was every fifteen seconds. At twenty to seven, she ordered a scotch and soda. Dudley was probably working a bit late or had had difficulty getting a taxi. He'd be full of apologies, which Isabel would say were quite unnecessary. She had tidied her apartment, and the coffee-maker was clean and ready, in case he would accept her invitation to come up for a final coffee at the end of the evening. She had brandy also, though she was not fond of it.

The music, gentle from the walls, was old Cole Porter songs. The voices and laughter around her gave her cheer, and the aroma of freshly broiled steaks began to make her hungry. The décor was old brown wood and polished brass, masculine but romantic, Isabel thought. She checked her appearance in the mirror above the row of closely set bottles. She was wearing her best 'little black frock' with a V-neck, a slender gold chain that she had inherited from her mother, earrings of jade. She had washed her hair early that morning, and she was looking her best. In a moment, she thought, glancing again at the door, Dudley would walk in hurriedly, looking around for her, spotting her and smiling when she raised her hand.

When Isabel next looked at her watch, she saw that it was a couple of minutes past 7.30. A painful shock went through her, making her almost shudder. Up to then, she had been able to believe he was just a little late, that a waiter would page her, calling out "Miss *Crane*?", to tell her that Mr Hall would be arriving at any minute, but now Isabel realized that he might not be arriving. She was on her second scotch which she had been sipping slowly so it would last, and she still had half of it.

"Waiting for somebody? — Buy you a drink in the meantime?" asked a heavy-set man on her left, the opposite side from the door side, whom Isabel had noticed observing her for several minutes.

"No, thanks," Isabel said with a quick smile, and looked away from him. She knew his type, just another lone wolf looking for a pick-up and maybe an easy, unimportant roll in the hay later. Hello and goodbye. Not her dish at all.

At about five minutes to eight, Isabel paid for her drinks and departed. She thought she had waited long enough. Either Dudley Hall didn't want to see her, or he had had a mishap. Isabel imagined a broken leg from a fall down some stairs, a mugging on the street which had left him unconscious. She knew these possibilities were most unlikely.

The next day Dudley Hall did telephone to make his excuses. He had been stuck at a meeting with his partner plus two other colleagues from six o'clock until nearly eight, he said, and it had been impossible to get away for two minutes to make a phone call, and he was terribly sorry.

"Oh — not so important. I understand," said Isabel pleasantly. She had rehearsed her words, in case he telephoned.

"I thought by seven-thirty or so you'd surely have left, so I didn't try to call The Brewery."

"Yes, I had left. Don't worry about it."

"Well — another time, maybe. Sorry about last night, Isabel."

They hung up, leaving Isabel with a sense of shock,

not knowing how the last few seconds had passed, causing them both to hang up so quickly.

The following Sunday morning, Isabel went to the Metropolitan Museum to browse for an hour or so, then she took a leisurely stroll in Central Park. It was a sunny spring morning. People were airing their dogs, and mothers and nurses — women in uniforms, nannies of wealthy families — pushed baby carriages or sat on benches chatting, with the carriages turned so the babies would get the most sun. Isabel's eyes drifted often from the trees, which she loved to gaze at, to the babies and toddlers learning to walk, their hands held by their fathers and mothers.

It had occurred to her that Dudley Hall was not going to call her again. She could telephone him easily, and invite him for a Sunday brunch or simply for a drink at her apartment. But she was afraid that might look too forward, as if she were trying too hard.

Dudley Hall did not come again to the office, because he had no need to, Isabel realized. Nevertheless, meeting him had been exciting, she couldn't deny that. Those few hours when she had thought she had a date with him — well, she'd *had* one — had been more than happy, she'd been ecstatic as she'd never been in her life that she could remember. She had felt a little the way she did when reading a good romance novel, but her date had been real. Dudley had meant to keep it, she was sure. He could have done better about phoning, but Isabel believed that he had been tied up.

In her evenings alone, doing some chore like washing drip-dry blouses and hanging them on the rack over the tub, Isabel re-lived those minutes in The Brewery, when she had been looking so well, and had been expecting Dudley to walk through the door at any second. That had been enchantment. Black magic. If she concentrated, or sometimes if she didn't, a thrill went over her as she imagined his tall figure, his eyes finding her after he came through the big brown door of The Brewery.

226

Eva Rosenau, a good friend of her mother's, called her up one evening and insisted on popping over, as she had just made a sauerbraten and wanted to give Isabel some. Isabel could hardly decline, as Eva lived nearby and could walk to Isabel's building, and besides, Eva had been so helpful with her mother, Isabel felt rather in her debt.

Eva arrived, bearing a heavy iron casserole. "I know you always loved sauerbraten, Isabel. Are you eating enough, my child? You look a little pale."

"Really? — I don't feel pale." Isabel smiled. The sauerbraten was still a bit warm and gave off a delicious smell of ginger gravy and well-cooked beef. "This does look divine, Eva," said Isabel, meaning it.

They put the meat and gravy into another pot so Eva could take her casserole home. Isabel washed the big pot at the sink. Then she offered Eva a glass of wine, which Eva always enjoyed.

Eva was about sixty and had three grown children, none of whom lived with her. She had never had a job, but she could do a lot of things — fix faulty plumbing, knit, make electrical repairs, and she even knew something about nursing and could give injections. She was also motherly, or so Isabel had always felt. She had dark curly hair, now half grey, was a bit stocky, and dressed as if she didn't care how she looked as long as she was covered. Now she complimented Isabel on how neat the apartment looked.

"Bet you're glad to see the last of those bedpans!" Eva said, laughing.

Isabel rolled her eyes upwards and tried to smile, not wanting to think about bedpans. She had chucked the two of them long ago.

"Are you going out enough?" asked Eva, in an armchair now with her glass of wine. "Not too lonely?"

Isabel assured her that she wasn't.

"Theo's coming for Sunday dinner, bringing a man friend from his office. Come have dinner with us, Isabel!

Around one. Not sauerbraten. Something different. Do you good, dear, and it's just two steps from here."

Theo was one of Eva's sons. "I'll — That's nice of you, Eva."

"*Nice?*" Eva frowned. "We'll expect you," she said firmly.

Isabel didn't go. She got up the courage to call Eva around ten on Sunday morning and to tell a small lie, which she disliked doing. She said she had extra work for the office to do at home, and though it wasn't a lot of work, she thought she should not interrupt it by going out at midday. It would have been easier to say she wasn't feeling well or had a cold, but in that case, Eva would have been over with some kind of medicine or hot soup.

Sunday afternoon Isabel tackled the apartment with a new, calmer determination. There were more of her mother's odds and ends to throw away, little things like old scarves that Isabel knew she would never wear. She moved the sofa to the other side of the room, nearer a front window, and put a settle between window and sofa to serve as an end table, a much better role for that object, and Isabel was sorry she hadn't thought of it before. "Settle" was not even the right word for these chair-tables, Isabel had found by accident when looking into the dictionary for something else. A settle had a back to it and was longer. Another, one of many, odd usage of her mother's. The sofa rearrangement caused a change in the position of the coffee table and an armchair, transforming the living room, making it look bigger and more cheerful. Isabel realized that she was lucky with her three-room apartment. It was in an old building, and the rent had gone up only slightly in the fifteen years since her family had had it. She could hardly have found a one-room-and-kitchenette these days for the rent she was paying now. Isabel was happy also because she had a plan for that Sunday evening.

Her plan, her intention, kept her in a good mood all the afternoon, even though she deliberately did not think hard about it. *Play it cool*, she told herself. Around five, she put a favourite Sinatra cassette on, and danced by herself.

By seven, she was in a large but rather cosy bar on Sixth Avenue in the upper 50s. Again she wore her pretty black dress with the V-neck, a jade or at least green-bead necklace, and no earrings. She pretended she had a date around 7.30, not with Dudley Hall necessarily, but with somebody. Again she sat at the bar and ordered a scotch and soda, sipped it slowly while she cast, from time to time, a glance at the door. And she looked at her watch calmly every once in a while. She knew no one was going to walk in who had a date with her, but she could look around at the mostly jolly crowd with a different feeling now, quite without anxiety, as if she were one of them. She could even chat with the businessman-type on the stool next to hers (though she didn't accept his invitation to have a drink on him), saying to him that she was waiting for someone. She did not feel in the least awkward or alone, as she had finally felt at The Brewery. During her second drink, she imagined her date: a blond man this time, around thirty-four, tall and athletic with a face just slightly creased from the cold winds he had braved when skiing. He'd have large hands and be rather the Scandinavian type. She looked for such a man when she next lifted her head and sought the faces of three or four men who were coming in the door. Isabel was aware that a couple of people around her had noticed, without interest, that she was awaiting someone. This made her feel infinitely more at ease than if she had been at the bar all by herself, as it were.

At a quarter to eight, she departed cheerfully, yet with an air of slight impatience which she affected for any observer, as if she had given up hope that the person she was waiting for would arrive.

Once at home, she put on more comfortable clothes and switched on the TV for a few minutes, feeling relaxed and happy, as if she'd had a pleasant drinks hour out somewhere. She prepared some dinner for herself, then mended a loose hook at the waist of one of her skirts, and then it was still early enough to read a few pages in her current romance novel, *A Caged Heart*, before she went to bed, taking the book with her.

Valerie remarked that she was looking happier. Isabel hadn't realized this, but she was glad to hear it. She was happier lately. Now she was going out — dressing up nicely of course — twice a week on her fantasy dates, as she liked to think of them. What was the harm? And she never ordered more than two drinks, so it was even an inexpensive way of entertaining herself, never more than six or seven dollars an evening. She had a hazy collection of men with whom she had had imaginary dates in the past weeks, as hazy as the faces of girls she had known in high-school, whose faces she was beginning to have trouble identifying when she looked into her graduation book, because most of the girls had been only a part of the coming and going and dropping-out landscape of the overcrowded school. The Scandinavian type and a dark man a bit like Dudley Hall did stand out to Isabel, because she had imagined that they had gone on from drinks to dinner, and then perhaps she had asked them back to her apartment. There could be a second date with the same man, of course. Isabel never imagined them in bed with her, though the men might have proposed this.

Isabel invited Eva Rosenau one Saturday for lunch, and served cold ham and potato salad and a good chilled white wine. Eva was pleased, appreciative, and she said she was glad Isabel was perking up, by which Isabel knew she meant that she no longer looked under the shadow of her mother's death. Isabel had finally thrown out the old curtains, not even wanting to use them for rags lest she be reminded of drearier days, and she had run up new light green curtains on her mother's sewing machine.

"Good huntin'!" Valerie said to Isabel, Valerie was off on her vacation. "Maybe you've got a secret heart interest now. Have you?"

Isabel was staying on at the office, taking her vacation last. "Is that all you think makes the world go round?" Isabel replied, but she felt the colour rise to her cheeks as if she had a secret boyfriend whose identity she would spring on the girls when she invited them to her engagement party. "You and Roger have a ball!" Valerie was going off with her steady boyfriend with whom she was now living.

Four days before Isabel was to get her two weeks' vacation, she was called to the telephone by Prissy who was at the reception desk. Isabel took it in another office.

"Willy," the voice said. "Remember me? Wilbur Miller from Nebraska?" He laughed.

Isabel suddenly remembered a man of about thirty, not very tall, not very handsome, who had come to the office a few days ago and had found some office space. She remembered that he had said, when he had given his name for her to write down, "Really Wilbur. Nobody's named Wilbur any more and nobody comes from Nebraska, but I do." Isabel said finally into the telephone, "Yes."

"Well — got any objections if I ask you out for dinner? Say Friday night? Just to say thanks, you know — Isabel."

"N-no. That's very nice of you, Mr Miller."

"Willy. I was thinking of a restaurant downtown. Greenwich Street. It's called the Imperial Fish. You like fish? Lobster?" Before she could answer, he went on. Should he pick her up at the office Friday, or would she prefer to meet him at the restaurant?

"I can meet you — where you said, if you give me the address."

He had the address for her. They agreed upon seven.

Isabel looked at the address and telephone number of the Imperial Fish, which she had written down. Now she remembered Wilbur Miller very well. He had an openness and informality that was unlike most New Yorkers, she recalled, and at the same time he had looked

231

full of self-confidence. He had wanted a two-room office, something to do with distribution of parts. Electronic parts? That didn't matter. She also remembered that she had felt an unusual awareness of him, something like friendliness and excitement at the same time. Funny. But she hadn't put herself out for him. She had smothered her feelings and even affected a little formality. Could Willy Miller of Nebraska be Mister Right? The knight on a white horse, as they said jokingly in some of the romances she read, with whom she was destined to spend the rest of her life?

Between then and Friday evening, Isabel's mind or memory shied away from what Willy Miller looked like, what his voice was like, though she well remembered. She was aware that her knees trembled, maybe her hands also, a couple of times on Friday.

Friday around six, Isabel dressed for her date with Willy Miller. She was not taking so much trouble with her appearance as she had for Dudley Hall, she thought, and it was true. A sleeveless dress of pale blue, because it was a warm evening, a raincoat of nearly transparent plastic, since rain was forecast, nice white sandals, and that was it.

She was in front of the Imperial Fish's blue-and-white striped awning at five past seven, and she glanced around for Willy among the people on the sidewalk, but he was probably in the restaurant, waiting for her. Isabel walked several paces in the uptown direction, then turned and strolled back, under the awning and past it. She wondered why she was hesitating. To make herself more interesting by being late? No. This evening with Willy could be just a nice evening, with dinner and conversation, and maybe coffee back at her apartment, maybe not.

What if she stood him up? She looked again at the awning and repressed a nervous laugh. He'd order a second drink, and keep glancing at the door, as she always did. He'd learn to know what it felt like. However, she had nothing whatsoever against Willy Miller. She simply realized that she didn't want to spend the evening with him, didn't want to make better acquaintance with him. She sensed that she could start an affair with him, which because she was older and wiser would be more important than the silly experience — She didn't know what to call that one-night affair with the second of her loves, who hadn't been even as important as the first, with whom she'd never been to bed. The second had been the married man.

She wanted to go back home. Or did she? Frowning, she stared at the door of the Imperial Fish. Should she go in and say, "Hello, Willy. Sorry I'm late"? Or "I'm sorry, Willy, but I don't want to keep this date."

I prefer my own dates, she might add. That was the truth.

A passerby bumped her shoulder, because she was standing still in the middle of the sidewalk. She set her teeth. *I'm going home*, she told herself, like a command, and she began to walk uptown in the direction of where she lived, and because she was in rather good clothes, she treated herself to a taxi.